The Xandra
Book Six
Iceworld

By

Herbert Grosshans

Published by
Melange Books, LLC
White Bear Lake, MN 55110
www.melange-books.com

ISBN: 978-1-61235-449-1 Print

Published in the United States of America.

Cover Art by: A. Bratt

The Xandra, Book Six - Iceworld
By Herbert Grosshans

Exploring a new world can be exciting and rewarding. Ten researchers are trying to unlock the mysteries of a planet plagued by fierce storms and harsh winters. They find more than mere excitement as they discover they are not alone.

* * * *

Visit Herbert's website:

http://hegro.shawwebspace.ca
http://hegro.blogspot.com/

Works also by and including Herbert Grosshans:
(Available at www.melange-books.com)

Stars In Chains 1, Slave
Stars In Chains 2: Liberator
Stardogs 1 & 2
The Xandra Series Books 1-5
Cliffs of Time
Orion the Hunt
Beyond the Stars Digest
Orion: Symbiont of Passion
Men of Eros
The Spider Wars, Books 1-3

Chapter One

Professor Tennenboum walked to the outer rim of the observatory to look at the star-speckled black void outside. The ancient alien space station curved away all around the tower, the only tower the Humans had adapted to support human life. Only three of the twelve towers studding the giant sphere could be partially seen from his location. The fourth planet of the star system ACG 671-397-D hung overhead like a huge, shiny soap bubble. He may never set foot on its surface. His destination lay elsewhere.

"Overwhelming, isn't it?"

He turned to glance at the woman who came up beside him. She was tall, slim, and beautiful, with long, red hair and lovely green eyes. "It certainly is," he said.

"Every time I look at that planet it seems to beckon to me." Her voice sounded almost dreamy.

"I haven't been down there, but I hear it is an ideal planet. One of the best we've discovered so far."

She chuckled. "The colonists named it Nu-Eden. Let's hope we don't find a snake to spoil it."

"There usually is one. Nothing ever turns out to be perfect." Tennenboum was pessimistic. "I remember Devil's Nest as it is called now. Did you know it was named Eden at first?"

"I don't know about Devil's Nest, but I know of at least three other planets starting out as Eden."

"Perhaps this one will be different." Tennenboum turned to walk back to his table. "Care to join me for dinner, Miss…I'm sorry, I don't know your name. I've seen you around, though." He smiled. "A beautiful woman like you does draw attention."

"Thank you for the compliment, Professor Tennenboum." She laughed at his puzzled face. "Everybody knows the head of the research team that is going down to the fifth planet." She held out a hand. "I'm Breanna McGuinness. I'm a xenologist."

"You study alien life forms. A xenologist and beautiful to boot. Too bad I didn't know about you before I put together my team. A good-looking woman is always a pleasant addition."

She pulled her eyebrows into a mock frown. "I hope the members of your team were selected for their qualifications and not because they are beautiful people."

"All of them are the best in their field." He smiled and took her arm. "Come, lovely Lady Breanna McGuinness, and let me have the pleasure of looking at you from across the table."

"Are you flirting with me, Professor Tennenboum?"

"I am an old man, young woman. My flirting days are over." He led her across the crowded room to his table and held the chair for her until she sat down. When she was comfortable he moved to the other side of the table and took the seat across from her.

"Thank you, Professor. You are a gentleman."

"Thank goodness one doesn't forget his manners with age." Looking around the room, he sighed. "I shall miss the comforts of the Station but then again…I'm looking forward to studying the fifth planet. It's a rugged world. Humans will probably never live on it, even though the air is breathable."

"I've read the preliminary reports from the exploration drones. That world is racked by violent storms and torrential rains. The snow-covered mountains are so high no Human will ever climb them. Doesn't sound like a pleasant place one would want to visit."

He smiled. "And yet…I have a feeling you'd probably give a lot to be part of the team. I'm surprised you didn't put your name on the list."

She shrugged. "I thought about it but decided to join the research team destined for Nu-Eden."

"Perhaps you'll be the one to discover the snake hiding in the grass." He looked at the darkened part of the transparent dome. The Primary was a blazing ball two hundred and fifty million km away, its glare dulled by the polarized invisible barrier designed to keep out the damaging rays and preventing the air from dissipating into the cold, airless eternal night.

"The people who built this space station must be millennia ahead of us. I wonder what happened to them," he mused. "This ancient artifact is the first real proof there are other space faring species out there. We just haven't found them yet."

"Maybe it is a good thing. If they are as quarrelsome as Humans and possibly as hostile we might regret meeting them," Breanna said.

"It will happen eventually. We may have to defend our place in the Galaxy."

Tennenboum studied her casually. "Would you like some wine?"

"Yes, please."

"Don't go away. I'll be back." He got up and strolled toward the bar, stopping along the way to exchange pleasantries with a couple of people who would be part of his team.

Douglas Roland was known to him personally, but the woman with him he knew only by name. Roland was a geologist. Tall and thin with a hooked nose and piercing eyes, he always reminded him of a large bird of prey.

The woman was as tall as Roland, with a sturdy built, like that of a body builder. Her face was soft and friendly. The most impressionable feature was her eyes. Bright blue, they lent her an air of aloofness. He tried to remember her name, but it only came to him as he walked away from their table.

Antje Swornson. She was an entomologist.

I hope there will be bugs for her to study.

As he wound his way between the tables, he perused the room. Of the approximately two hundred crewmembers and researchers on the Station only about a quarter sat at the tables, chatting and eating. Their conversations seemed low and almost subdued, drifting through the observatory like the soft droning of the air circulating system.

He couldn't blame them. Even now after being on the space station for months it took his breath away every time he stepped out of the elevator onto the deck. No struts or beams to indicate a barrier existed above and around him. Had it not been for the darkened part the illusion of nothing but empty space between the stars and the observer would have been nearly perfect.

Humans did not possess this technology. After discovering the abandoned giant sphere circulating the planet below them, they took possession of it but had not been able to access its sealed interior.

The giant space station was approximately one point five km in diameter. Twelve towers protruded from it at regular intervals. The towers were one hundred fifty meters high and sixty meters wide.

The engineers on the huge Mother ship carrying colonists in cryogenic suspension to distant planetary systems isolated one of the towers from the rest of the space station and turned it into livable space for Humans.

When they found the giant orb it wasn't completely dead. They detected a power source in the central core, which created a low level of gravity on the outside and inside of the sphere. They couldn't tap into that power, so they installed a separate power system in the tower and brought it back to life. An elevator traveled from the lowest level through twenty-five floors to the observatory.

The Mother ship was gone now, searching for other suitable planets. The engineers managed to do their job in a relatively short time.

I guess our technology isn't so primitive after all.

He interrupted his musings and waved to the bartender. “Two glasses of red wine, please.”

“Sure, Professor. When are you leaving us?”

Tennenboum gave the young man a friendly smile. “Hi, Anthony. Not for a couple of weeks. We have to wait until the weather is favorable for a landing. Right now, there is a thunderstorm ravaging the area we’ve selected for setting up the research station.”

“Can’t you just move it somewhere else? I mean…that is a huge planet.” Anthony’s face took on a dreamy expression. “I wish I could come with you. What an adventure that would be.” He sighed. “But I’m stuck here on the Station. They won’t even let me down to Nu-Eden.”

Tennenboum laughed at the young man’s enthusiasm. “I don’t believe we have need for a bartender.”

“I’m also a good cook and I’m quite strong. I work out every day. I could do chores like chopping wood.”

Still laughing, Tennenboum said, “We’ll be using our own power generators for heat and power. I hope we never have to resort to such primitive methods as using wood to cook our food and heat the Station. I’m afraid there isn’t a job for a woodcutter, either.”

“Too bad. I thought I might be able to convince you. What’s one more person on the shuttle? I’m used to cramped quarters and I can survive on very little food.” He filled two glasses with red wine. “Enjoy, Professor. When you come back we may have run out of wine, unless the colonists are starting to produce their own.”

“They’ll have more important things to occupy their time, survival being one of them.” He reached across the counter and slapped Anthony’s arm. “Take care, young man. Perhaps your destiny lies elsewhere. Possibly even on Nu-Eden. Who knows?”

Anthony heaved a loud sigh. “I wanted to see the stars, but here I am stuck serving drinks, just like at home on Earth. Nothing much has changed.”

Tennenboum chuckled softly. “The view is much better here. Besides, you’ll be a rich young man when your contract is finished in five years. You can live out the rest of your life in comfort.” He looked back at the table where he had left Breanna. “I’d better return to my dinner companion or she might think I abandoned her.”

“That’s Breanna McGuinness,” Anthony said wistfully.

“You know her?”

Even in the dim light washing the observatory it was evident Anthony was blushing. “Barely,” he said, trying to sound casual and uninterested. “She’s quite beautiful. Is she on your team?”

"No. She has other ambitions." Tennenboum turned and made his way back to his table. Breanna watched him as he walked toward her, carrying one glass in each hand, trying not to spill the precious liquid. She smiled when he sat down, but he seemed to detect a touch of annoyance in her green eyes.

"Forgive me for leaving you like this," he said. "By the way, I've met an admirer of yours."

Breanna seemed amused when she said, "You mean Anthony, the bartender? He's asked me for a date more than once but I'm not interested. He's too young for me. Besides, I have no interest right now in a serious relationship. It would only distract me from my work."

"Don't use your work as an excuse to avoid making a commitment, young lady. Life goes by too fast." He remembered his youth with regretful thoughts; remembered his first and only love…Elisa. He had truly loved her, but his work had been more important.

We'll get married when I come back for Alpha Centauri. Five years isn't such a long time to wait when we have our whole life ahead of us.

He signed on for another two years. When he came back she had married another man.

"Are you married, Professor Tennenboum?"

Her voice broke into his thoughts and brought him back to the present. "No." He smiled ruefully. "There was no room in my life for a wife."

Her green eyes regarded him with a thoughtful expression. "Maybe there is no room in mine for a husband."

"As long as you are happy and never have regrets with the life you lead there is nothing wrong with that, but as you get older your priorities may change. I miss the children I never had. I miss not having someone who calls me Dad. I'll never rock a grandchild on my knees." He looked up from the menu in the tabletop he had been studying. "Are you ready for dinner?"

She nodded. He pressed his thumb against the small order screen in the center of the table. "Mock turkey is on the menu tonight. I can't wait to eat some real meat again some day."

Chapter Two

They were flying blind and had to rely entirely on the autopilot to bring the space shuttle through the thick clouds and to a safe landing. Lightning bolts hit the outer shell of the craft and knocked out a couple of screens. The shuttle rocked violently and suddenly dropped with gut wrenching speed. The gravity cocoon kept the passengers inside the vessel from receiving serious injury and losing the contents of their stomachs.

Nobody spoke. Everyone kept watching the screens in the front. Even though the human pilot sat in his chair, he didn't touch any controls and let the automatic pilot do its job.

The two lost screens sprang back to life as the computer repaired the damaged circuits. One screen showed a gray sky, the other one peaks of snow-covered mountains.

"We've broken through the first level of clouds," the pilot announced. "We will be landing in thirty-five minutes. Hang on for a bit of a rough ride."

A few of the passengers chuckled. "How much rougher can it get?" Yules Bonnet asked. He was a young, thin man, sporting a small square mustache. It made him look comical, like a character out of a play. His high and nasal voice didn't help either. Had it not been for the mustache drawing attention to his face, he would have given the impression of just an ordinary guy not worth a second look.

Tennenboum knew this to be an illusion. Bonnet possessed a brilliant mind, capable of doing complex calculations in his head. He could see the missing pieces of a puzzle as clearly as if they were laid out in front of him.

Too bad he has this annoying voice. I hope it won't become an irritating factor with the other team members.

Tennenboum watched the terrain displayed on the screen. The picture was clear. It wasn't an accurate representation of the conditions outside but a computer-generated image, without the turbulence and second level cloud cover obscuring the view onto the rugged surface below.

Strong winds buffeted the spacecraft and the stabilizing system worked overtime to keep it on a straight course. On the screen, the mountains disappeared and were replaced by what looked like relatively flat terrain with a river and a huge lake.

The craft lost altitude quickly, reducing speed at the same time until it came to a complete stop.

Everyone applauded and laughed to ease the tension in the passenger cabin.

"It seems we've survived the landing," the pilot said, chuckling. "Be patient for a little while longer. Once we have released the capsule containing the supplies and building materials for your temporary shelter, the shuttle will settle down on a more appropriate spot."

"What's it like out there?" one of the women asked.

"According to the computer it is a balmy twelve degrees Celsius."

The woman laughed. "Almost warm enough to go swimming in the lake."

"I didn't bring a bathing suit," another woman said.

She reminded Tennenboum of Breanna McGuinness with her red hair and green eyes. Her name was Beth McGregor. She was the chemist in the team.

"I didn't bring one either." The first woman laughed.

Alena Bronsky. She was the oldest of the five women. Tennenboum picked her because of her extensive experience with alien planets. According to her resume, she spent three years on Alpha Centauri IV, one year on Sirius V, and two years on Hell's Playground, a planet with extreme weather conditions, similar to the one they just landed on. He figured she'd be a valuable asset.

As long as she doesn't take off her clothes we should be fine.

She could not be called beautiful. Not in Professor Tennenboum's book. She was short and frumpy-looking, with a square, coarse face, and her hair cut like that of a man. Not a woman who would arouse a man's interest. One thing she had in her favor…her voice. Soft and gentle, a man could listen to it all day long.

Tennenboum smiled. With closed eyes, assuming it's possible to listen to a woman talking for that long.

He felt a gentle rocking as the capsule attached to the belly of the shuttle dropped away. Then the craft moved forward and descended fully to touch the ground. A shiver ran through the cabin, and he felt the soft pressure of the gravity cocoon release its hold on his body.

He stretched and cleared his throat. "Nobody leaves the ship until the area has been scanned for dangerous life forms and deemed safe by the AI," he called out. He knew everyone was impatient and eager to step onto the alien soil, especially since all of them had been cooped up in the space station for months, and another week in the cramped quarters of the shuttle.

He knew he was. He couldn't wait to feel solid ground under his feet again and see the sky, even if it was as gray and cloudy as the one on this planet.

None of the team had visited Nu-Eden. Captain Cunningham was a cautious man. Only a select few of the researchers had been allowed to go to that mysterious planet. All indications showed it to be an ideal world, ready to be claimed for humanity. A thousand colonists were already on it, but another thousand were still waiting to be brought out of cryogenic suspension. They'd be waiting for five years. Only when the first thousand flourished would the Captain revive the others.

"No threats detected in the immediate area surrounding the shuttle," the pleasant female voice of the shuttle's AI announced.

A rush of cold air entered the cabin as the door to the airlock slid open.

All the members of the team could barely contain their eagerness to leave the ship, but they all waited until Professor Tennenboum stepped into the airlock before they left their seats.

He was the head of the research team and the oldest. It went without saying that he would be the first to touch the surface of this new world.

The first Human.

Before this, soil and air samples had already been taken and analyzed by robotic research drones to make certain they were safe for Humans to be handled and breathed.

Tennenboum took an experimental shallow breath and inhaled the alien air. It smelled fresh, crisp, laced with unfamiliar scents and odors, none of them unpleasant. When he looked across the foreign and yet strangely familiar land stretching around him he saw what appeared to be grass covering the ground.

Straight ahead the surface of the lake glittered, extending as far as he could see. It was not a quiet lake. Whitecaps topped the windswept waves as they rolled toward shore. To his left he saw a forest of tall trees with leafy, low hanging branches. A wide river flowed into the lake to his right. In the distance, he saw mountains rising into the cloudy sky.

"I didn't think it would be so beautiful," a woman's voice said behind him.

"Looks peaceful," another one said.

He recognized Beth McGregor's voice. "I hate to burst your bubble but looks can be deceiving," he said. "There may be no large animals in the area but watch out for the small ones, like insects, worms, reptiles."

"It is too cold for reptiles," Anthony Renaldo said. He should know. He was the zoologist.

"Different planets produce different life forms," Douglas Roland warned. "The rules for one world aren't necessarily valid on another one."

Tennenboum began descending the steps, taking care not to slip and fall. It wouldn't do to enter this new world rolling down the steps. He smiled, realizing he was claiming this planet for humanity. Humans would change it, upset the balance of nature just by being here, and bring new ideas, new problems.

He would bring his sense of humor.

The alien grass bent the way grass bends when stepped on. The ground felt hard, cushioned by the crushed vegetation under his boots. He took a few steps and then waited for the rest of the team to join him. Two of the men began walking toward the lake. He stopped them before they strolled away too far.

"Please stay with the group. I don't want anyone getting lost. Before we begin exploring, there are a few priorities. The most important one is the erection of the shelter."

"Isn't that the job of the construction crew? I'm an archeologist not a construction worker."

Tennenboum threw the man an annoyed look. "Professor Maisoneuve, for your information, the construction crew will put together the main building and the labs. The temporary shelter is our responsibility...unless we want to sleep under the stars."

"Who the hell decided that? Nobody made me aware of it. I don't like it when others make decisions where I'm involved without informing me first." Maisoneuve shook himself and stared into the cloudy sky. "I'm not sure if I am going to like it on this planet. Will we ever see any stars?"

"Well, you are free to return with the shuttle," Tennenboum said. "Nobody forces you to stay but be advised, should you decide to return you will work with the construction crew on the main building until then. You look fit enough for that job."

Maisoneuve's face was a cold mask when he looked at Tennenboum. "You may be the team leader, Professor Tennenboum, but I joined voluntarily and don't have to take..." He stopped talking and shrugged his broad shoulders. "There is nothing waiting for me on the Station, so I might as well stay here."

"All right." Tennenboum looked around the assembled members of the team. "Are there any other objections?"

The majority of the men and women seemed uneasy under his angry gaze, embarrassed by the hostile exchange between Maisoneuve and him. He sighed, annoyed at himself for letting Maisoneuve make him loose his temper, but then again...he was the leader and should be treated with respect. He didn't need some ambitious young upstart undermine his authority...especially not at the beginning of the project.

The capsule with the supplies for the shelter lay near half a dozen other huge oval shaped objects. Each one was filled to capacity with the materials needed to build the research station. They had been brought to this planet on previous unmanned shuttle trips. It would take the building crew a few weeks to put the prefab pieces together.

One of the construction workers had already moved to the site and was busy unlocking the doors to the first capsule.

Tennenboum spotted a small cluster of trees nearby and decided it would make a good spot for the shelter. "Over there," he said. "It shouldn't take more than a few hours to build that thing. We should be able to easily finish it before nightfall. Tonight we will be warm and cozy. Tomorrow we can start mapping the immediate area."

* * * *

They did manage to finish their temporary shelter before darkness fell, and everyone was happy to move in. The shelter provided them adequate protection from the elements and the built-in heaters generated warmth and comfort, especially since the temperature dropped down to near zero Celsius during the night.

Even with only eleven people space was, of course, tight. They slept on collapsible cots, barely wide enough for some of the larger men.

The nine construction workers and the pilot slept inside the shuttle.

Everyone woke early the next morning, eager to go outside and begin exploring. The air greeting them was crisp and smelled of snow.

"What about a latrine?" Jennifer Ratzenberger asked.

"It was supposed to be built yesterday," Tennenboum said. "Otherwise we'll have to look for a secluded spot somewhere near."

"I suggest we don't introduce too many of our germs and bacteria into this world until we know more about it. A latrine to process our bodily waste is of utmost importance."

"You are right, of course, Doctor Ratzenberger," Tennenboum agreed. "Just by our presence here we are already introducing alien micro organisms into the ecosystem, but I agree we should be more careful. Why don't you go and talk to Mr. Armand. He's the construction foreman. If they haven't put it together yet, tell them to make it a priority project. In the meantime I suggest we use the toilet in the shuttle."

"Where can we wash up?" Alena Bronsky asked.

"We will all go down to the lake. We know the water is safe to use for washing but don't drink it. It needs to be boiled first. We've brought plenty of clean drinking water and food to last until we are fully set up to begin processing and using local stuff. I really don't need to remind anyone to be careful, but I'm saying it again. Don't touch, don't smell, don't eat and drink anything until it has been determined safe and harmless."

The construction crew was already busy working when the group of eager scientists made their way to the lake. Everyone wore insulated pants and jackets for protection against the cold wind blowing across the lake.

The lakeshore was rugged in places, but as luck would have it, below them was a beautiful beach of white sand.

Roland, who was the first one to climb down the steep incline to the water surface, stopped and looked at Tennenboum. "I can see by the waterline on those rocks that the water level in this lake rises at certain times of the year, most likely in spring when the snow begins to melt. From the images I saw on the screens, the riverbed is far below the dry land. Another indication of fluctuating water levels."

Tennenboum nodded. "I agree. As long as the land doesn't get flooded it shouldn't matter to us."

"There is no guarantee it won't," Roland said.

"Don't worry about water levels now," Renaldo said. "Let's just get down there and check out the water."

"I'll second that." Beth pushed past Roland, closely followed by Alena. The women were the first ones to reach the beach. Laughing, they dug their boots into the soft sand.

"I really wouldn't mind taking a dip," Alena said, "but I think I'll stick to washing only my hands."

"I dare you," Renaldo said, grinning.

Alena laughed and made motions to take off her jacket.

"Nobody enters that water until we know there aren't any dangerous creatures lurking below the surface," Tennenboum ordered.

"I was only kidding, Professor. You wouldn't get me into that ice bucket."

"I can't wait until the showers are installed," Beth said. She pushed back the hood of her jacked and shook her red hair. "My hair is a mess. It needs washing."

"I can't wait either. I will feel much safer overall when the whole research station is finished," Regina Seagul said. "I've never cared much for camping outside."

Tennenboum watched with amusement as the petite woman daintily put her hands into the water and scooped up a handful. Closing her eyes, she splashed a little into her face. "It's cold," she said, giving her body a little shake.

"You people should be on guard."

Tennenboum turned around at the sound of the voice and watched the construction foreman climbing down the riverbank. He carried a laser rifle. Jennifer Ratzenberger climbed down behind him, trying to keep pace with the big man.

"Any problems, Mr. Armand?" Tennenboum asked

Armand nodded. "One of my men spotted a large animal coming out of the forest this morning. He didn't get a good look at it but he said it was as large as a tiger, even looked like one. I suggest you have someone with a weapon standing guard at all times."

"An alien life-form?" Renaldo asked, excitement in his voice. "That is fantastic news."

"That may be so," Armand said, "but it also means we could be in great danger. Where there is one there usually are more. Be careful."

"We don't know if it is dangerous," Alena protested. "I've never seen a tiger in real life, only on pictures, but I know they were powerful and ferocious beasts. Just because this creature looked like a tiger doesn't mean it is a carnivorous predator. It could be an herbivore…a plant eater."

"Always assume the worst, Miss," Armand said, while his eyes scanned the surrounding area. "I've hunted animals on other planets. Some of the least dangerous looking ones turned out to be the most vicious. I've been attacked by tiny, beautiful birds sporting long, wicked beaks and by cute looking woolly balls with stingers as long as your arm."

"The only dangerous animals I ever saw were in a zoo on Earth, and they looked pretty tame to me, even the tigers," Bonnet said. His nasal voice sounded even more irritating than usual.

"There are no more wild animals on Earth, sir." Armand's words were polite, but his voice carried a note of contempt. It was easy to tell he didn't think much of the assembled group of overeducated eggheads, as the workers called the scientists when talking among themselves.

"I don't know if any of my colleagues is comfortable handling a weapon," Professor Tennenboum said. "I for one have a healthy respect for guns. Could you possibly spare one of your men, Mr. Armand?"

Armand shook his head. "I'm afraid not. We need every man to finish this project on time, but I'll tell Prowler. Perhaps he can help you out." He walked away, back to the plastasteel structure that would soon be the research station, providing comfort and safety for the team.

"Didn't anyone think of bringing weapons for our protection?" Maisoneuve asked belligerently. He looked at Tennenboum. "You are the leader, Professor. Our safety is part of your responsibilities."

"We've brought weapons, plenty of them, but I didn't think there would be any need for them. The preliminary surveys of the planet didn't report any dangerous large animals."

"The surveys were taken from space and by drones flying high above the surface. I also know that only a small part of the planet was studied," Maisoneuve said.

"I can't dispute that, Professor Maisoneuve. We were mostly concerned if this planet could support human life. As Miss Bronsky suggested, we don't know if the animal the man saw is actually dangerous. If he even saw one. Sometimes our imagination plays tricks with our minds." Tennenboum didn't believe his own words. "If everyone is done washing up we'll go back to the shelter. Should danger threaten, we can take refuge inside the shelter."

Everybody seemed subdued when they headed back for the small temporary structure. Some stared toward the forest; some had their eyes on the sky as if expecting to see a flock of tiny, beautiful birds with wicked beaks bursting out of the clouds.

From the shuttle, two men carrying rifles came walking toward them…Prowler, the pilot, and a black man Tennenboum knew as Irwin Hunter.

"Armand tells me you may need protection from a possible predator one of his men spotted," Prowler drawled.

"He did. We have no proof what the man saw was actually anything threatening," Tennenboum said.

"Nevertheless, we'd better take precautions." Prowler looked toward the forest. "Hunter and I will take turns standing guard. Hunter is the electronics expert and electrician. There is nothing for him to do right now. Once he is needed, I'll be the only one standing guard. I can do it until we leave. After that…" he shrugged. "I'm afraid you'll be on your own. Perhaps you can request a couple of armed personnel to be sent down with the next shipment of supplies."

"I will take your suggestion into consideration." Tennenboum cursed silently for not thinking of it himself.

I'm a geo-physicist, a scientist, damn it! Not an organizer.

The sky above looked grayer than before and the wind seemed to have increased in strength. It had changed direction and was blowing from the mountains, bringing with it icy air and the smell of snow.

"We will have to establish north and begin doing some preliminary mapping so we are able to navigate without getting lost," he told the team. "We can't let any real or imaginary threats demoralize us."

"There is no chance of getting lost if we hang around camp all day long and sitting on our butts," Antje Swornson said.

Tennenboum gave the tall woman a sharp look, surprised by her remark. She had spoken few words since they landed.

"Don't worry about having to hang around the camp, Doctor Swornson. We will take short excursion trips. After all that is what why we came here…to explore, not to sit on our butts." He spoke calmly, trying not to show his annoyance.

The woman smiled. Her bright blue eyes sparkled mischievously. "I was trying to make light of the situation, Professor. No need to ream me out."

"What's for breakfast?" Alena piped up.

Her unexpected question broke the tension and everyone laughed.

"Yes, what are we having for breakfast?" Beth echoed.

"I want bacon and eggs and a cup of coffee," Regina said, laughing.

"Women!" Renaldo threw his hands up in mock disgust. "We're surrounded by vicious predators and the women want to eat."

Tennenboum straightened his shoulders and let out a deep sigh. Maybe he was overreacting by getting annoyed so easily. It wasn't their fault he had overlooked safety precautions. Maisoneuve was right…he was the leader and it was his responsibility to think of everything.

"Since you're the one who seems to be the hungriest, Miss Bronsky, I delegate you to prepare this morning's breakfast," he said, trying to put a cheerful note into his request.

"I'll give her a hand," Beth said.

The two women headed for the containers holding the food packages. They'd be living off concentrates until the food synthesizer was operational.

* * * *

The days went by slowly. The team couldn't do much until the research station was completed. They needed the computers, the instruments, and the comfortable work area inside the protective walls. Roland, who was not only a geologist but also a cartographer and topographer, took the Landroamer, accompanied by Maisoneuve and Alena Bronsky, to start mapping the immediate area. Even though Alena was a chemist, she had experience with alien geography and what's more, she handled the Landroamer as well as any man.

Maisoneuve went along as a guard armed with one of the laser rifles from the shuttle's armory. He had admitted to Tennenboum that he was not a stranger to most weapons and not afraid to use a laser.

Professor Tennenboum was not unhappy about having him out of his hair for a while. He was surprised when Maisoneuve actually volunteered for the job.

The rest of the team was busy taking samples of the soil and alien plants. Bonnet began dictating notes into his portable Analyzer on weather conditions, the air, and other information connected with the weather.

Tennenboum used his time to go over the survey reports of the drones. He had read them a couple of times before, but it wouldn't hurt to refresh his memory.

Standing outside, looking toward the forest, as he did every day, he pondered over the sighting one of the construction workers reported. Nobody had seen anything since that first day, and he questioned if large animals actually existed on this planet.

Sighing, he strolled over to the construction site. The building was beginning to take shape. He'd seen the plans for the research station, but he was pleasantly surprised how large it actually was. Inside the protective walls of plastasteel they would find safety and comfort, even if conditions turned nasty outside.

The bottom floor was designed for storing equipment and supplies. The kitchen and mess hall, a large common room, an exercise area, an entertainment room, and the laboratories would occupy the main floor. The sleeping cubicles on the upper floor would be small but large enough for two bunks, a desk, and a closet for the occupants' personal belongings. There would also be showers and lavatories, something everybody was eagerly waiting for.

The whole station was designed to be completely isolated from the ecosystem of the planet. No waste products would pollute the alien environment.

All of the components for the station had been prefabricated on Earth and packaged into capsules ready to be delivered to their final destination.

He was a bit surprised to see how high the egg-shaped structure was above ground. It rested on telescopic metal supports and girders. An elevator inside a tower was the only means to gain access to the station.

He spotted Armand studying a large computer screen. "How are things progressing?" he asked.

Armand looked up from his plans and gave Tennenboum a nod. "We are actually a bit ahead of schedule," he said. "Those engineers on Earth are a bunch of geniuses. Everything is designed so precise it makes assembling this giant egg almost too easy. The pieces all fit together like the pieces of a well-designed puzzle. A child could do it."

Tennenboum chuckled. "Don't be so modest, Mr. Armand. I think it takes a little more than a child's brain to build something like this. Take some of the credit."

"Maybe a little." Armand smiled. "I have a good crew. I couldn't do it without these men."

"I don't want to criticize but was it necessary to have it so high off the ground?"

"That was the suggestion of the engineers on the Station. According to the computer analysis they are expecting immense amounts of snow and they fear the whole valley may be flooded in the spring." Armand looked up and into the gray sky. "This is not a friendly planet. How long are you planning to stay here?"

"A year. Perhaps as little longer. It all depends how things progress and what we discover."

"Do you think we will ever colonize this planet?"

Tennenboum shrugged. "That again depends. We Humans can adapt to all kinds of conditions. It is not such a bad world. The air is breathable and, as far as we can tell from preliminary tests, doesn't contain any harmful elements.

The water is clean and should be usable. We haven't discovered any large indigenous life forms, but they exist, I have no doubts." He smiled. "I don't mean to dispute what your man might have seen, however, until we have had more sightings or, better yet, recordings of the animal he claims to have seen, we can only assume its existence."

"You can be certain what Hemming saw was real. This is not the first planet we've worked on. We have been trained to spot and recognize anything that could prove dangerous to us." Armand went back to studying his screen. "Now, if you'll excuse me, Professor, I have work to do." He favored Tennenboum with a friendly smile. "We don't want to fall behind and make a liar out of me. You wouldn't want that on your conscience."

"No. I certainly don't." Tennenboum walked away with a chuckle. He was beginning to feel much better.

The clanking of hammers, wrenches, and the humming of power tools and construction machinery seemed almost natural by now, but he knew it was an intrusion into the normal sounds of this world they were beginning to invade.

Local life forms, if they existed, would be shying away from this area the strangers from another world dared to disturb. The more curious would be making an appearance once they got used to the sounds and sights of the intruders, and the bolder ones would challenge their right to be here.

It was only a matter of time.

Armand was right. The need to be on guard at all times was not something to be taken lightly.

Chapter Three

Anthony Renaldo was the first one to spot an object flying in the sky. It was only fitting since he was a zoologist. Even though his specialty was the study of reptiles, he had extensive knowledge of most known species still existing on Earth and of discovered animals on some of the colonized planets.

As it happened, he carried an image recorder and managed to get a few pictures before the object disappeared in the clouds. Regina was as excited as he was. Being a xenologist, her interests lay in intelligent life forms. There was a possibility whatever Renaldo recorded could be intelligent, or display some form of intelligence.

"It looks like a giant bird," she said.

"Could it have been an artificial artifact? Something built by intelligent beings?" Jennifer wondered.

Renaldo shrugged. "We'll have to wait until the computer is operational. Then we can magnify it and get a better look."

"If it was a bird it was huge, like the Roc in our old legends," Regina said.

"Let's hope it wasn't a Roc," Renaldo said. "It would mean other huge life forms exist on this planet. Large animals like that could pose a serious threat to us."

"If that thing was artificial then we have even more to worry about," Maisoneuve warned.

"We haven't seen any evidence of intelligent beings populating this planet," Tennenboum cautioned them. "Of course, that doesn't mean there aren't any."

"Let's assume it was a bird. Shouldn't there be any small birds around? What about other animals or insects?"

They all looked at the woman who had spoken. She shrugged and smiled. Her teeth gleamed white against her black skin. "I'm a nurse," she said, "I know nothing about the birds and the bees."

"I doubt that, Miss Sherbo," Renaldo said, laughing.

They all chuckled.

Tennenboum couldn't help but laugh when he looked into the young nurse's innocent looking face. Maybe she doesn't know about the birds and the bees. Highly unlikely but not impossible.

Her name was Vendy Sherbo. She wasn't part of the research team. Her assignment was for two or three months, depending when the shuttle with the second team arrived. She'd be replaced by Dr. Liss, who was a biologist but also an accomplished GP.

"It is too cold for insects," Antje Swornson explained. "As for birds and other small animals? Well, I'm not an expert. I'm an entomologist. If it comes to insects ask me, but Doctor Renaldo is the more knowledgeable person to answer your question. I believe they'll make an appearance soon enough…if they indeed exist. Am I right, Doctor?"

"You are quite correct, Doctor Swornson," Renaldo said. "We've been dropping alien objects into their environment and producing unfamiliar noises for weeks now. Our arrival has sent them into hiding, but they'll be back."

"I grew up on a small farm in Brazil. I miss the singing of birds." Vendy looked up into the rolling clouds. "I also miss the blue sky with no clouds hiding the sun. Will we ever see the sun here?"

Yules Bonnet coughed delicately beside her. "I'm afraid you won't be able to see our sun on this planet, except for on a clear night. It'll be just another star, but eventually the Primary of this system should break through the clouds."

"You're the weatherman," Vendy said, heaving a deep sigh. "You should know."

"I'm not a weatherman," Bonnet said, almost indignant. "I prefer to be called a meteorologist."

Vendy rolled her eyes. "What's the difference? Meteorologist…weatherman. Can you tell us when the clouds will go away?"

Bonnet pressed a finger against his upper lip. "If I had more data I would be able to create a chart. On the basis of that chart I could make a prediction. Quite accurate, actually."

Vendy giggled. "You talk funny. Did anybody ever tell you that?"

"Not to my face, but I've heard people commenting behind my back. I'm used to it. There is nothing I can do about my voice." He looked her up and down. Then he cracked a smile. "Anybody ever tell you you're cute?"

"All the time." She broke into cheery laughter. "You're kinda cute yourself, Doctor Bonnet. I like that square patch of hair under your nose."

"It's called a mustache, young Lady."

"A mustache? Who would have guessed?" She giggled. "And please don't call me young Lady. My name is Vendy."

Everybody had been listening to their conversation, not quite knowing where it would lead, but now they all smiled. Some laughed. Tennenboum let out a breath he didn't know he was holding. Bonnet was an odd fellow, but it seems he and the young nurse hit it off. Too bad she wouldn't be staying long. She was a breath of fresh air desperately needed among this assembly of uptight scientists.

He pulled the collar of his windbreaker tighter around his neck. A strong wind blew from the direction of the lake. With it came the smell of seaweed and other odors.

"I smell fish," Vendy said, wrinkling her nose.

"There is a distasteful reek in the air," Renaldo admitted. "It could very well be from reptilian life forms living in the lake. Possibly even fish."

Tennenboum's attention was diverted by the group of construction workers heading for the lake and he wondered what they were up to. As he watched he saw a couple of them remove their clothing. Stark naked, they entered the water and began splashing each other while their comrades laughed and cheered them on.

Damn it! I would have thought Armand was smarter than that. This is not a good example for my people.

He stomped toward the water, followed by his team, probably equally curious and wondering. As they neared the lake a third construction worker undressed and joined the two in the water.

Tennenboum slowed his approach and cursed again. He had not been aware that one of the workers was a woman.

She was as tall and sturdy as Antje Swornson. Her breasts, while not overly large, were firm and full, like the rest of her body, and her long legs muscular and slim. She jumped into the water, laughing and shaking her shoulder-length black hair.

He reached the group and grabbed Armand by the shoulder.

"What the hell are you people thinking? There might be dangerous creatures in the water. I told my team not to go in and here you are ignoring my orders!"

Armand gave Tennenboum an annoyed look. Then he shrugged. "Zydyk went fishing last night and he caught a fish-like creature. It didn't appear to be dangerous. I believe the water is safe. Besides, you have no authority over my men."

Tennenboum pointed at the woman in the water. "That is not a man."

"Oh, you've noticed?" Armand chuckled. "That is Cara Gunn."

The two men came out of the water, shivering. "It is damn cold," one of them said, his teeth shattering. He looked back at the woman. "She doesn't seem to mind." He grinned. "Of course, when you're as hot-blooded as Cara you'd probably consider this foggen ice bucket a hot-tub."

She laughed. "I heard that, Hemming. Even I can only take just so much. I'm coming out, too, but this was refreshing."

Tennenboum watched her walking back to shore, her nude body glistening, looking like a goddess or warrior woman out of Earth legends. He had to admit she awoke feelings in him he could not afford to have. Not at his age. He was fifty-five years old and she was probably less than half his age.

He had one consolation. When he looked at the other men he saw the same desire in their eyes.

"Well, back to work," Armand said.

"Aren't you going in, Nelson?" Cara asked while rubbing her body with a small towel. Watching her voluptuous body twist and turn didn't help to calm Tennenboum's state of mind.

Armand laughed good-humouredly. "I don't think so. Just seeing Han and Hemming turning blue is enough for me."

* * * *

"While I have no real objections if some of your people want to stay until the next supply shuttle comes back, I do have some reservations." Tennenboum looked at the three construction workers who had expressed an interest in staying. He knew them by name, but otherwise he knew little about them.

The big man with the friendly face was Jerry Kullmann. He laughed a lot and was fond of telling jokes, most of them considered inappropriate in some people's mind.

Edmund Zydyk was small and wiry, prone to scowling, but he seemed to enjoy fishing. He had been the first one to catch a fish in the lake. A small fish it had been but nevertheless it was the first creature caught by a Human on this world. He wanted to stay and catch a big one.

Then there was Cara Gunn.

Armand saw his gaze, obviously guessing his thoughts. "I admit she is an independent person and a bit of a maverick when it comes to protocol and regulations, but she is a good worker and smart," he said. She grew up on Ceres. Her parents were miners. If she had been given the opportunity she would have been a scientist, like you, Professor."

I hope she won't present me with any problems. "All right," he said. "They can stay if they want to, but they will have to help out with the chores and they will accept me as the Station Master. I hope they know this."

Armand smiled. "They understand. You won't have any problems." He looked toward the mountains and then into the sky. "The weather conditions are favorable. We'll lift off early tomorrow morning. Wong and Hunter should have the communications tower finished by this afternoon. You can call the space station tonight and put in your first report, Professor."

"So far, we don't have much to report, except that the facilities are working and we are all still in good health. Will you be returning with the next supply shuttle, Mr. Armand?"

Armand shook his head. "Probably not, unless Captain Cunningham orders me to be on it. As far as I know, he wants me to go down to Nu-Eden and help with the erection of buildings there."

Tennenboum chuckled. "You could stay here and help exploring this planet. You might find it interesting since you are a hunter and somewhat of an adventurer."

"I'd rather go to Nu-Eden." Armand grinned. "I like the weather there better. This is the beginning of summer and it is cold. I can only imagine how the winter will be. As I understand, it takes over two years for this planet to complete its journey around the Primary, which means longer seasons. The winter might be as long as a whole norm-year."

"That could very well be. It will also mean a longer summer with warmer weather. Eventually we'll have to adapt our calendar to this planet and give every month more days."

"Those are things your team will have to work out or whoever decides to make this place home." Armand shook himself. "I wouldn't exactly call this warm, Professor. I like to pull up my sleeves when I'm working. By that I mean literally pull them up."

"I guess Miss Gunn is probably the only one who doesn't think it is cold here," Tennenboum said, recalling the sight of her naked body as she splashed around in the cold water of the lake. Something she had been doing almost every morning before she started her workday.

Laughing softly, Armand threw a look at the tall woman, who seemed to be in deep conversation with Vendy Sherbo. "She is used to cooler temperatures. The tunnels on Ceres are cold. This is like a holiday for her."

"A working holiday, I hope," Tennenboum remarked, a little sarcastically. "We can't afford to have freeloaders."

"She'll earn her keep, Professor." Armand winked. "She might be a good catalyst to keep the men on your team awake and eager to get up in the morning. I've seen the way they look at her."

"So have I." Tennenboum suppressed a sigh. Then he smiled. "What I mean I've also seen them looking."

Armand grinned but didn't comment.

Tennenboum studied the oblong structure looming above them, sparkling silvery in the harsh rays of the Primary that had decided to break through the thick cover of clouds for a few days.

Like an egg left behind by a giant bird, ready to hatch and eager to invade an unsuspecting planet.

He saw Hunter coming out of the elevator tower. The black man spotted them and headed in their direction. “We’re done,” he said when he was close, beaming with obvious satisfaction. “Wong is giving the system one last checkup. The transmitter is ready to go, Professor. You can try to contact the space station. You shouldn’t get much atmospheric interference. If you wait about half an hour conditions should be nearly perfect. According to Wong, the Station will be in a favorable position.”

“Thank you, Hunter.” Tennenboum smiled. “I was told you’re the best.”

Hunter made a little bow, shrugged, and grinned. “I’m also the only one here who can set up a system like that.”

“That’s why I’m happy to know you’ll stay for a while. In case the system crashes.”

“There isn’t much chance of that, Professor. Wong connected the electrical system to a self-repairing program monitored by the Mother-computer. Repair-drones and microbots inside the walls will do continous maintenance to keep everything operating smoothly.” Hunter sounded smug and proud. “Once the system is up and running there isn’t much work for me anymore.”

“I see. Then why are you staying?”

“Glitches can happen. Nothing is ever one hundred percent foolproof. I’m staying to make sure they don’t happen. View me as an insurance policy.” His dark eyes rested on Tennenboum’s face. “Computers are not infallible, Professor. They will never take the place of a Human.”

Tennenboum laughed. “And yet you keep an invisible companion strapped to your wrist.”

Hunter looked at the tiny device. “This? It keeps me focused and sane. It talks to me and I can talk to it without wondering if I’m going insane talking to myself. I use it to record my personal experiences for future references. Besides, it is a genius when it comes to solving mathematical problems and also a fountain of stored knowledge.” He smiled. “I have to admit, Humans do have certain limits. I have mine.”

“I’m glad to finally hear you say that, Hunter,” Armand said. “I was beginning to think you were some kind of mechanical construct. This is the first time I’ve seen you smile and in a happy mood since we landed.”

“There was nothing to smile about, Boss. I didn’t like this place in the beginning. Too gloomy, not enough sunshine. I wasn’t looking forward to spending three or four months on this forsaken planet.”

“So why smile today?”

“I’m finished with my job and the sun is shining. Suddenly things don’t look so bad anymore. I might even like it here.”

"Does the fact that Cara is staying have anything to do with your good mood?"

Hunter chuckled. "Whatever gave you that idea, Boss?"

"I've seen you two sticking your heads together. Don't think I missed it. I'm trained to notice those things."

"I like her. Is there a rule against that?"

Armand shook his head. "No rule and I couldn't care less. Just be careful. She is like a rogue comet. Unpredictable. I'd hate to see you get burned."

"It makes me feel all soft inside to know you care about my welfare, Boss. Don't worry, I won't get burned." His lips curved into a big smile. "Perhaps you should worry about her. I might be a volcano ready to explode."

"Don't overestimate yourself, Hunter." It was Armand's turn to grin. "Just make sure when you explode the fire is contained inside a safe vessel."

"I'll remember that, Boss."

Tennenboum had been listening to their friendly bantering. He looked at his watch. "I believe I will go and try to contact the space station. Wish me luck."

"Tell the Captain I'll be on my way tomorrow and to have the welcome committee ready in about a week," Armand said.

Tennenboum walked away, waving with one hand. "I will tell him to open a bottle of his finest Scotch for you. You did a great job."

As he headed for the finished research station, Vendy called after him, "When can we move in, Professor?"

He stopped and turned around. "Tell everyone to pack up their belongings and move into their new home."

He stepped into the elevator and took it up.

Chapter Four

An excerpt from Irwin Hunter's personal log.
June 30th, 2985

It has been exactly forty days since we landed on this forsaken planet. Even though Doctor Bonnet is trying hard to find a way to predict the weather, so far he has not been successful. It is unpredictable. Today it actually warmed up and we've recorded sixteen degrees Celsius. If we're lucky we might even get temperatures in the twenties when July and August come around.

Last week we had a storm. I've never experienced so much rain, such high winds, and so many lightning strikes. It was frightening. I'm afraid to think what the winter will be like. I am just glad that I won't be around for that. The shuttle with another batch of scientists is scheduled for August. I will be leaving this place for good and it won't be too soon.

Zydyk has been trying his luck to land a big fish, but until now he hasn't caught anything larger than five pounds. These critters have an uncanny resemblance to the fish I used to catch on Emerald when I was a kid. Makes one wonder and think about the Universe, God, and how Humans and other creatures started out on the different planets. Is there a common dominator? Hemming was the one who apparently saw a large cat-like creature the first day we were here. Nobody else saw it, but Hemming wouldn't make up something like that. We haven't seen one or anything like it since, but that doesn't mean they don't exist. We've discovered quite a number of small animals, even some bird-like flying creatures. None of them have proved dangerous. Where there are small animals there should be large ones, especially the predatory kind. It is only a matter of time until we stumble across them.

Will we find Humans or humanoids? It would be exciting to be here to witness it.

There is not much to do for me. Everything is working fine as far as lights and power goes. The transmitter is also working. Professor Tennenboum is complaining about the static but I can't do anything about that. The atmosphere on this planet is full of static electricity and electromagnetic radiation. It creates havoc with communication.

I don't have anything to do with the computers. That is Wong's department. He is satisfied with his children, as he calls the drones and bots. Sometimes I think he is in love with the computer that runs the station. He even calls it Mother when he communicates with it.

Talking about love...I think I'm in love with Cara Gunn. That woman is hot. I've had sex with her a few times and she nearly fried my brains when she caused me to climax inside her. She wants to feel my sperm shooting into her. I told her I didn't want to get her pregnant, but she assures me she had anti-pregnancy shots. They are good for at least three years.

I don't know if she screws anyone else. She says she doesn't but I'm not quite sure about that. I've seen Professor Tennenboum checking her out when she goes swimming in the lake, but I'm not too worried about him. He's too old for her. She is only twenty-three and he is more than twice her age. She wouldn't go for an old guy like him, but I could be wrong about that. She is unpredictable. Just like the weather. I am thirteen years her senior, but she told me it didn't matter.

The only other men I worry about are Wong, Professor Maisoneuve, and Kullmann. All three are close to my age. Wong is my friend. I don't think he would go behind my back. He knows about Cara and me because he is my roommate. Kullmann I'm not sure about. He is amiable, jokes around all the time, and acts uninterested, but I've seen him sneak peaks at her. Then again...what healthy, horny man wouldn't?

Maisoneuve is a rebel. He hates authority and does pretty much what he wants. He and Professor Tennenboum are rubbing each other constantly. I don't trust him. I told Cara to watch him and never be alone with him or without a weapon when they take the Landroamer into the wilderness. He is a big, strong man and should he decide to rape her she'd be helpless. I don't believe he has any scruples and wouldn't hesitate to kill her should she make a fuss.

Of course, there is a good chance I am overreacting, but I'm a suspicious guy by nature and I don't trust people.

Tomorrow I'll be going out with Doctor Roland in the Landroamer. He is the mapmaker and a pretty damn good one. He is very meticulous and loves what he does. I'll be driving the Roamer and also go along as a guard. Professor Tennenboum insists that nobody goes anywhere without a weapon. Usually I'm the one who guards the area around the station, but when I'm not there Wong takes over my job.

I enjoy the outings with Doctor Roland. At first impression he seems uptight and cold. He has these piercing black eyes and seems to look right through you, but he is a really nice guy when you get to know him.

I'm looking forward to tomorrow.

Chapter Five

When sixteen people live together in close proximity and on an alien planet filled with unknown dangers it is hard for two people to find some privacy. Hunter was lucky. He shared his cabin with Wong, who gave him the privacy he needed.

"How about you spending some time in the reading room? Cara is coming over for a bit."

Wong gave Hunter a speculative look. "You know, one of these days I'm going to ask you for a favor, my friend, and you'd better deliver. You owe me big." He grinned. "Are you horny again? You two just fucked your brains out two nights ago."

"We don't fuck. We make love."

"What's the difference?"

"A lot but you wouldn't know it. You should ask Regina or Beth if they want to join you in your cabin. Maybe then you'll find out what I'm talking about. They're both good-looking women." Hunter squinted at Wong. "Or haven't you noticed?"

"They're scientists. They have no time for playing house."

"You'll never know until you ask them. You might be surprised. Even scientists need a piece of tail sometimes. Now go, she'll be here any minute."

Just as Wong reached for the door handle, someone knocked against the door from the outside. He opened it and looked at the woman standing in the corridor. "Hello, Cara. Hunter is quite tired today. Maybe I can be of service."

Cara laughed merrily. "Let me pass before I slug you one, little man." She threw him a look from under lowered lashes. "One day I'll surprise you and take you up on your offer."

He moved aside to let her into the room and leered at her. "I'm ready now. How about a threesome?"

She put her finger on his nose. "Maybe next time. Now go away!"

"Promises. All I ever get is promises."

"I have a promise for you, lover," Hunter called from his bunk. "If you're not gone in ten seconds I'll create a short circuit in one of your drones and blame it on you."

"I'm going. I hope you both blow up in one great ball of fire. Then I'll have this room all to myself." Wong closed the door behind him. Even though the doors and walls were reasonably soundproof Hunter could still hear his muffled laughter in the corridor.

Cara sighed. "I thought he'd never leave. Does he always talk this much?"

"Sometimes even more." Hunter held out a hand. "Take off your clothes and come here."

He watched her as she opened the top button of her blouse. With deliberate slowness she opened another button and then another one until her blouse fell open. Slipping it off her shoulders, she bared her breasts to his gaze. He reached for her, but she eluded his grasp.

"Not yet," she whispered huskily.

Then she pushed her pants past her hips, revealing lacey panties. Her thick Venus mound was clearly visible through the thin material. Stepping out of her pants one leg at a time, she struck a pose to let his eyes feast on her voluptuous body. She knew he liked to look at her, and he appreciated that.

"You are so beautiful," he said, his voice thick with desire. He felt his penis rising inside his pants. "I'm a lucky guy."

Hooking her fingers into the top of her panties, she slowly rolled them down her smooth belly to expose the puffy lips of her pussy. Wriggling her legs she let the panties slip down until they pooled around her ankles. Then she kicked them away and moved in front of him, her long legs spread apart. "Lick me," she commanded.

He put his hands on her round buttocks and pulled her to him. Putting his lips on her shaved pubis, he pushed his tongue between her labia and began licking her. She grabbed his hair and pulled his head against her belly.

"That feels so good," she moaned loudly. "Put your tongue inside me."

Entering her moist vagina, he moved his tongue in and out of her. She exhaled sharply and cried out when she experienced a small orgasm. "I can't wait any longer," she gasped. With feverish haste, she opened his belt and pulled his pants down to his knees to free his erect penis. Straddling him, she sat in his lap and rubbed her clit on his hard mast.

She was wet and slippery and snapped her lower body back and forth erratically. He held her hips and pushed up, sliding with ease into her soft sheath. She moaned, sounding like a wounded fawn. Rotating her hips, she milked him enthusiastically. He crushed her to him and let her have her way, enjoying the feel of her moving buttocks in his hands.

After experiencing a couple of orgasms, she released him and tugged on his shirt. “I want you naked so I can feel your hard chest against my breasts,” she breathed.

“Then we have the same desire. I want to feel your soft breasts against my chest,” he said, helping her with the shirt.

She climbed onto his bunk and lay on her back, legs apart. He moved between them and let her guide him back into her warm, moist vessel. With a deep groan, he pushed into her and fucked her with steady strokes.

They didn’t speak words but communicated with their bodies, hammering against each other for a long time. Once in a while she would whimper softly when an orgasm shook her body. He stopped moving and held her in his strong arms until she ceased shaking. Then he resumed his lovemaking.

After experiencing one of her orgasms, she whispered, “Take me from behind.”

He kissed her and pulled out of her. She slipped off the bed, stood on the floor, and rested her upper body on the bunk. He stepped behind her, guided his penis between her quivering round cheeks, and eased it back into her greased pussy. She pushed against him, taking him deep into her.

He clamped his hands around her moving hips and forcefully pounded his groin against her buttocks, flattening them with every thrust.

It didn’t take long before she had another powerful orgasm. Letting out a loud squeal, she doused him with her discharge. “That was wonderful,” she exclaimed after calming down. “I just love that fat black cock of yours. Now, let me sit on you so I can make you come inside me.”

He laughed softly and stretched out on his bunk. She climbed on top of him. He watched with anticipation as she lowered her sex-organ onto his strutting cock. She loved to tease him with her pussy. Taking only his engorged head between her thick labia, she closed her eyes and caressed his penis with her clitoris. Her mouth opened and her breath came in little gasps as she brought herself to another orgasm.

With a loud cry, she sank into his lap and slipped her satiny sheath over his tingling pole. He knew he was nearing the end of his control. From deep inside him the tremor rose and rolled like a tidal wave through his system. Digging his fingers into her breasts, he pushed up. She knew that he was about to come and began squeezing his penis with the inside walls of her pussy.

His loud grunts of pleasure echoed from the walls as he exploded inside her clutching pussy. She pressed her buttocks into his groin, shaking above him as her own pleasure overcame her. After what seemed an eternity, she collapsed on top of him, her breasts soft and spongy against his heaving chest, her thick hair spilling across his face. Her breath came in loud gasps and they lay like that for a long time.

"That was the best one yet," she finally said, still breathing hard. "You are a wild beast, Hunter. I thought I was having sex with a bull the way you bellowed. It's a lucky thing these walls are soundproof."

He laughed into her hair. "You're not exactly a tame little pussycat, more like a crazy passionate wildcat and I love every part of your delectable body." He blew away strands of her hair and licked her neck. "You taste salty, but I love even that."

She kissed him on the lips. Then she rolled off him and snuggled against him, one leg thrown across his lower body. "Do you love only my body or do you love me, Irwin?"

He stroked her hair. "I love you, Cara. The fact that you have a beautiful body helps, of course, but I love your free and wild spirit. I love listening to your voice and take great enjoyment in watching you walk. I can't get enough of you, ever. You're in my thoughts all the time and I was hoping we could make our arrangement more permanent."

She lay silent in his embrace for a long time, stroking his chest with her fingers.

Just when he thought she had gone to sleep, she said, "I was afraid you would say that, Irwin. I love you too, but I'm not ready to make a commitment…not yet. Sex with you is great, mind-blowing, and I enjoy it immensely. I feel comfortable with you and when I'm with you I am happy, but I do not want to bind myself to one man. I'm sorry and I hope you understand."

"I'm trying to." He didn't know what else to say. He had hoped for more, hoped for some kind of assurance that he was the only man in her life right now.

"Don't be disappointed," she said, kissing him gently. "I do love you, you know."

"Are you fucking another man?" He said it without thinking and felt sorry after the words left his lips.

She sat up and stared at him, an angry look in her face. "It would be none of your business if I did. To answer your question, no, I'm not fucking another man."

He sighed. "I apologize for asking. It just came out because, I guess, it bothered me."

He face softened. She stroked his cheek. "I understand. Maybe I should be flattered that you care so much. I never had anyone care for me. Life on the asteroids is hard. There is not much time or opportunity for socializing and creating friendships. We spent most of our time trying to survive."

Her hand fondled his penis. She laughed when she felt it reacting in her hand. "I think someone is trying to tell me something."

She stroked him until he had an erection then she slid on top of him and sheathed him with her warm, moist pussy. “Maybe this will calm you down,” she whispered. She moved her lower body with gentle gyrations in his lap.

He moaned and closed his eyes, accepting the gift she gave him, almost certain in his knowledge this might be the last time for a while…perhaps forever.

* * * *

Coming out of a dream he forgot as soon as he opened his eyes, he looked at Wong, who was already dressed and staring down on him. Something in Wong’s face made him ask, “What are you gawking at?”

“I’m surprised you’re asking, Hunter.”

He felt someone stirring beside him and became aware of a warm naked body touching his. When he looked, he saw the exposed body of Cara lying next to him.

“Shit!” he cursed, looking for the thin cover that had slipped away.

“Too late,” Wong said. “I’ve seen everything and more.”

Cara moaned softly and sat up. Rubbing her eyes, she looked first at Hunter and then at Wong. “Hi, Wong. Is anything wrong?” She sounded sleepy, like someone not fully awake.

“Not really, except that you’re in the wrong room and the wrong bed.”

She seemed to wake up. Looking down at her exposed breasts, she giggled. “I’m naked and you are staring at me.” She made no attempts to cover her breasts or the rest of her nude body.

Hunter finally found the blanket and pulled it over his and part of Cara’s body. “I will have a good talk with you later, Wong. You’re a horny voyeur. Now look away!”

“Don’t be so harsh with your friend. I don’t mind if he looks at me.” She smiled. “I’m not ashamed of my body.”

“But I mind.” Hunter glared at Wong.

Wong chuckled. “I’ve seen her naked before. Everybody has. Every morning down by the lake. So what’s the big deal? She doesn’t belong to you, Hunter.”

Cara pushed away the covers and climbed out of the bunk. Stretching her nude body, she yawned. “I guess I’ll go and take a shower. I feel a bit grimy and still sleepy.” She giggled. “You two boys feel like joining me in the shower? It could be fun.”

Hunter stared at her as she pushed out her breasts and buttocks, turning her body lazily. “What’s wrong with you, Cara?” he asked angrily.

Her face was cool when she looked at him. “Nothing is wrong with me, Hunter. I’ve made a decision, that’s all.” She bent down and took her time picking up her clothes. He could see her swollen labia clearly below her white round cheeks. So could Wong.

Angry and fuming at her behavior, he pulled the covers over his head and turned toward the wall. He heard the soft rustling of her clothes as she slipped into them. He didn't look up when the door opened and she walked out.

"She's gone," Wong said softly. Then he chuckled. "I guess you didn't satisfy her last night."

"Oh, shut up!"

"You don't have to be mad at me, Hunter. I'm not the one who had a woman in my bed all night. Imagine my surprise when I looked into your bunk this morning and saw a pair of naked buttocks staring at me. Not yours but Cara's. Not that I mind. She does have a nice ass."

Hunter glared at him, anger boiling inside him. Then he suddenly relaxed and laughed. "You are right. She has a nice ass. Everything about her is nice. And you are correct when you said she doesn't belong to me. I have a feeling it's over between us."

"Why?"

Hunter shrugged and swung his feet onto the floor. "She's not ready for a commitment. Her words not mine. Too bad, I really like her."

"Maybe she'll come around again."

"Maybe, but I doubt that. She's…Cara, a free spirit who doesn't want to be tamed. I love that about her, but it is not something working in my favor. I guess I should be happy with what she gave me." He searched for his clothes and found them under the only chair in the room. "I'll hit the showers. See you later."

Wong nodded. "I'm going to check up on Mother. Just to make sure she's all right."

"It's not a she, Wong. It's a computer. A construct. Don't treat it like a human being."

"You should be the last person to talk that way. You have an invisible companion you call Dawn strapped to your wrist. I never asked you why you call it that."

Hunter hesitated, embarrassed to tell Wong.

"Well?"

"If you must know, Dawn was the name of a girl I once knew. A long time ago."

"You loved her?"

"Damn it, yes, I loved her. She broke my heart when she left me for another man." His voice couldn't hide the bitterness.

"That's why you're so angry with Cara. You don't trust women."

"No, I don't.

* * * *

Professor Tennenboum studied the map on the large computer screen. “You’ve done an excellent job, Doctor Roland.”

“I could have done a better job had I the use of an airborne vehicle. Why don’t we have one?”

“Captain Cunningham didn’t think it was necessary. He needs every shuttle to explore Nu-Eden. That is his priority. By the way, where did you say you saw those ruins?”

Roland pointed to a spot. “Right about here. We didn’t have much time to do any exploring because it was late in the day and we saw them only from afar through our binoculars. I wouldn’t mind going there and spending a couple of days.” He pulled his thin lips into a smile. His dark piercing eyes stared at Tennenboum. “I want you to keep that off the records until we are sure those are actual ruins. The ground there is quite hard and the terrain rough. They could have been nothing but an interesting rock formation.”

“We can’t assume anything. I am as interested as you in making certain. Let’s plan on going there the day after tomorrow and spend a few days checking out the area. I’m coming with you.” He paused and rubbed his chin. “I think we should take Maisoneuve with us…as much as I despise that man. He is an archeologist and the best candidate for this discovery.”

“I have to agree, especially since he was the one who actually discovered the…what we assume to be…ruins. He would never forgive us if he wouldn’t be part of the team. I suggest we also take Hunter. His experience as an outdoorsman will make him a valuable asset should we decide to stay there longer. Besides, I trust him driving the Landroamer.”

“How about taking Bonnet along? He can see things others can’t. He might be able to fill in the missing pieces.”

Roland chuckled. “As long as he doesn’t talk too much I have no problem. His voice always reminds me of the sound you hear when you rub two pieces of sandpaper against each other. It gets annoying after a while.”

“There is that but he is a capable man. That’s why I picked him as a member of this team.” Tennenboum looked thoughtful. “He and Vendy Sherbo seem to have taken a liking to each other. He indicated he might go back with the shuttle because of her. I’d hate to see that happening.”

Roland lifted one thin shoulder. “He hasn’t been too successful in predicting the weather. I wouldn’t miss him.”

Chapter Six

It looked like the sunny weather would stay with them for the rest of the day. It was the middle of August according to the old calendar and the temperature might even break the record of plus twenty-two from the previous day by a degree or two.

"Can we expect any rain in the next few days?" Roland asked, addressing Bonnet who sat in the backseat behind Maisoneuve.

Bonnet shrugged. "The weather on this planet is not easy to predict. We haven't been here long enough for me to make an accurate model. As far as I can see the prospect of a few warm sunny days is good."

"That makes me feel much better, Doctor Bonnet. It is good to have an expert with us. Of course, anyone can make that prediction just by looking at the clouds in the sky. Today there are only a few small ones. I'd say we have a thirty percent chance of rain. Thirty percent is always a good number. It provides us with an open door in case it does rain." Roland looked at Tennenboum and winked.

Tennenboum didn't react to Roland's remark and gesture and turned his head back to stare out of the front windshield. He had no intentions in taking sides. He knew both men quite well by now. Roland didn't care much for Bonnet and he made it known as often as possible. Maybe it had not been such a good idea to take Bonnet along.

On the other hand, Bonnet didn't seem to take Roland's contemptuous remarks too seriously, a fact Tennenboum appreciated. His respect for the young man had grown over time, but he had to admit Bonnet sometimes tended to complain and whine a bit too much. "I suggest we take the weather as it comes. Nothing we can do about it anyway," he said. "I for one am enjoying these warm temperatures and the sunshine." He kept his tone light. "How about you, Mr. Hunter? You are an outdoorsman and should appreciate this good weather."

Hunter chuckled, taking his eyes off the rocky ground for a moment to glance at Tennenboum. "As much as you, Professor. Thank you for taking me along. It will be a nice change spending a few days outdoors and sleeping in a tent. I'm looking forward to sitting around a campfire instead of watching holograms all night."

"I fully agree. I can't wait to get a closer look at those ruins," Maisoneuve rumbled. "Finally something decent to study."

Tennenboum leaned back in his seat and relaxed.

As long as you're all happy.

The terrain changed from a flat grassy prairie to gently rising mounds of packed soil and sand, covered with large and small rocks. Cactus-like plants grew in large clumps over most of the hilly land. The few trees they saw were low-growing and covered with spindly branches, unlike in the forest where the trees were tall and the vegetation thick, not easily penetrated with the Landroamer.

Thinking about the forest made Tennenboum wonder about something. "Is there a reason we are traveling so far away from the forest?"

"Yes, there is. A very good reason. I guess you don't remember the map?" Roland asked. When Tennenboum shook his head, he said, "There is a huge swamp coming up running alongside the forest. We got stuck there once and we had a hard time getting out of the quagmire."

"You never told me."

Roland chuckled softly. "I can't burden you with everything that happens, Professor."

"I appreciate that but some things should be put into the reports for future reference."

"Well, you know about it now." Roland pointed out of the open window. "There are those deer I told you about."

Tennenboum squinted against the sun and looked across the rolling land. At first he didn't see them, but then his eyes adjusted and he let out a soft grunt. "That is quite a large herd."

"I estimate possibly around eighty to a hundred animals."

Tennenboum reached for his binoculars and looked through them. The screen inside created the illusion of the observer practically standing among the animals. He had the sensation he could almost touch them. "They don't seem to be as large as the deer I am familiar with."

"No, in fact they are not much larger than a big dog, but they display an uncanny resemblance to the Cervidae family. At least that is what Mr. Hunter told me. He is quite knowledgeable when it comes to game animals, but Doctor Renaldo would be better able to categorize them."

"Did Doctor Renaldo get a chance to study them?"

"No. It's only been a few days since we spotted the first ones. I haven't talked to him about it."

"He'll be excited. Maybe I should have asked him to come along."

"There will be plenty of time for him to study and catalog all of the animals we've discovered so far."

"No predators yet?"

"No large ones but they are there, I'm certain of it. By their very nature they have to be elusive and cautious."

"I'm still wondering about the tiger-like animal Hemming apparently saw during our first days here," Tennenboum mused. "Why haven't we seen it since?"

"If he indeed spotted one it could have been a lonely predator on the prowl and it moved away again," Hunter ventured. "Predatory animals are territorial and roam large areas. They are usually more intelligent than the animals they prey on and this one may have perceived us as a threat in need to be studied. Just because we haven't seen it doesn't mean it isn't around. It may be watching us right now...from a distance; perhaps hiding behind one of those cactus-like plants."

"I've done some hunting in my time and I know a little bit about animals," Maisoneuve said. "Predators are cautious by nature and forever wary about confronting other, possibly larger and stronger, predators. You'll never see them unless they want to be seen."

"That is true," Hunter agreed. "Of course, they are also very curious and if they are large and confident enough they will make an appearance and challenge an intruder into their territory."

"I wouldn't complain if I never saw any dangerous animals," Bonnet said.

"Unfortunately, were there are animals like these deer there will inevitably also be predators who feed on them. That is the way things are everywhere. There has to be a balance, otherwise these plant eaters would over-breed in a short time." Maisoneuve almost sounded like a lecturer.

"It seems the deer are on the way to the grassland," Tennenboum mused. "There certainly isn't much to eat for them in this terrain."

"You're right. They may be migrating at this time of year," Hunter agreed. "We might see more herds like this one."

Tennenboum put down his binoculars. "I guess we'd better move on. I'm curious to get to the site where you saw the ruins."

"Alleged ruins," Roland cautioned. "As I already pointed out, they may have been nothing more than rocks. I hope none of you will be disappointed."

"If nothing else we did get some time away from the station." Hunter stirred the Landroamer across the rugged terrain. His thick lips bared white teeth. "I wouldn't mind doing a bit of hunting if time permits. It would be nice to broil some fresh steaks over a fire."

Bonnet let out a snort of disgust. "Why is it that some people only think of killing one when they see beautiful animals like these? We can survive without eating meat."

"I gather you don't eat meat?" Hunter ventured.

"No, I don't."

"I've seen you eat meat," Roland said, somewhat gleefully, apparently happy to trip up Bonnet.

"That's different. You know as well as I that the meat from the food synthesizer is artificial and doesn't come from live animals." Bonnet spoke loudly, sounding almost like an irritated woman with his high, nasal voice. He was obviously quite aware of the fact Roland was needling him.

"But the steaks look and taste like real steaks." Roland grinned, not giving up. "How do you know someone like Hunter here didn't substitute the artificial meat with real meat?" He gave Hunter a conspiratorial wink.

"My stomach would know, believe me. A lifetime of not eating meat conditions one's body." Bonnet forced a chuckle. "I'm surprised you don't know that, Doctor Roland. You seem to be knowledgeable about everything else…even how to predict the weather."

"Touché," Maisoneuve said, applauding. "If you gentlemen are finished sparring, perhaps we can discuss something else?"

"I agree." Tennenboum heaved a silent sigh. He turned around in his seat to look at Maisoneuve. "I understand you were one of the archeologists who discovered ruins of an ancient civilization on Thunderball."

Maisoneuve nodded. "Yes, I was."

"I'd like to hear more about that." Even though Maisoneuve had been annoying and belligerent in the beginning, he seemed to have mellowed somewhat and actually kept his temper under control. Tennenboum was determined to keep it friendly between them. He made every effort not to antagonize the man, who, to his surprise, turned out to be quite amiable and helpful.

"Well, there really isn't much to tell. As far as we could determine, those ruins dated back about fifty thousand years. According to our findings, they belonged to a race of intelligent reptilian beings that worked metals and lived in large communities. We don't know why they disappeared. We couldn't find any descendants." Maisoneuve stared at the bleak landscape outside the window on his side. "It's been ten years for me since that first discovery. Even though I was on the team, my research was never acknowledged. That's why I'm so excited about this find. I hope I'll get a chance to do a more intensive study should there really be some ruins."

"At least you wouldn't have any competition with your studies," Tennenboum said. "All the credit will go to you. There should be some satisfaction in that."

Maisoneuve laughed good-humoredly. "Sometimes even I get lucky."

The Landroamer traveled over rough terrain at the moment and Hunter slowed down to avoid colliding with some of the larger boulders. The ground was solid but covered with rocks of all sizes as if thrown there by a giant's careless hand.

"I wouldn't want to travel this way by night," Tennenboum commented.

"That's why we didn't check out those ruins," Roland said. "Traveling by night is too dangerous. Not only is the terrain treacherous, but we don't know what kind of night creatures we might run across." He chuckled. "There are no roads across this barren stretch of land...yet."

"I doubt there'll ever be any roads here," Bonnet said. "This place is not friendly."

"That's because we don't know much about it. Once we've mapped this whole area, get to know the safe and unsafe places and keep records of what types of animals inhabit the land and air, it will become familiar and seem less hostile." Roland pointed at one of the tall spiny plants nearby. "See the bright-red furry ball on top of that plant? We don't know yet what it is. Hunter thinks it is an animal living in symbiosis with the plant. I believe it is part of the plant...a part that gathers food for the plant. We've observed it jumping to the ground, catch one of the small rodents we've also discovered and then return to its place."

"Why would you think it is part of the plant?" Tennenboum asked.

"Because I may have seen a thin strand connecting the furry ball with the plant."

"May have seen? You're not sure?"

Roland shook his head. "I can't be certain of what I saw. We didn't dare go too close to the plant because we have not determined if it is harmless to Humans. This is a job for Doctor Ratzenberger or Doctor Renaldo."

"You've done the right thing to stay away," Tennenboum agreed. "We can't be too careful. The most beautiful, harmless looking plant may turn out to be extremely dangerous. That is the reason we are here...to study and record our findings so the people who come after us can walk around safely and be aware of the dangers."

"Do you really believe some day Humans might live on this planet?" Bonnet was looking out of the rear window at the cactus-like plant with the furry red ball. "If that thing on top is part of the plant then we're looking at a meat-eating plant."

"One that may only eat small rodents," Tennenboum said. "Should that be the case we have nothing to fear from it. As to your first question...we can only speculate. This planet is not ideal but it would support human life. Humans adapt to all kinds of conditions. Take for example the Inuit on Earth who survived in a hostile environment, living in igloos built from blocks of snow. In the long winter they didn't see the sun for months, yet they continued to exist, eating raw meat and fish in the winter and berries in the short summer."

"Lucky for Doctor Bonnet he wasn't born an Inuit," Roland said, chuckling. "He would have never survived on a diet of whale blubber."

Maisoneuve let out a rumbling laugh. "Even though I don't mind a good piece of broiled meat I think even I would draw the line at eating raw whale meat."

Tennenboum shook his head, annoyed at Roland for not giving up poking fun at Bonnet. "The only whales on Earth are in the Sanctuaries and I doubt if any of us will ever get a chance to eat whale meat, raw or cooked," he said, trying to smooth out things. The last thing he needed was dissention among the small team. He was beginning to doubt the wisdom of bringing Bonnet along on this trip. Perhaps it would have been better had he left him behind and brought Jennifer Ratzenberger instead. She was a biologist and would have been able to begin cataloging the different animals they encountered so far.

He shrugged and looked at Hunter who was concentrating on keeping the Landroamer on a steady course. "You've been this way before with Doctor Roland, haven't you Mr. Hunter?"

Hunter nodded, keeping his eyes on the non-existent road. "I have, that's why I'm so careful driving right now. I know what lies ahead, but we'll be leaving this particular stretch behind soon, Professor. I'll be happy to join in the conversation then." He smiled and glanced sideways. "Sorry if I sound abrupt but I need to concentrate on my driving."

Tennenboum smiled back. "Our lives are in your capable hands, Mr. Hunter. I won't bother you with more questions."

They drove on in silence, each of the men contemplating his thoughts. Tennenboum didn't mind relaxing for a while and just watching the landscape outside go by. As Hunter promised, the boulders were disappearing and the ground didn't look so dry and hard anymore. Stunted trees and shrubs were replacing the cactus-like vegetation, and patches of grass sprouted from the sandy soil. The grass became thicker and taller as they drove on.

When they topped a hill, Tennenboum saw the river he remembered from Roland's map. A carpet of lush green grass covered the ground on each side of the river. "It seems this region is much more fertile than the area around the station," he remarked.

"It seems that way," Roland agreed.

As they neared the river, Hunter turned the Landroamer and drove in a northerly direction, keeping the river to the right. "We saw a flock of water birds here the last time," Hunter said.

As if the confirm his words, a dark cloud of winged creatures burst out of the high grass ahead of them and circled above them, emitting high-pitched cries and shrill whistles.

"I think they are annoyed at us for disturbing them." Hunter craned his neck to look at the flock. "They are large enough to make a good meal. There are certainly plenty of them."

"Is that all you think of, Mr. Hunter?" Bonnet asked. "Do you ever look at a creature without the desire to shoot it?"

"Of course I do. I wouldn't shoot a songbird, for instance. But if it is a food animal I want to eat it. After all…I am a hunter." He chuckled. "I have to live up to my name. Hunting is in my blood. My father taught me how to hunt when I was barely old enough to hold a rifle. And my grandfather taught my father. We've been hunters for many generations." He laughed cheerfully. "Pun intended."

"Where did you do all of your hunting?" Maisoneuve asked.

"On Emerald. I grew up there."

"Emerald, huh?" Maisoneuve mused. "That's a harsh planet. I assume your parents farmed there?"

"That's correct. Actually, my great-grandfather moved there when the planet was first opened up for colonization. Much has changed since then, of course. We are quite modern and civilized now."

"Good hunting there?"

"Emerald boasts huge forests and vast savannahs. They are teeming with game animals." Hunter chuckled. "Some are quite nasty and are providing a hunter with great challenges."

"Sounds interesting. When this is all over I might visit your home planet and do some hunting. Perhaps you can be my guide."

"That all sounds so barbaric," Bonnet said. "I don't believe in killing animals for food and certainly not for what some people call sport. We Humans should have evolved and outgrown such uncivilized behavior by now."

"I like hunting," Maisoneuve said. "And as for not killing for food…well, when you're starving and desperate you will kill to stay alive, unless you don't possess a strong will to survive. A couple of years ago I was with an exploration team on Apollo Three when our shuttle went down on a bare island in the middle of a huge lake. The island was used as a breeding ground by cuddly looking amphibians. They were friendly and curious. When we ran out of rations we had no choice but to kill a few of these cuddly creatures. They didn't even taste good, but they kept us alive."

"I would rather die than kill another creature," Bonnet said with conviction.

"That of course is your choice." Maisoneuve shook his head, obviously not agreeing with Bonnet's principles. "I choose to live. Since the beginning of time one creature has killed another one to survive. Carnivores eat only meat, herbivores only vegetable matter. Omnivores eat both. Humans are omnivores and that is a fact. Even you can't deny that, Doctor Bonnet. That's how nature designed it, on Earth and on other planets."

"That may be so, but I still won't eat meat," Bonnet said stubbornly.

"Which also is your choice, but don't force others to live by your philosophy."

"I agree," Roland said. "Not everyone..." he stopped talking in mid-sentence. Then he pointed out of the window on his side. "Something moved over there. I hope what I believe I saw was only a figment of my imagination."

Tennenboum turned around in his seat to look at Roland. "What do you believe you saw?"

"I only saw a glimpse of what looked like a head covered with shaggy hair, but it scared the crap out of me. The head was large and the gaping jaws were filled with long teeth." Roland stared out of the window. "Whatever it was...that head belonged to a huge animal."

"Stop the Roamer," Tennenboum ordered Hunter. "I want to check it out."

"I would advise against investigating on foot," Maisoneuve cautioned.

"I have no such intentions." Tennenboum studied the terrain. "Can you take us there with the Landroamer, Mr. Hunter?"

"I can try. The grass is tall in that direction but I believe we shouldn't have any problems navigating through the grass, as long as we don't come across any boulders. I'm familiar with this stretch since I've traveled this way before, but we never ventured too close to the river." He turned the steering wheel and headed in the direction Roland indicated.

He drove slowly, watching the ground and their surroundings. The windows were down, letting in the smells and sounds from outside. Tennenboum was suddenly aware of the warm air brushing across his face but also of the silence. He remembered hearing all kinds of noises only a short time before.

He was startled by an earsplitting roar and by the shaggy-haired creature bounding into their path out of a thick clump of shrubbery.

"What the hell is that?" Maisoneuve cursed from the seat behind him.

Tennenboum could only stare at the nightmarish creature glaring at them. He knew it had to be of the same species as the one Hemming spotted that first day, and he easily saw it could be mistaken for a tiger but only at first glance. The creature confronting them was much larger; it had six powerful legs with huge paws capable of disemboweling a man with one swipe, and dagger-long teeth that would have been the envy of the most ferocious tiger prowling the jungles on Earth a thousand years ago.

The animal roared again and swung its head back and forth, beating the ground with its tail.

"This is incredible," Roland said. "I think it's challenging us."

"It's huge," Bonnet said. "And look at those claws. Are we safe in here?"

"Quite," Tennenboum assured him.

"What about that spiny ball on the end of its tail? It looks hard enough to smash our windshield."

"No chance of that," Hunter said. "These Landroamers are built tough and nearly impossible to damage, unless we receive a direct hit from a rocket launcher." He smiled. "I would suggest though we close all the windows."

"You might want to shoot this one, Mr. Hunter," Bonnet said. "That shaggy head with its giant canines should make a great trophy on your wall."

Hunter didn't take the bait. "It wouldn't be much of a sport. I like to stalk my prey. Makes it much more challenging."

"And shoot it from a safe distance?" Bonnet laughed. "I don't see much challenge in that. Now…facing this beast armed with maybe only a primitive spear like our ancestors did would be a bit of a challenge."

"Be my guest, Doctor Bonnet," Hunter said. "I'll take a backseat and let you do the honors. This is one trophy I won't even attempt to bag."

"Gentlemen, gentlemen, please." Tennenboum was getting annoyed at the constant bickering between the men. "This is not the time to fling provocations at each other. We have an immediate problem do deal with. How about someone making a recording of this creature? Don't you have the image recorder, Doctor Roland?"

"Yes, I do. Sorry, Professor. I was taken by surprise." Roland lifted the recorder hanging from his neck and pointed it at the angry beast. At that moment a second snarling creature appeared behind the first one, roaring and gnashing its teeth.

"Unbelievable," Roland exclaimed. "At first we don't see any and suddenly there are two of them."

"Either we've interrupted them having dinner," Maisoneuve said, "or we are trespassing into their territory."

"I believe neither." Tennenboum watched in amazement as a small furry bundle tumbled out of the thicket and stood on six shaky legs, staring at them out of large, round eyes. Then a second and a third one joined their sibling, bumping into each other as they tried to reach their parents.

"Seems we've stumbled across a whole family of them." Hunter held up his wrist, the small screen of his device facing the group of felines. "I will have Dawn analyze the behavior of these animals."

Tennenboum knew that by Dawn Hunter meant the personal computer he had strapped to his wrist, a sophisticated device with an artificial intelligence, capable of making decisions and of carrying on intelligent conversations. He wondered how Hunter had come by the expensive and uncommon gadget.

"They are so cute and cuddly," Bonnet said.

"As cute and cuddly as most newly born creatures," Hunter said, chuckling softly. "They'll grow up and turn into savage beasts…just like their parents."

Tennenboum ducked out of reflex when one of the large felines rushed toward their vehicle, jumped and landed on the roof, the spiny ball on the end of its tail smashing into the windshield with a dull thud. The sound of sharp claws scratching across the roof made him hold his breath. "I hope you weren't wrong about the sturdiness of the Landroamer, Mr. Hunter," he shouted trying to make himself heard above the beast's enraged roar.

"I've been wrong before," Hunter shouted back when the hard knob walloped the windshield again, causing it to vibrate with the alarming tinkling of breaking glass. Fortunately the windshield didn't crack.

"That doesn't sound encouraging," Roland commented with a loud voice. "A few more hits like that and it'll scoop us out of here like oysters from their shells."

"I don't believe these beasts like oysters. I have the strong impression they are meat eaters." Maisoneuve's laugh sounded almost as loud as the roaring beast.

"Maybe they are vegetarians like Doctor Bonnet," Roland said when the animal on the roof stopped roaring for a second.

"None of that now, gentlemen," Tennenboum said sharply. "I suggest we execute a fast retreat. Hopefully, we'll lose our new passenger before it manages to poke a hole through the roof or crack our windshield."

Hunter put the gears in reverse. As the Landroamer rolled backward, the beast on the roof let out one more defiant roar before it jumped to the ground. It stood watching them out of yellow eyes, growling loudly and pounding the ground with its spiny knob.

"It seems this fellow has won its first confrontation with the new kid on the block," Maisoneuve commented. "I'll bet it will remember this victory."

"It probably will," Hunter agreed.

"I wonder why it attacked us with such ferocity," Roland observed.

"Because we were a threat to its family. Always use extreme caution when approaching a female with young. It was the first thing my father taught me.

Never come between a mother and her offspring. Even a usually peaceful animal will defend its young…to the death if necessary," Hunter said.

Tennenboum studied the snarling catlike creature. "These are not peaceful animals," he mused. "I am really happy we didn't decide to go for a little stroll down to the river. To meet this family in the open would have been disastrous for us."

"From now on I won't leave the Landroamer without carrying a weapon," Maisoneuve announced.

"I'm not so sure if I want to leave the safety of the Roamer at all," Bonnet said.

"Nonsense." Tennenboum felt irritated by Bonnet's statement. "We can't stay in here forever. If we want to explore this place we'll have to do so outside. Let's not panic because of this one encounter. This is the first time we ran across them. They can't be that numerous, otherwise we would have seen them a long time ago. I'm not counting the one Hemming saw."

"In any case now we know he didn't make it up," Roland said. "We also know at least another one of these beasts is near the base."

"Unless he saw one of these two. One thing is certain though…they do come close to the base."

"A sobering thought," Bonnet said, "but I still don't see why we should consider killing one when we see them. There is no reason to believe they are usually aggressive. As you said yourself they are only protecting their young."

Tennenboum suppressed the urge to make a comment, but Hunter, Maisoneuve, and Roland roared with laughter.

"You can't really be so naïve, Doctor Bonnet," Maisoneuve said, shaking his head. "Look at those teeth and those paws tipped with razor-sharp claws. They are not the teeth and claws of a harmless vegetarian. They are meant for ripping and tearing. These definitely are meat eaters, my friend. Carnivorus Incarnatus."

"What the hell does that mean?" Bonnet asked loudly.

Maisoneuve chuckled. "It means they are the embodiment of a Carnivore." He laughed at Bonnet's puzzled look. "Carnivorus Incarnatus. Sounds so Latin doesn't it?"

"There is no such word in Latin."

"I know so I made it up." Maisoneuve grinned. "Come on, Doctor Bonnet, lighten up, broaden your horizon, and accept the universe as it is. It will make life much easier for you and the people you associate with. You can't condemn others for their views and their opinions and you can't expect everyone to live according to your principles and personal choices."

"I don't expect that at all but at the same time others should respect my principles."

“I do and I’m sure everyone else does too. I promise I won’t bring up the subject again, and I hope you won’t either.” Maisoneuve looked at Tennenboum. “What do you want us to do, Professor? Do you want us to shoot one so we can dissect it?”

Tennenboum shook his head. “They are no danger to us as long as we are inside the Landroamer and there is no need to kill one just so we can study them. The only thing we have to consider from now on is the fact they exist and we must take care when we move around outside.”

“We’ll have to give them a name and I’m not talking about the ridiculous one Professor Maisoneuve came up with,” Bonnet said.

“How about Tigers,” Tennenboum suggested.

“Sure. Why not? They do resemble the tigers on Earth if you want to ignore the two additional legs.” Bonnet seemed satisfied.

“Doctor Renaldo is the zoologist. He should be the one giving them a proper name,” Roland said.

“We’ll see. Until then it is Tigers.” Tennenboum didn’t feel like starting another discussion.

The giant cat was still watching them, its long snout open, canines gleaming white in powerful jaws. It crouched on its four hind legs ready to spring into action should this strange intruder decide to come closer again. The outside microphones transmitted the rumbling growl coming from the beast’s throat, and it sounded terrifying.

Tennenboum had no intentions to test the animal’s tolerance. “Pull back a little more, Mr. Hunter, and then drive around their den.”

Hunter followed Tennenboum’s orders. Once they were far enough away, he changed the direction of the Landroamer and made a large circle around the hideout of the Tigers.

“Keep your eyes on our surroundings, gentlemen,” Tennenboum said. “It is possible the native inhabitants are loosing their shyness and will be making more appearances. These cats may not be the only dangerous predators around.”

“I can’t agree more, Professor,” Hunter said.

They drove in silence for about an hour, when Hunter suddenly pointed, “See those ragged silhouettes in the distance? Those are the ruins.” His teeth gleamed white as he smiled. “Alleged ruins,” he added, looking at Roland.

Chapter Seven

It took them nearly another two hours to reach the site. Everyone was excited to discover Dr. Roland and his team had not been wrong with their assumption.

What they found were indeed ruins…remains of structures built by intelligent life forms.

Maisoneuve was the first one to reach the low walls of what once had been a small building. He rubbed his large hand across the gray stones…almost like a lover's caress. Wind and water had worn them smooth in places and pitted with tiny holes in others. "No question about it, these are ruins of a home built by intelligent people," he said, grinning with pleasure. It was obvious he could barely contain himself.

"Intelligent, yes," Bonnet commented, "but were they people?"

"I'm only using it as a figure of speech." Maisoneuve examined the wall closer. "They could have been human or at least humanoid. This hole in the wall is a window, and this large rectangle used to be an entrance, closed off with nothing more than a piece of animal hide…or maybe a door made from tree branches to keep out animals."

"How old do you think these ruins are, Professor?" Tennenboum asked.

"From the looks of the worn stones at least a thousand years old, but I could be wrong. I don't know what kind of extreme weather conditions exist on this planet. Does it hail often? Is the rainwater sometimes acid? Alkaline? I don't have a clue, but I'm anxious to find out everything I can about these ruins."

"One thing is clear…what we found here means this planet was at one time populated by a race of beings intelligent enough to erect dwellings to live in, to protect them from the elements and most likely also from dangerous predators," Roland said. "That of course raises the question are they still around?"

"Maybe they were visitors from another planet," Bonnet mused.

"They wouldn't build solid homes like this one, not if they were only visitors." Tennenboum dismissed the idea.

"It is possible they were stranded and forced to stay."

"There may be descendants," Hunter suggested.

"What if there were only males or females?" Bonnet carried on with his theory. "They'd live out their lives and that would be the end of them."

"I doubt this was built by stranded aliens." Maisoneuve looked around. "There are more ruins over there. Seems to me this used to be a village."

"What happened to the people or their descendants who lived here?" Hunter asked.

"Either they died out if we want to adopt Doctor Bonnet's theory or they just moved somewhere else," Tennenboum mused.

"And that could mean they are still around and we need to be on guard." Hunter threw a look at the not so distant forest, his eyes wary, and his posture tense. "They may not be friendly."

"They can't afford to be friendly…not with those Tigers around." Roland hunched his thin shoulders and craned his neck, like a sparrow suddenly aware of a predatory bird circling in the sky. "We've been fortunate we haven't run across them yet, as naïve and unprepared as we've been."

"Let's not draw any hasty conclusions," Tennenboum warned. "If we should run into any indigenous people, we don't want it to be a hostile meeting. It would not be in our best interest. We must never forget it is their planet and we are the uninvited guests."

"I'm only saying we should be careful," Roland protested.

"And we will be." Tennenboum raised a hand, his index finger up, as if giving a lecture. "I don't want to have a repeat of our home planet, Earth's, history here. It is full of examples of what can happen when advanced civilizations come in contact with more primitive societies. Look at the Americas…the native population was considered subhuman and nearly wiped out in many cases. The natives in Africa were captured and used as slaves for centuries. Humans don't have a good record."

"I'd like to believe we have outgrown all that," Maisoneuve growled. He glanced at Roland. "Of course, some of us apparently haven't. Prejudice toward those who are a little different is still alive and prevalent with some people."

Tennenboum knew Maisoneuve was referring to the animosity between Roland and Bonnet but didn't comment. Sometimes it was best to leave things alone. It was ironic to hear Maisoneuve making that remark. He was not exactly the epitome of tolerance. "As long as we are all on the same wave length here," he said, "everything will go well."

"Don't worry, Professor Tennenboum. We are all Ambassadors of Good Will here," Bonnet said. He threw a look at Roland. "Right, Doctor Roland?"

Tennenboum suppressed a smile, feeling guilty. Listening to Bonnet's nasal voice and seeing the small square mustache quivering on his upper lip made it sometimes difficult to take the man seriously.

"Right, Roland?" Bonnet said again.

Roland gave him a condescending look. "If you say so, Bonnet."

Tennenboum shrugged and followed Maisoneuve, who started to walk away from the group. "I suppose you're quite excited about our find," he said. "There is nobody here who will dispute your right to investigate these ruins. The credit will be all yours."

Maisoneuve chuckled. "In a way it is academic. By the time I will be able to publish my findings too many years will have past on Earth to make a great impact. Other researchers will discover perhaps more important evidence of alien civilizations closer to Earth and the people I would really like to impress may not be alive anymore or not care about me."

"Ah, don't be so pessimistic, Professor." Tennenboum favored the big man with a smile. "You'll be a famous man some day. I have a feeling this planet has many mysterious places waiting to be discovered and you have a front seat to it all." He turned when he heard the crunching of small rocks by someone dislodging them with his boots.

"Gentlemen, I suggest we should think about setting up our shelter. It is getting dark." Hunter sounded concerned. "Ruins like this attract predators, especially during the night."

Tennenboum nodded. "You're right. In fact, my stomach tells me it is time for some food. I wouldn't mind having something to eat and being inside the protective walls of the shelter before dark."

It was obvious Maisoneuve forced himself to leave the ruins. He touched one of the crumbling pillars holding up a partially collapsed roof with an almost loving gesture.

"It will still be here tomorrow, Maisoneuve," Tennenboum said, gently. "We'll give you enough time to study this place."

Maisoneuve grinned sadly. "There is enough material here to keep me and a whole team busy for years. You can't give me those years."

"No, I can't do that," Tennenboum agreed. "But we'll stay a few days…that I can do. Perhaps at a later date we can set up a small research station here and you can spend more time."

"I'm almost positive these are not the only ruins," Hunter said. "There will be more sites like this. Maybe we'll even find a village still used by indigenous peoples. That would be more exciting than this assembly of dead rocks."

"Not to me," Maisoneuve said. "I study dead things. I would almost prefer we'd never find any survivors."

It didn't take long to erect the shelter. Tennenboum had slept in similar constructions before, but it never failed to amaze him to see the folded walls open up and metamorphose into a structure large enough to house a dozen people comfortably. From afar it looked like the silvery halve of a giant soap bubble stuck onto the rocky ground. An oval opening provided entry into the bubble, only to close almost immediately behind the intruder, open barely long enough to allow a glimpse of the interior. Of course, Tennenboum knew what it looked like inside.

A floor made from tough elastic material kept out unwanted visitors who might want to sneak in using the ground as an entrance. A fixture in the ceiling provided light. An air-conditioning unit cooled down the air, and heating elements in the walls created warmth should it get cold.

There was plenty of room for the five sleeping cots Hunter retrieved from the storage area of the Landroamer, and Tennenboum was grateful for Hunter's foresight to load them into the Roamer in the first place. At his age sleeping on the ground was not his idea of comfort.

The walls of the shelter were tough enough to protect the sleepers from the elements and from predators. Even the claws of the Tigers wouldn't be able to rip the fabric into shreds…at least Tennenboum hoped so.

It was dark by the time everything was ready, but they installed a powerful floodlight to illuminate the area in front of the shelter. Tennenboum felt edgy, listening to the sounds of the night dwellers, imagining a pack of hungry Tigers prowling their camp at a safe distance, waiting for the lights and the campfire to be extinguished so they could move in to sample the meat of the alien intruders into their world.

The night was much noisier than back at the research station. Even though he didn't hear any frightening roars or anything advertising the presence of large predators, the shrill cries and chirpings of small creatures made him aware this planet was not devoid of life.

"I wish there would have been an opportunity to bag one of those deer." Roland interrupted the silence between the men. "We could have roasted a few succulent pieces of meat over this fire instead of just staring into the flames." He reached for one of the sandwiches in the cooler and held it against his nose. "Smells like real sausage but knowing it is nothing but plant fibers somehow makes it less exciting to eat."

"Tastes fine to me," Bonnet said. "I don't feel guilty eating it, because I know it comes from a plant. No living animal had to give up its life force so I could live."

Maisoneuve grunted, "Let's not start that again, gentlemen. I want to enjoy being out here in the wilderness, breathing fresh air, and hearing the sounds of life all around me. Tomorrow I have an exciting task ahead of me. I'm thrilled and happy, so please don't spoil my mood by making me listen to you two bickering over petty issues."

"It's not…" Bonnet started.

Tennenboum interrupted him. "I have to take sides with Professor Maisoneuve. We have made an important discovery and we should all concentrate on finding out as much as we can about these ruins. What kind of beings left them behind, are their descendants still around, and so forth. Those are the most important issues at hand right now."

"What about the Tigers? I'd say they are equally important," Hunter said.

"Perhaps even more so." Roland gave Hunter a nod of agreement. "They could pose great danger to us. In fact, I feel a bit uneasy and vulnerable right now sitting here in the open."

"They are not necessarily night-hunters," Maisoneuve said. "We might be safer from them during the night than during the day."

"If they're like the great cats I'm familiar with they will hunt by night," Hunter cautioned. "Tonight I'll set up a Guard-Dog just to be on the safe side."

"I hope you all have large bladders," Maisoneuve joked. "It may not be safe to go outside during the night."

"That could pose a bit of a problem. I usually have to get up at least once." Bonnet's voice sounded even higher than usual.

"We'll leave one of the flood lamps from the Landroamer on. That should keep the beasts away…I hope," Tennenboum said, trying to exude confidence he didn't feel.

I hope I can sleep through the night. The thought of having to step too far away from the safety of the shelter doesn't exactly get me excited.

The fire crackled and glowing sparks exploded when someone threw another piece of wood onto the glowing coals, startling Tennenboum, and he realized he must have dozed off for a short moment. He lifted his head and listened intently to the sounds surrounding them, staring into the darkness beyond the circle of light. He drew a few deep breaths to calm his nerves. The smell of the burning wood was strong in his nostrils, masking the by now familiar odors in the air of this alien planet. He remembered the air on Earth, polluted and poisoned through overpopulation and the clearing of oxygen-producing boreal forests and jungles centuries ago.

Everything seemed suddenly so unreal. Here he was, sitting around a campfire, afraid to walk away from it, worried about something nobody on Earth worried about anymore…being attacked by a ferocious predator…other than another Human.

The only fierce animals surviving on Earth lived in the reserves and didn't pose any threat. It was different here on this new world. Animals roamed free and needed to be feared. Until now they hadn't been concerned, but things had changed. Now they knew the forest and plains were not peaceful. Man was not the only dangerous animal on this planet.

He sighed and looked at the others. "I think it's time we call it a night. I'm suddenly quite tired."

"I'm going to stay awhile watching the fire," Hunter said.

* * * *

It rained the next day. Not much but enough to make it uncomfortable. Maisoneuve was not to be deterred by it. He slipped into his raingear and headed for the ruins of the first building. Hunter slung his laser rifle across his shoulder and accompanied him. He grinned at the others before he followed the Professor. "Somebody has to keep an eye on him. He'll be so engrossed in his studies he'll ignore everything else around him. Besides, sitting inside these walls will only make me claustrophobic."

"I have no such problems," Bonnet said. "This rain will give me the opportunity so set up my equipment and the chance to go through my charts."

Roland chuckled. "Perhaps some day you'll have enough data so you can predict the weather more accurately. You never saw this rain coming."

"That's because my charts are not complete," Bonnet retorted.

Hunter let out a snort. "Well, I'll be out of here. You gentlemen enjoy the weather inside this shelter. It looks like a storm is coming." He laughed and stepped outside.

Tennenboum shook his head. Hunter was right. This bickering between Bonnet and Roland had to stop before it became too intolerable. Not for the first time he regretted bringing Bonnet along. Even though he liked the young man, there was something about him that brought out negative vibes in others, especially in Roland. Of course, Roland was not exactly Mister Charming himself.

I should have left them both at the research station. Unfortunately, Roland is the cartographer, and he knows the lay of the land. Without him, we'd probably get lost out here.

"I'm going to work on my maps," Roland said, drawing a silent prayer of thanks from Tennenboum to whatever gods resided on this planet.

He sat down in front of one of the fold-down desks they managed to install the day before. Taking his personal computer out of his pack, he put the small device on the narrow desktop. Activating it, he watched the softly glowing energy cube expanding. It took only moments until he was locked into the main computer at the station. He might as well make use of the time he had here. There was nothing he could do outside…nothing he felt like doing in the rain anyway.

As he stared into the vortex of swirling colors, waiting for the computer to register his identity, a short chiming sound announced somebody was trying to contact him. A moment later the three-dimensional image of Wong's head materialized inside the cube. "Hello, Professor," Wong said. "My bots alerted me to somebody breaking into Mother and I wondered who it could be."

Tennenboum chuckled. "I'm not breaking in, and besides, who else but me would be connecting to the home computer?"

"Who else indeed?" A wide grin cracked Wong's features. "I've been hanging around in the communication's room waiting for some signs of life. I don't have much to do around here. What's my friend Hunter up to? I envy him for being out there with you."

"Hunter is fine. Actually, he and Professor Maisoneuve are digging around in some ruins we've discovered," Tennenboum said casually, knowing the reaction he'd get from Wong. Even though Wong was not an official member of the research team, he was nevertheless quite interested in everything going on around him. This planet intrigued him...one of the reasons he didn't go back to the space station with the construction crew.

"Ruins?" Wong exclaimed, excitement clearly in his expression and voice. "You have actually discovered ruins?"

Tennenboum nodded, smiling.

"Now I'm really jealous of Hunter. I wish I could be there with you."

"Maybe next time, Mr. Wong. We'll probably need you as a guard, because we encountered some possibly dangerous predators. We'll explain everything in more detail when we get back. Anything interesting happened since we've been gone?"

"Nothing special, except Captain Cunningham contacted us last night. He is sending down another team of researchers. Twenty of them. A lieutenant Striker will be the team leader."

"When?"

"In about a couple of weeks. The Captain will let you know when the shuttle leaves."

"Thanks for the info. We'll make sure we're back by then." He chuckled. "Professor Maisoneuve won't be happy. We'll probably have to pry him away from his ruins and tie him up."

Wong grinned. "Is there anything else we need to know, Professor?"

Tennenboum shook his head. "Nothing that won't keep. Now, if you don't mind, I'll sign off, but I'll stay connected to the mainframe. I need to work on some stuff."

"Sure. No problem." Wong's image faded and was replaced by a jumble of spinning colors. When his own face took shape inside the field, Tennenboum leaned back.

"How can I help you, Professor?" the AI asked in Tennenboum's voice.

"Switch to silent mode," Tennenboum instructed.

"As you wish, Professor." The face dissolved and a small keyboard appeared on his desk. He let his fingers slide across the letters and numbers and watched the information emerging on the flat screen inside the energy cube.

* * * *

"I feel I'm wasting my time hanging around here," Roland said on the morning of the fifth day. "I wouldn't mind driving on so I can expand my maps."

Tennenboum agreed. His own feeling of agitation had been building up for a couple of days and he was not against a change in scenery. "I'll talk to Professor Maisoneuve."

The rain lasted only one day and the weather was pleasant. Maisoneuve was happy and in his glory. Tennenboum hated to spoil his good mood.

"How's the digging going?"

Maisoneuve rose inside the small square hole he had cut out with his laser and dusted off his knees. "The ground is packed and quite hard in this area. Most of it is rock, but I believe I'll soon be through. According to my readings, there is a large airspace underneath here, quite likely an underground storage area. I'm hoping to find some artifacts that have been untouched by the elements."

"Well, I wish you luck." Tennenboum hesitated. "The team is getting a bit edgy, especially Doctor Roland. He wants to get on with his surveys. We want to move on."

Maisoneuve shrugged his massive shoulders. "I can't stop you. You're the team leader. Go ahead and do what you must. I'll be fine here." He grinned lopsidedly. "Just don't forget to pick me up when you head back home."

Tennenboum was a bit surprised how calmly Maisoneuve took the news. "You'll be alone here," he said.

"That's okay. I know how to take care of myself." He patted the laser pistol on his hip. "Besides, we haven't seen any signs of the Tigers or any other dangerous animals." His gaze wandered to the silvery dome. "Are you taking the shelter with you?"

"No. We'll probably leave it here permanently. I'm sure you'll want to come back for a longer period of time, perhaps with Miss Seagul. She studies alien life forms. She may be interested in finding out more about the people who built this."

"Miss Seagul hates camping."

"She'll get used to it."

"She may not be inclined to coming out here. You know...just me and her."

"I'll try to persuade Miss Bronsky to join you also. Alien planets are her favorite research objects. She can tuck you in every night and sing you a lullaby. She has a beautiful voice, but I guess you know that." Tennenboum chuckled when he saw Maisoneuve's expression.

"She's a lesbian. I'd rather have Miss Seagul tuck me in." Maisoneuve wiped his brow with one large hand. "It's getting damn hot out here under the sun. Make sure you leave me enough water and food."

"You can have one of the water coolers and a case of rations. Besides, we won't be gone long. I want to be back at the station in a week. We're expecting guests."

"That's right, the shuttle bringing more scientists. I'm looking forward to their arrival. Maybe I'll get a colleague who can share my findings."

Tennenboum didn't know if Maisoneuve was being sarcastic, but he assumed it. "Don't worry, Professor, you'll be the head of this research. Nobody will take the glory away from you. This is your baby."

"Well, that's good. When are you leaving?"

"Today. It's still early enough to put some distance between this place and our next destination…wherever that will be." Tennenboum gave Maisoneuve a friendly smile and walked back to the shelter. The other men were already packing up their belongings.

An hour later they were on their way. When Tennenboum looked in the rearview mirror, he saw Maisoneuve busy with his digging.

I guess he doesn't miss us. The man is not someone who needs company when he's working on a project. I hope he'll be all right.

After driving in silence for about forty-five minutes, Hunter turned the Roamer toward the river. It had changed direction a while back and was flowing in an easterly direction now. Their goal was to follow the edge of the forest, heading north. "This is the best spot to cross. The river seems calmer here and doesn't look too deep, judging by the rocks sticking above the surface," Hunter explained his decision. He drove down the gentle slope and into the water. There were a couple of times when Tennenboum thought they would get stuck but they made it across safely.

"You told us the other day you got stuck in a swamp," Tennenboum said, addressing Roland. "How did that happen? We had no problem getting across the river."

"The Landroamer was built to float on water but driving through a swamp is a different story. It was like driving through quicksand. Also, there were too many obstructions like dead trees, rocks, and other tough vegetation. I hope we'll be able to skirt the swamp." Roland studied the terrain between them and the distant forest through his binoculars. "From the looks of it we should be fine."

It was late afternoon, when Roland tapped Hunter on the shoulder. "I'd like to stop for awhile and take more readings."

Hunter complied and slowed down, bringing the Roamer to a complete halt. "Good idea. I wouldn't mind walking around and stretching my legs a bit."

Everyone left the vehicle. Tennenboum took a few deep breaths and exhaled slowly, enjoying the fresh, warm air. After breathing artificial air for months on the space station it was such a pleasure to breathe air produced by plants.

"It's beautiful, isn't it?" Hunter said beside him.

"It sure is. It reminds me of the reserves on the African continent, except the air here is cleaner and fresher. Any moment now I expect a herd of Wildebeest racing across the savannah, followed by a couple of lions hunting them."

"We haven't seen any Earth-lions yet, only a family of local Tigers. We should be careful from now on, though. This high grass can hide anything," Hunter cautioned, scanning the area, his rifle ready in his hands.

Tennenboum couldn't argue with that. Hunter was an experienced outdoorsman and to be taken seriously. Scientists tended to become complacent sometimes, too engrossed in their studies to be aware of their surroundings. That's why it was important to have people like Hunter among a team. They kept everyone safe and on their toes if necessary. He turned his head when he heard someone shouting. Seeing Bonnet, who had walked away and climbed the small hill ahead of them, waving his arms frantically, he said, "I wonder what Doctor Bonnet wants."

Bonnet came back running, still waving his arms. "There are people down there," he shouted, his voice high and excited.

"What do you mean by people?" Tennenboum asked, a sudden cold shiver running down his spine.

"They look like people and they are in trouble. It seems they're being attacked by a couple of those Tigers."

Tennenboum and Hunter looked at each other. They both began running up the hill at the same time.

Chapter Eight

Hunter reached the top of the hill before Tennenboum did. He let out a string of curses. Tennenboum joined him a moment later and stared at the scene not far away.

Bonnet had been right…a small group of what looked like people in furs were fighting two of those giant cats.

"We have to help them," Hunter said. "They don't stand a chance against those ferocious beasts."

"I agree," Tennenboum said. "I'll get my rifle."

"I'll come with you," Bonnet said.

"Mr. Hunter, please interface your Companion with the Landroamer's monitor. Let's go, Doctor Bonnet."

They both ran back to the Landroamer and retrieved the weapons.

"What's going on," Roland asked, watching them with a puzzled expression.

"We found people," Bonnet shouted. "They need our help." He ran back up the hill, swinging his rifle.

Roland gave Tennenboum a questioning stare. "What's he babbling about?"

"He's not babbling just excited," Tennenboum said. "Bring the Landroamer to the top of the hill and stay there…inside it. Watch us on the monitor and stay alert. We'll call you if we need your assistance and then you come to get us, guns blazing if necessary…not before. Okay?"

Roland nodded, obviously a bit confused. "Okay. Be careful."

Tennenboum followed Bonnet without filling in Roland. As soon as Roland turned on the monitor and saw the images transmitted from Hunter he would understand. Bonnet and Hunter waited impatiently for him. All three men ran toward the group of strangers, their rifles ready. As they came closer, Tennenboum saw the group of fur-clad beings looked indeed human, but he wondered suddenly if they had misread the situation. One of the Tigers was struggling to free itself from the ropes tied to two of its legs and to its knobby tail. Three of the aliens held on to the ends of the ropes.

Another three used long spears to jab at the second Tiger.

Maybe they're hunters and we are interfering.

But then he realized that two of the aliens confronting the Tiger were females. Their upper garments had fallen open, exposing their breasts, and they seemed to move sluggishly, their jabbing spears hardly touching the enraged animal. He also saw one man lying on the ground, unmoving, his spear beside him. The ground was wet and red from his blood where he lay.

Hunter was the first one to react. He aimed his rifle at the spitting, roaring Tiger and fired one energy bolt into its broad chest. The giant animal staggered but didn't fall. Tennenboum shot it in the head, burning off part of the thick skull. Another bolt from Hunter's rifle hit the spine right behind the head, causing the great predator to collapse. Its spiny tail kept pounding the ground for a few long heart-stopping moments, and finally a violent shudder shook the body and it lay still.

Tennenboum heard the high crackling sound of a rifle being discharged beside him, followed by a triumphant shout from Bonnet. He turned to look at the second Tiger and saw it struggling feebly to stay on its feet, but Bonnet's bolt of energy had severed the spine of the predator, paralyzing it. He became aware of his heart beating in his chest and his breath coming in great gasps. The run down the hill and the ensuing battle made his adrenal glands pump his system full of stimulants, but now they demanded payment. Bending forward, he put his hands on his knees and tried to still his beating heart and catch his breath. He lifted his head when he heard Hunter talking.

"We're friends," Hunter was saying.

Tennenboum straightened out and looked at the aliens. They stood gaping at them, their spears lifted. He shouldered his rifle and spread both of his empty hands, following Hunter's example in the, he hoped, universal gesture that signified they meant no harm.

"Friends," Hunter said again, keeping his voice low and neutral. He bent and put his weapon on the ground. Pointing at the wounded man, he said, "It seems he needs help. I can help him." Without waiting for a response he slowly walked over to the injured man and squatted down beside him.

Tennenboum studied the aliens and realized how closely they resembled Humans. The men had handsome faces and the two women were quite beautiful…one of them looked young. The likeness of the women and the age difference made him guess they were mother and daughter.

One of the men opened his mouth to display short but sharp fangs. His golden eyes glittered under a ridged forehead and he let out a harsh, warbling sound, clearly a warning when Hunter touched the thigh of the injured man.

"No need to worry," Tennenboum said, smiling, hoping baring teeth wasn't regarded as a hostile expression. "He won't hurt your friend."

"This man is hurt badly," Hunter said. "He'll bleed to death if I don't treat his wound. It needs to be disinfected and mended. I'll need the med kit from the Landroamer."

"I'll get it," Bonnet volunteered.

"Hurry up." Hunter's voice sounded urgent. "We don't have much time."

Bonnet hurried away. Tennenboum watched the natives who in turn were watching him and Hunter, but none of them made any threatening moves. "I hope you can save this man's life, Mr. Hunter. If he dies we may get blamed for it."

"If Doctor Bonnet doesn't drag his feet we may be lucky and perform a small miracle. My only concern is the blood this man already lost."

It seemed like hours had gone by when Bonnet came running back carrying the bag with the medical supplies. He nearly collapsed when he threw the bag down beside Hunter. "I tried to run as fast as I could," he gasped, sinking to the ground where he knelt trying to gulp air into his lungs.

Hunter opened the bag and took out some stuff.

"Anything I can do?" Tennenboum asked.

"You could hold the fur away from the wound while I do my job," Hunter suggested.

Tennenboum knelt on the other side of the native and peeled back the fur, exposing his thigh. He held his breath when he saw the wound. Razor-sharp claws had left a gaping, deep cleft of shredded meat. Miraculously the claws had missed the major artery, but the wound was still bleeding profusely. Tennenboum looked into the man's golden eyes and gave him an encouraging smile. "We'll fix you up," he said soothingly.

The man didn't say anything. Even though his lined face was slack, his eyes were alert. He moaned softly when Hunter gave him a local anesthetic but relaxed almost immediately when the drug took effect.

After spraying the thigh with disinfectant foam, Hunter applied a coat of artificial flesh, closing the wound. "I hope his metabolism is similar to ours," he murmured as he sprayed on the castfoam. He leaned back and waited for the foam to harden. It took only a couple of minutes until a hard but flexible cast encased the thigh, preventing it from further injury. The transparent cast would eventually dissolve as the wound healed.

Checking his handiwork, Hunter let out a deep sigh. "That's all I can do for him. His body will have to do the rest, but I believe we've been successful."

"You have been successful," Tennenboum said, feeling great respect for Hunter at the moment. "I did nothing. By the way, where did you learn how to do this with such efficiency?"

"It's part of my job training as an Electrician. Sometimes we work under hazardous conditions where injuries are quite common. Basic medical knowledge is a requirement."

"You never cease to amaze me, Mr. Hunter. Is there anything you're not good at?"

Hunter grinned, throwing a glance at Bonnet. "Quite a few things. I can't run as fast as Doctor Bonnet, for instance."

Bonnet chuckled, obviously pleased, still breathing hard. "Necessity and panic lent me wings." He came over and patted Hunter's back.

"Congratulations, Mr. Hunter, your quick action probably saved this man's life. I believe it will be of tremendous help in our relationship with the indigenous people of this planet."

Hunter grinned. "I don't want to needle you, Doctor Bonnet, but I'm surprised you shot that animal. I mean...you don't believe in killing."

"I don't believe in killing for sport or even for food, but there are times when I have to sacrifice my principles to save another human being's life." His smile was apologetic. "I am not perfect, Mr. Hunter, but I try to stay true to my beliefs. I may have saved a man's life, but right now I do feel remorse for taking the life of another living entity, even one as ferocious as this one."

The man on the ground stirred and then he sat up. His hand moved to his thigh and touched it. He looked at the Humans and spoke a few short words. Of course, they didn't understand what he said.

Tennenboum smiled and said, "If you just thanked us for saving your life you're welcome."

Examining his thigh more closely, the man knocked his knuckles against the hard cast and moved his toes. Then he stood up and bent the knee of his injured leg. Shaking his head, he looked at Tennenboum. His mouth opened in what was clearly a smile. Bending down he picked up his discarded spear but aimed it into the sky. His golden eyes regarded the Humans silently for a moment. Holding up his left hand, he spread his fingers and spoke a few words.

Not knowing what the spread fingers signified, Tennenboum nevertheless repeated the gesture. The man nodded and turned away to look at the other members in his group. Pointing at the Humans, he uttered a string of short syllables. They sounded rapid and urgent in Tennenboum's ears.

The older woman rushed up to him and looked into his face. Then she slapped his cheeks gently a few times. The man laughed and touched her chin. Turning his attention back to the Humans, he pointed first at himself and said something, and then he repeated the gesture with the older woman and then the younger one, who stood studying Hunter with more than just passing interest.

"I think he just introduced himself and the women. If I'm not mistaken they are his wife and his daughter." Hunter spoke into the gadget on his left wrist, "Dawn, can you analyze language and gestures. What did the man say?"

"Insufficient data, but the male's name is Uroo. The older female is presumably his mate. He called her Sagela, and the young female is Arlee, seemingly his daughter. Keep them talking."

The sophistication of the Companion strapped to Hunter's wrist amazed Tennenboum every time he saw Hunter using it. It was hooked up to Hunter's nervous system and it saw through his eyes and heard through his ears. Not for the first time he wondered how Hunter got a hold of it. Devices like that were expensive and usually only used by law enforcement agencies and the Military, and sometimes by criminals.

Apparently there was more to Hunter than was obvious at first glance.

The natives turned their attention to the carcasses of the Tigers. They skinned them expertly and cut some of the meat into chunks, which they wrapped into leather skins. As Tennenboum surveyed the surrounding area he became aware of a number of black-coated animals as large as small horses tied to trees not far away. He also saw a few tents made from animal hides nestled among the trees.

Either this is a small tribe or a party of hunters. I'm leaning toward the latter. There are not enough females in the group to make it a tribe.

The natives worked in silence, but it didn't take them long to finish their task. Tennenboum noticed they used knives made from sharp stones. The men and the women alike wore sleeveless shirts fashioned from thin furs, closed in the front with braided strips of leather. Around their hips, they wore leather kilts that reached down to just above their knees. The spears were tipped with shards of white bones, sharpened to almost needle-thin points.

Hunter and Bonnet had also been studying the silent group. "They're stone age people," Bonnet said.

"It seems so, but I think they are more advanced than that," Tennenboum said. "They use animals for transportation and they are quite skilled. Even though the knives they use are stone, observe their intricate shape and sharpness."

"Flint is apparently sharper than a surgeon's scalpel," Hunter said. "They had no trouble cutting through the thick fur and skin of the Tigers."

"They're keeping the meat. It means they are meat eaters. Do they eat it raw or do you think they have fire?" Bonnet wondered.

"It would be nice if we could communicate with them," Tennenboum said.

"If we can get them to talk, Dawn can analyze their language, and we might be able to learn a few simple phrases." Hunter walked up to the young woman and said, "Did anyone ever tell you you're beautiful. I'd like to get to know you better."

Bonnet snorted beside Tennenboum. "I don't believe I've ever heard anything stupider than that. This is not a party where you can pick up a woman, Hunter. Besides, only a bubblehead would fall for such a dumb line."

"I'm not trying to pick her up. I want her to talk and I didn't know what else to say. She doesn't understand me anyway," Hunter defended his action. When he looked at Bonnet, he grinned. "You're wrong though, Doctor Bonnet. I've made contact with quite a few women using that very same line. Women don't really care what you say, as long as you make the effort."

Bonnet sighed and looked at Tennenboum. "I didn't know he was so shallow."

Tennenboum couldn't help but laugh when he saw Bonnet's expression. He's actually quite funny. He should have become a comedian instead of a meteorologist. But then he became serious. "I wouldn't get too close to her, Mr. Hunter. We don't know their customs, and we don't want to offend them by breaking some taboo. Perhaps she's already attached to one of these men."

Hunter took a step backward. "Sorry. I hadn't thought of that." He made a little bow to the young woman. "I meant no offense."

She smiled and bowed also. Turning to the older man, she laughed and said something. He looked at Hunter and nodded. His lips parted, revealing sharp fangs. He suddenly appeared hostile, like a wolf warning a potential rival, but when he spoke his words came out soft and non-threatening.

"I hope he didn't just marry you two," Bonnet said. "Then we really have a problem."

The young woman came up to Hunter and looked into his face. Pointing to her forehead, she said, "Arlee."

"Arlee?" Nodding, he smiled and poked his chest. "Hunter."

She laughed, laid a hand on his chest, and said, "Hunter." The she touched her own chest and said, "Arlee."

"Well, now we know for sure her name is Arlee. She demonstrated intelligence by imitating Hunter's gesture, because it seems her people point to their forehead and not their chest when they introduce themselves," Bonnet whispered beside Tennenboum.

"I believe you're on the right track, Mr. Hunter," Tennenboum said. "Get her to talk but don't get too intimate with your gestures, okay?"

"Sure, Professor. Maybe she'll take me to their camp where she can explain things to me. Keep her in familiar surroundings, you know." Hunter pointed at the tents and started walking toward the camp. "I'm interested in the way you live," he said to the young woman.

She seemed to understand his intention but obviously needed her father's approval, because she looked at him and spoke a few words. He answered with a string of short syllables and pounded his belly. She giggled and led Hunter away.

"I don't even want to guess what they talked about," Tennenboum said.

"Like I said before, let's hope Hunter didn't enter into an agreement with that young alien female he may not be able or willing to keep." Bonnet sounded pessimistic.

Tennenboum brought his attention back to the alien men. Two of them were rolling up the skins, while the other two tried to break off the long teeth of the Tigers with the use of a primitive hammer, which was nothing but a rock tied to a short wooden handle.

"They don't have metals," he said.

The group of aliens was ready to move on. With one last look at the remnants of the Tigers, the four men headed for their camp, carrying the bounty on their shoulders. Uroo, who was obviously the leader, looked at Tennenboum and Bonnet and said something. He underlined his words with a gesture Tennenboum had no problem understanding. "He's inviting us to their camp," he said to Bonnet.

"Then I suggest we follow the invitation."

"We need to inform Doctor Roland of this." Tennenboum activated his wrist-communicator. Roland responded immediately. His voice sounded anxious in Tennenboum's ear. "What is happening?"

"Everything is fine," Tennenboum assured him. "We'll be joining our new friends in their camp. Stay put but keep watching."

"Okay. Be careful."

Tennenboum didn't answer. He followed Bonnet who was already walking beside the older native and his mate.

His name is Uroo. I mustn't forget it. And her name is Sagela…I believe.

When they arrived at the camp, Hunter and Arlee were standing beside the tethered animals. Arlee was talking with gestures and words while Hunter seemed to be listening intently. Tennenboum knew that in reality Hunter's Companion was doing most of the listening, at the same time analyzing everything the young woman said and did. He also knew that everything Hunter's gadget recorded was transmitted to the monitor in the Landroamer.

Tennenboum was fascinated by the animals. Stocky, their bodies covered with a thick black coat, they did indeed look like small horses. Uroo saw him studying the animals. He pointed at them and said, "Leeas."

"Ah," Tennenboum said, nodding. "Leeas." He smiled. "I never told you my name. I am Tennenboum." Pointing at his chest, he repeated, "Tennenboum."

Uroo showed his teeth. Then he put a finger on Tennenboum's chest. "Tenbum."

Bonnet snickered beside him. When Uroo looked in his direction, Bonnet touched his chest. "Bonnet."

Uroo nodded gravely. "Bawnt," he repeated.

"Close enough." Bonnet laughed his high little nasal laugh. Tennenboum hoped their new allies didn't find it as irritating as he did.

Hunter and his young female companion came strolling back to the main camp. "I've learned a few things," he said. "They call those horse-like animals Leeas."

"We know that already," Tennenboum said. "What else have you learned?"

"This group is out here hunting. As far as I can understand they don't live in a permanent place. They are nomads but their main tribe is far from here. I think these people are all related...at least that's what Dawn deducts from the information she gathered."

Tennenboum spotted half-burned and charcoaled pieces of wood gathered inside a small circle of rocks beside one of the tents, clearly remnants of a fire. There were also a few clay pots piled up in a heap near the fire pit. "It seems they do have fire, Doctor Bonnet," he said.

"I'm not surprised, actually. Their knives are made from flint stones." Bonnet chuckled softly. "Were there are sparks there is fire. I notice they do pottery."

One of the natives brought an armful of dried twigs and branches. He broke them into smaller pieces and began building a small pyramid around a ball of what looked like wool. Then he cracked two small rocks against each other to create a shower of sparks and it took only a few tries before the wool-like substance caught fire.

"He makes it look easy," Bonnet said.

Another man pounded a couple of sticks into the ground on each side of the fire. Both sticks were forked at the top. The fire was burning quite nicely now, and the one who made the fire put a few heavier pieces of wood into it.

Every one was busy doing something. Sagela speared some of the Tiger meat onto a long, straight branch. When she was done she laid it across the fire. The natives kept silent most of the time. Only once in a while they would talk to each other in short sentences.

"It's hard to learn their language," Hunter commented. "They don't talk much."

Tennenboum saw Uroo watching the Humans with obvious interest. He's probably just as intrigued in us as we are in him and his people.

Uroo must have noticed he was being observed and smiled. Then he came over and uttered a few words. Tennenboum shook his head and spread his hands, indicating he didn't understand, and hoping the gesture didn't have some other meaning in their language.

The alien man thought for a moment. He pointed at the meat above the fire and then at Tennenboum. Putting the fingers of his left hand between his lips he made chewing motions and swallowed.

"I believe he's inviting us for supper," Bonnet said.

Tennenboum laughed softly. "I believe the same thing." Looking at Uroo, he nodded and said, "We'll accept."

"I don't eat meat." Bonnet sounded upset, almost panicky.

"We'll deal with that when we sit down to eat." Tennenboum didn't let Bonnet's eating habits discourage him from taking advantage of the opportunity to learn more about the natives.

Uroo looked pleased. He spoke to the woman who had come to join him and the strangers in their midst. She let out a little laugh, stepped close to Tennenboum and gently touched his chin. Surprised by her gesture, he wasn't sure what it meant or how to respond. On an impulse, he touched her chin fleetingly with one finger. She smiled and stepped back.

I guess it was the right thing to do.

The woman turned and walked to one of the tents. She disappeared inside. Uroo also walked away to talk to one of the other men.

"How does Dawn interpret what just happened?" Tennenboum asked Hunter.

The black man closed his eyes for a moment. Tennenboum didn't quite know how exactly the interaction between Hunter and the artificial intelligence inhabiting the electronic gadget on his wrist worked, but obviously Hunter was communicating with it in silence.

Opening his eyes, Hunter said, "She thinks it's a gesture of trust or even a show of affection. It seems the woman likes you, Professor."

"Not too much, I hope," Tennenboum murmured. "After all, she is the mate of the leader of this tribe."

"So it seems," Hunter said.

Chapter Nine

Roland did not sound overly enthusiastic when Tennenboum told him they would be spending the night with the group of natives.

"I won't be able to stay awake all night and wait for a signal from you should something go wrong," he complained.

"I don't believe we are in any danger here," Tennenboum soothed his fears. "Not much is going on now anyway. Just keep the monitor on standby. I'll contact you if anything happens." He moved his legs to get into a more comfortable position. Sitting with his legs crossed under him was not something he was used to and he noticed with satisfaction that Bonnet fidgeted around as much as he did. Hunter was the only one of the Humans who looked comfortable sitting on the bare, hard ground.

One of the men cut off a small portion of meat with his flint knife and handed it to Tennenboum. He accepted it with a nod and a Thank-you. The meat was charred and still hot…and greasy. He blew on it and moved it from one hand to the other until it didn't burn his fingers. Sniffing, he detected a strange odor, but he bit into it and ripped off a small piece with his teeth. Chewing it, he found it tough and gamy. Not exactly a gourmet meal.

When he glanced over at Hunter, he noticed that he seemed to eat his meat with gusto. Either he liked it or he put on a show for the benefit of their hosts. Bonnet on the other hand looked with disgust at the greasy chunk of meat between his fingers. His eyes searched out Tennenboum and he mouthed, "I can't eat this."

Tennenboum felt sorry for the man but shrugged and avoided to look at him. It's his problem not mine. He made the choice not to eat meat and now he must deal with it.

"Not bad," Hunter commented. "The meat tastes pretty much like the meat from the great cats on Emerald." He chuckled. "And it's just as tough."

"I'm glad you're happy, Mr. Hunter," Bonnet said. "You finally got your wish to eat some steaks."

"This isn't exactly a steak, Doctor Bonnet." Hunter sounded jovial. "But it will have to do…for now. Perhaps I'll get to eat a piece of meat from the more tender parts of these animals." He glanced at the young alien woman sitting beside him, and grinned. "Who knows I might even get a chance to give her a taste of a different kind of meat. I can sense a scorching fire burning inside this alien girl and she wants me. I'd like to roast my meat inside her hot oven."

Bonnet grunted something under his breath. "As long as you don't get your piece of meat burnt inside her hot oven, my friend. I advise caution. These people are different from us and we can't assume they have the same customs and habits as we Humans. They may look like us, but are they like us?"

"She's female and I am a male. I'm quite certain their sexual habits are no different from ours."

"Don't be so sure. She might rip out your throat when you try to penetrate her or, in case she let's you, she'll drain you of your blood after you've satisfied your animal desires and when you least expect anything. Have you taken a good look at her teeth? They were meant for ripping or perhaps for puncturing your artery. Maybe she's got teeth inside her vagina."

"You have a fertile and morbid imagination, Doctor Bonnet." Hunter turned to Arlee when she tried to put a small piece of roasted meat between his lips. She laughed and pushed her finger into his mouth when he opened it.

Bonnet let out a loud groan. "You should tell this sexually enraged bull to keep his organ inside his pants, Professor Tennenboum. He's putting us all in danger. I don't feel like being roasted over that fire. We know nothing about these people. They might just be fattening us up for their next celebration. How do we know the rest of their tribe won't be dropping in for dinner soon?"

Tennenboum shook his head. "Don't become paranoid, Doctor Bonnet. I don't believe they are cannibals." He gave Hunter a thoughtful look. "Doctor Bonnet is right, Mr. Hunter. Don't rush things. Sure, it seems this young alien woman is all over you, but be careful how you interpret her actions. Aside from Uroo's mate she is the only other female among these men. It is highly likely one of them has already claimed her or possibly plans to claim her."

"Her actions seem pretty clear to me," Hunter said. "Rejecting her may cause even more trouble than accepting her obvious invitation. And from what I observe, none of the others is even remotely interested in her."

"All right." Tennenboum made a motion with his hand, indicating he didn't worry too much. "Do what you think is best, but keep a level head." When someone touched his shoulder, he looked up and realized Sagela had come up behind him. Her teeth gleamed dully in the flickering light of the fire and he became acutely aware of her long incisors. For an insane moment he expected her to bend forward and sink her teeth into his neck.

Now I'm becoming paranoid.

The woman held something in her hand. She offered it to him and when he took it from her he realized that it was a piece of bread. He smiled and said, "Thank you."

Before she moved on her other hand touched his neck and lingered for a moment. Her fingers felt warm on his skin, and when she stroked him briefly her gesture sent a delicious shiver through his body. It had been a while since a woman touched him so intimately.

He bit into the bread and found it hard and bland tasting, but he swallowed it, concentrating on eating the bread, trying hard not to show his discomfort.

Damn it. What am I thinking? She is the mate of their leader and therefore untouchable. Explorers have been murdered before by indigenous people for getting involved with their women.

She came back shortly after and handed him a gourd. He was thirsty and drank from it. Expecting water, he was surprised when he swallowed the strong but pleasant tasting liquid. Sagela touched his cheek and said something with a low soft voice. He looked into her golden eyes and thought he saw something there he shouldn't be seeing.

I'd better watch myself. I'm beginning to imagine things.

He swallowed another large mouthful from the potent drink, knowing deep inside him it may not be a good idea to drink too much. Already he felt his head going somewhat fuzzy.

The alien men didn't seem to pay attention to him. Even Uroo appeared uninterested in what his mate was doing. They passed a large gourd around, taking long swigs from it. Judging by their laughing and hooting they seemed in good spirits.

"They are happy," Bonnet said beside him.

"Probably telling each other tall stories about heroism and valiant deeds they performed," Tennenboum mumbled, his words coming out a little slurred.

"Perhaps they include us in their tales. In their eyes we're probably gods come down to rescue them." Bonnet laughed noisily. "What is in this drink? I'm feeling funny."

"You're drunk," Tennenboum said, taking another swig from his gourd. Wiping his mouth, he burped. "It does taste great, though."

"Sure does." Bonnet's high-pitched laughter sounded like the cackle of an old witch. "I think I'll have to get up and follow the call of nature."

Tennenboum heard him getting to his feet and watched him stumble toward the trees. The touch of a gentle hand on his shoulder caused him to turn and stare at the woman. She smiled and knelt beside him. Then she bent forward and kissed him fleetingly. Rising, she pulled him up. Standing on wobbly legs, he pressed his fingers against his temples when a wave of dizziness threatened to overcome him, but it passed quickly.

Damn it! I believe I'm drunk.

The woman took his hand and dragged him with her toward one of the tents. He followed her like a docile dog, not questioning what she had in mind.

It was dark inside the tent and he let her push him into the mass of soft furs covering the floor. Her hands went to the belt on his pants and fumbled with it. Her nearness made his head swim and he let her unbuckle the belt. When her warm fingers touched his naked belly, he gasped and helped her push down his pants.

Her fingers curled around his rising penis and began to stroke him gently with one hand. By the sound of rustling he knew she was slipping out of her own clothes and when his hands reached out, he touched one of her naked breasts. She let out a soft hissing sound and pushed him onto his back.

He wished he could see her, but it was too dark to make out her features. The entrance to the tent was still open and he saw her silhouette against the rosy light of the campfire outside. He heard the laughing of the alien men sitting around the fire and hoped nobody noticed his and the woman's absence.

His penis had grown hard inside her stroking hand. That and the alcohol he had consumed made him forget where he was. He didn't care about breaking any taboos or the men who were close enough to hear what was going on inside the tent. Neither did he worry that the barbarian leader of the group might react violently should he discover his mate fucking a stranger, even if this stranger had saved his life. The only thing on his mind was the woman straddling him and all he wanted right now was to plunge his aching cock into her soft, inviting cunt.

Her soft, naked buttocks touched his thighs as she sank into his lap. Rocking back and forth with slow movements, she rubbed her pussy over his straining organ. He groaned and grabbed her moving hips.

"Don't tease me," he moaned loudly, trying to push his member into her, but she held him pinned to the ground with her weight and kept rubbing herself against him. Her breath came faster as she increased her tempo, snapping her lower body to and fro.

Crying out, she suddenly stopped moving and sat quivering in his lap, emitting loud clucking sounds. He felt warm liquid dousing his pubic area and knew she was experiencing an orgasm. It was comforting to know that she reacted just like any human woman.

He was afraid her noisy exclamation would surely attract the attention of the others outside but nobody seemed to notice. If they did, they didn't react. Nobody came to investigate.

Greatly turned on by her expletive reaction he nearly came, but even in his befuddled state he had enough control to suppress the urge. He didn't want to waste the unexpected opportunity ejaculating onto his own belly before experiencing the heat of this alien woman's passion while locked in her embrace and joined to her body.

She stopped her ecstatic cries and slipped from him. Disappointed, he lay there, cursing silently for not giving in to his own desire. In the near-darkness he saw her kneeling beside him. Her long hair fell into his face when she bent over him and searched his mouth. Pressing her lips over his, she kissed him feverishly.

Grabbing his penis, she pulled on it. Then she slapped her buttocks and uttered a few, breathless words. Somehow he understood what she wanted. Getting to his feet, he knelt behind her and put his hand between her slightly spread thighs. She moaned deeply when he found her labia and pushed one finger into her. She clamped her thighs together and bucked in front of him.

"I guess I assumed right," he murmured. "For a moment there I was afraid you may not have an opening." He pulled his finger out of her wet pussy and spread her thighs with one hand. Putting his swollen penis between her soft cheeks, he moved it lower until his engorged head touched the entrance to her vagina. Snapping his hips forward, he penetrated her easily. She emitted a loud cry as he pushed deep into her dripping, hot sheath and continued to sob as he moved slowly back and forth. Pushing back against him she took him deep into her with every thrust.

"You have a hot cunt," he groaned and held on to her hips, steadying his own movements. "I only wish you wouldn't be so noisy."

The alcohol and whatever else was in the drink gave him stamina he never knew he possessed. Even though there were moments when Sagela's frantically rotating pelvis and clutching tight sheath made it difficult for him not to explode inside her, he managed to stay focused on his goal to enjoy the gift she made him as long as possible. The joy and pleasure he felt was so exquisite he didn't want it to end…ever. His hands moved up her naked body and closed over her breasts. They felt as smooth and soft as those of any human woman's breast he remembered touching.

When he nearly lost it at one point, he pulled out and let the moment pass. She hissed softly and turned onto her back, reaching for his penis. He moved between her spread thighs. Entering her again, he was pleased to find his control was back. Sagela sobbed happily and wrapped her legs around his lower torso, grinding her hips forcefully against his.

It seems no matter what we humanoids look like, what planet we were born on, and what customs we may have to follow, when it comes to sexual intercourse we all speak the same language. It is a common bond we have.

Her fingers raked his back and he knew he would have welts as evidence of her great passion, but he didn't care. It was small payment for the exquisite pleasure he found in her arms. Grunting and moaning loudly, he moved between her clutching strong thighs for a long time, lost in a world of pleasure he didn't remember ever enjoying with any woman. Of course, he barely remembered the last time he had sex and he felt regret for the missed joy all these years.

It only fleetingly occurred to him that his action may have dire consequences. He may have to pay dearly for the bliss he was experiencing. After all, he was fucking a woman who belonged to another man.

Finally, he couldn't suppress the desire to reach the ultimate moment. He felt it building up deep inside him, like the soft breath of a summer breeze that grew into a raging winter storm. It roared through his body like a hurricane. His hot fluid left him with the explosive force of an erupting volcano. Shuddering in Sagela's crushing embrace and shouting his elation, he filled her alien vessel with his seed, barely aware of her cries of ecstasy as she accepted his gift…the gift of a stranger to her world.

Spent, he collapsed into her arms and lay gasping for breath on top of her soft body. Suddenly he felt exhausted and wanted nothing but sleep. She stroked his back and neck with gentle hands and made happy cooing sounds. Closing his eyes, he listened to her soothing voice, tired but content.

* * * *

Tennenboum found himself lying alone on the thick furs. When he lifted his head, he became aware of soft light falling through the partially closed flap of the tent. Sitting up, he put his hand to his head and moaned.

Damn it! What happened last night? Was I dreaming or did I actually have sex with an alien woman?

He was naked. His clothing lay in an untidy heap in the corner of the tent. A sudden chill made him reach for his clothing.

What the hell was I thinking?

He was afraid to go outside and face the man he had betrayed. Looking around, he didn't see his laser rifle. It was probably still lying beside the campfire, unless someone picked it up. He shuddered to think what a weapon like that could do in unskilled hands.

Buckling his belt, he hesitated before he pulled aside the flap covering the entrance. Shrugging, he stepped outside. The sun had already risen past the tops of the trees and the bright light caused him to squint. The first man he saw was Bonnet. He sat near the fire, his back toward him. Hunter was nowhere to be seen.

Across from Bonnet sat Uroo, the leader of the group of natives…and the mate of the woman he screwed. He lifted his head and stared at Tennenboum out of golden eyes. His lips curled up, exposing sharp teeth and he waved with his hand, indicating Tennenboum should join them by the fire.

Still hesitating, Tennenboum walked slowly toward the two men, wondering what was going to happen next. From the corner of his eyes he saw Sagela coming out of the forest, carrying a small bundle of firewood.

What do you say to a man whose woman you fucked and how do you act toward her the morning after?

Uroo watched him coming closer. He stayed silent, only motioned again for Tennenboum to take a seat. Sagela threw down her bundle of wood and picked a few pieces to add them to the fire. Coming near Tennenboum, she touched his chin. Then she walked away, smiling.

Uroo let out a couple of clucking sounds but didn't say anything. Bonnet gave Tennenboum a look of what could only be described as contempt. Lowering himself down beside him, Tennenboum didn't know what to say but couldn't stand the silence. "What's for breakfast?" he asked.

Bonnet shrugged. "Perhaps a cup of that foul brew they offered us for supper."

"It was potent, wasn't it," Tennenboum said, putting his hand against his forehead. "I think my head is going to explode."

"I thought it exploded last night," Bonnet said, sarcasm clearly in his voice. "Or was that your other head, Professor?"

Tennenboum sighed deeply. "You know don't you?"

"Everyone knows. You two sounded like a pair of angry combatants. The walls of a tent are not soundproof. For a while I thought you were killing each other, but you weren't fighting, of course. You realize you were fucking the wife of the man sitting across from us, don't you?"

"I know. I have no idea what made me do what I did."

Bonnet laughed his nasal, high-pitched laugh. "Perhaps you let the wrong head lead you on? I hope none of us looses his head over this, Professor. All I can say is was it worth it?"

"You have no idea." Tennenboum allowed himself a crooked smile. "You have no idea, my friend."

Sagela returned with a large leather bag. She opened it and took out a piece of the dried bread Tennenboum had tasted the night before. She handed it to Uroo and then she gave a piece to Tennenboum and another one to Bonnet. Sitting down beside Uroo, she began eating. Her golden eyes seemed to study Tennenboum, but she didn't say anything.

"They sure don't have a varied menu," Bonnet murmured.

"Better than charred Tiger meat," Tennenboum said. "By the way, did you consume some of the meat?"

"You know I'm a vegetarian. I couldn't eat it. I spit it out when no one was looking. Besides, everyone was too busy drinking or listening to you. Nobody paid attention to me."

"Where is Hunter?"

"Probably screwing that young wildcat."

"He's still in one of the tents?"

"No. I saw him walking with her into the forest last night. After your performance last night he almost surely wanted more privacy. He hasn't returned yet." Bonnet bit into his piece of bread.

Tennenboum's eyes fell on Uroo, who had been sitting silently across from him, eating his meager breakfast, and watching the two Humans. He wanted to apologize to the alien man and cursed his inability to do so.

Uroo smiled and said something to Sagela. She let out a silvery laugh and touched his chin with one hand.

"I wish I could understand what they're saying," Bonnet said. "It seems none of them has any issues with you this morning. I'm surprised how easily they're accepting what happened between you and her. Any normal Earthman would be furious to witness his wife screwing another man. Just because you saved his life doesn't mean now you can do anything you want. Nobody is that generous."

"Has it ever occurred to you she may not be his wife?" Tennenboum asked.

"Well, Hunter's invisible companion said she was."

"Are you going to trust an artificial intelligence to evaluate a situation correctly?" Tennenboum challenged the other man.

"No, I'm not, but there is a good chance she is his wife, mate, companion or whatever they call their sexual partners," Bonnet mused. "This is an unknown planet with inhabitants we know nothing about. Their moral standards and traditions are most likely completely different from ours. We cannot judge them by our ways of life. Maybe it's his way of saying thank you for saving my life. Centuries ago on Earth in the more primitive societies a host would offer his wife to his guest for the night as a welcome gift."

"Maybe I would have angered and insulted them had I not accepted her invitation," Tennenboum said.

"Now you're trying to justify what you did, Professor." Bonnet chuckled softly. "But I have to agree. There is that possibility."

Uroo rose suddenly from his sitting position. He glared at Tennenboum and uttered a few loud, harsh sounding words.

In his right hand he suddenly held a flint knife.

Chapter Ten

Maisoneuve didn't really mind being alone. In a way he was a loner. Sometimes he found it difficult correlating with others. He hated authority, didn't like being ordered around, and reacted with hostility when people tried to tell him how he should do his job. He was not a good team player, and he was aware of that. Somehow he got off on the wrong foot from the beginning with Professor Tennenboum, but he had tried hard to play along and it seemed he and Tennenboum had found a way to keep the peace.

Nevertheless, he was not unhappy when his companions left him alone for a few days. He had everything he needed…enough food and water to last him a month, and his job to keep him busy. If he ran out of food, he had his rifle and confidence in his ability to bag one of the small deer-like herbivores roaming the prairie, should the eventuality arise that the others were held up somewhere and wouldn't be back for a while.

Of course, the thought occurred to him that he might be in deep trouble, should anything happen to them and the Landroamer. Getting back to the research station would be a long trek on foot, aside from the fact he may get himself lost in the wilderness. Not for the first time he questioned why the research team had been supplied with only one Landroamer.

Pushing the thoughts aside, he headed back to his dig site. The hole was nearly one meter deep and one across. Progress was slow. The ground consisted of hard soil mixed with large and small rocks, and his laser cut only a few centimeters deep into the ground. He cut out small squares and then used a pick to smash them into little pieces. Then he lifted them out of the hole with a spade.

He had to be more alert the deeper he dug down. According to his instruments, the ceiling of the cave underneath him was about two meters thick on this spot, thicker on others. He didn't want to take a sudden drop into the underground cavern. If the fall didn't kill him, he'd be trapped and surely severely injured.

The rope he secured to one of the columns lay on the ground and he hooked the other end into his belt. It should keep him from falling into the hole should it suddenly cave in.

Kneeling on the edge of the hole, he began cutting small cubes out of the rock. In a way it would have been nice, to have a helper who could do this backbreaking work and free up time for him to do other, more productive tasks.

After a couple hours of cutting, he stopped and sat up, wiping the perspiration from his brows. His back and knees were beginning to ache from kneeling bent over. He took a sip of water from his canteen.

Judging by the position of the sun in the sky, it was close to quitting time. It would be dark in about two hours and he didn't want to sit outside by himself after the sun went down.

The power supply in his laser cutter probably wouldn't last longer than another half-hour. He could replace it with the one being charged by the solar-converter, but he'd rather start with a full one in the morning.

He decided to stop for the day, when he heard a deep squawking sound coming from nearby. Grabbing his laser rifle, he rose and swung around.

At first he only saw a giant bird, the size of an ostrich, with a short neck topped by a large head. Its beak was thick and black, and the muscular clawed feet looked like they could inflict serious damage to a defenseless man.

Maisoneuve was anything but defenseless. He lifted his rifle, ready to use it should the creature decide to attack him.

Then he saw the rider on the bird.

It was a man, dressed in furs, his muscular arms bare. He carried a bow in one hand.

Maisoneuve stood erect, watchful of the stranger. He didn't want to make the first aggressive move, but he was ready to use his rifle, confident to emerge the victor in a possible conflict. Bows and arrows are no match for a laser rifle.

The giant bird scratched the soil with one foot and clucked its beak menacingly, but the rider didn't act hostile. He seemed as surprised to see Maisoneuve as he was to be confronted by a human-looking individual on this alien planet.

As the two men looked at each other, two more birds carrying riders appeared from behind the ruins. They stopped beside the first rider.

Maisoneuve was careful not to move erratically. He wasn't worried facing three opponents. Before they could nock an arrow they'd be dead, but he didn't want to kill them in cold blood. It would be murder.

One of the men slid from his steed and put his bow onto the ground in front of him. Spreading his arms, he began walking toward Maisoneuve. Watching the other two carefully, Maisoneuve didn't think they'd ambush him while he was busy scrutinizing the one approaching him.

On an impulse, he laid his own weapon on the ground. He still had the gun strapped to his hip. These were primitive people; they wouldn't recognize a laser gun as a weapon.

As the alien came closer, Maisoneuve noticed that his eyes were not human. They were large and glittered with purple fire in his handsome face. His body was muscular and well proportioned. He walked softly on fur-clad feet and carried himself with confidence that nearly bordered on arrogance.

He stopped a couple of meters in front of Maisoneuve and smiled, keeping his arms away from his body and the palms of his hands facing forward.

Maisoneuve imitated the gesture and said, "I'm pleased to meet you, even though it is totally unexpected."

The other man tilted his head. Then he slapped his right fist against his left shoulder and said, "Rasa."

Not quite knowing if the man had just introduced himself as Rasa, or if it was just some kind of greeting ritual, Maisoneuve took a chance and repeated the gesture.

"Maisoneuve."

"Maisoneuve," the man repeated, pronouncing it clearly but with a slight accent. Then he pointed back at his companions and said, "Stasro. Marca."

Maisoneuve nodded. "I understand. Your friends are called Stasro and Marca," putting emphasis on the two names.

Rasa spread his arms with his hands open, and said, "Arula."

"Arula," Maisoneuve said, also spreading his arms. "Arula. Peace."

I hope that's what he meant. I don't think he wants to give me hug.

Apparently satisfied with his answer, the alien man turned around and waved to his companions. They followed his request and rode their two-legged steeds slowly into the open space, leaving the rider-less bird behind.

Rasa shook his head, muttered something under his breath and trotted back to get his steed and his discarded bow.

Maisoneuve chuckled, imagining Rasa calling his two buddies idiots for not bringing his belongings with them. *I like them already. Their behavior is so typically human.*

The two newcomers were younger than Rasa. When Rasa came back, his mount in tow and his bow in his hand, he pointed at the taller of the two and said, "Stasro." Then, with a thumb in the other one's direction, "Marca."

Both younger men grinned and punched their fists into their left shoulder. Their purple eyes studied Maisoneuve with unveiled curiosity. He noticed that all three men had their long, black hair tied into a ponytail. He also saw each one wore a ring in his left ear. The rings reflected the rays of the sinking sun and he realized they were made from gold.

They know how to work metals. They can't be as primitive as they appear.

Stasro and Marca jumped from their steeds, displaying great agility and strength. All three men were powerfully built, with wide shoulders and muscular thighs. A wide, thick leather belt circled their narrow hips, holding their short pants made from animal skins in place. The carved handle of a long knife protruded from a sheath hanging on each belt, and Maisoneuve bet the blade was iron. His assumption was pretty much confirmed when he looked at the tips of the arrows inside a quiver they carried on their backs. They were definitely made from iron.

Suddenly he didn't feel as confident and smug as he had before. By the looks of it these three were hunters or possibly warriors and capable of overcoming even an enemy armed with modern weapons. For all he knew they possessed the ability to move faster than he could aim and fire his laser rifle. They didn't seem to be intimidated the least by him. Either they had met people like him before or they considered themselves his equals, possibly even superior, since they were three and he was alone.

None of them appeared hostile or aggressive, and he didn't sense any danger, but he kept up his guard. They were strangers and he was an intruder into their world. Good will could easily turn ugly should they feel threatened by him or his presence.

They looked around the site. When they saw the tent, they displayed more than just faint interested. After tying their mounts onto a couple of the ancient columns, all three men walked over to inspect the tent.

Rasa touched the fabric with his fingers, clearly impressed.

Maisoneuve knew they were anxious to see the inside and, with a bit of reluctance, he made a motion with his hand indicating they should enter. They didn't hesitate to follow his invitation.

Stasro seemed intrigued by the computer terminal on Professor Tennenboum's desk. Even the desk was part of his examination. He looked at Maisoneuve and said something, but Maisoneuve only shrugged. "It's a computer. Even if I explained it to you, you wouldn't have the faintest idea what I'm talking about, providing you could understand my language. Of course, you don't and I have no idea what you're saying, either," he said.

The young man gave him a friendly smile, as if he understood. He turned away and spoke to the older man, Rasa, who was examining the cots and the super-thin material of the sleeping bags.

That should baffle you guys for a while. "We sleep in those bags. They may look thin but they insulate us against heat and cold."

The three aliens seemed satisfied with their inspection. They left the tent, walked over to the fire pit and threw down the leather bags they had slung across their shoulders. Maisoneuve had a small mountain of branches piled up nearby which he collected early in the morning to make sure they were dry by evening.

In the meantime the sun had disappeared behind the forest and it was getting dark. The reddish color of the sky was beginning to fade away to make room for the star-speckled black roof of the night.

Time to get the fire started and prepare supper.

He had no idea what his new friends were going to eat. He didn't know if they carried anything in their bags.

Debating if he should set up a flood-lamp to light up the camp, he decided to do it, even if it meant scaring his visitors a little. Maybe he'd gain some respect and awe from them.

He flicked on the switch to energize the lamp hanging from a pole near the tent. Bright light flooded the area in front of the tent. The expected reaction didn't happen, causing Maisoneuve to be somewhat disappointed. The men made a few sounds he could have interpreted as amazement, but otherwise they didn't seem overly impressed. Marca, the smaller and youngest of the three, put a ball of dried moss and some branches into the pit and proceeded to smash a couple of flint stones together. It didn't take long until he had minute flames licking the dry moss. Feeding small branches into the flames he had a good fire going in a short time. It was obvious he was quite skilled in the art of making fire.

Rasa opened his bag and took out a bundle of large leaves. Wrapped inside was a chunk of dark meat. Pulling an arrow from his quiver, he speared the meat onto it and, squatting in front of the fire, he held the meat into the flames.

His companions did the same, and soon the dripping fat from the broiling meat sizzled in the flaring-up flames. The pungent aroma of the burning fat drifted into Maisoneuve's nostrils and he was hoping they wouldn't offer him a piece of meat.

He went inside the tent and retrieved one of the prepared food packages from the shelf. Ripping it open, he poured the dry contents into a small container, added water from the water cooler, and energized the heating element in the bottom of the container. It took only a few of minutes to heat his supper. Armed with a spoon he went outside to join his new companions.

They were still turning their arrows in the flames. The meat was getting dark, black in places, and Maisoneuve had no doubts that it would be tough and dry by the time it was done.

He spooned out his food, aware of the three men watching him, probably wondering what he was eating.

I'll never complain again about these food rations we have to eat. This is probably a gourmet meal compared to what you guys are eating.

They drank water from flexible balloons, most likely animal bladders. It proved again to Maisoneuve that primitive people everywhere progressed the same way. They made use of the materials and animals available to them. It only made sense. He had been to a few Earth-type planets and it surprised him every time how similar conditions were on these planets and how all life forms seemed related. Studying the three men, he speculated. Except for their large, purple eyes, they were human in appearance, but he wasn't sure if they could be considered human. Could their species breed with human women? Could a human man impregnate one of their women? Were there females? What would children from these unions look like? Would they have their large eyes?

He was suddenly struck by the revelation that this was a monumental occasion. He was actually in the company of three alien males who seemed quite intelligent. They represented a race equal to Humans…or nearly equal. It was important this encounter ended peacefully, and it was up to him to make certain it did.

Once their meat was broiled, the men ate it with gusto, chewing it carefully, while staring into the flames. Their strange, purple eyes looked even larger in the flickering light from the fire, reminding Maisoneuve of the giant lemurs roaming the Madagascar Reserve on Earth. Like the lemurs they could probably see better in the dark than the Humans.

After they finished eating, the three aliens curled up near the fire and went to sleep.

Maisoneuve sat still deep in thought, surprised they trusted him, but then he shrugged, shut off the light, and went into his tent. He lay listening for noises from the outside. The sounds from the nearby forest and the presence of the alien men sleeping by the fire kept him awake for some time, but his tired body demanded rest and he drifted into an uneasy slumber from which he awoke many times during the night.

He was aroused from his deep sleep that finally came by someone shaking his shoulder. Coming out of a vivid dream he opened his eyes and looked into the face of Rasa.

Chapter Eleven

An excerpt from Irwin Hunter's personal log
August 19, 2985

We've finally met the indigenous people of this planet. Their species is called Sras. I've learned quite a few words from Arlee. She is young and beautiful and as wild as a female Sirkrris, fortunately not as deadly…I hope.

Sirkrris is their word for the fierce predators we encountered a few days ago. We named them Tigers, because they do possess a certain resemblance to the tigers of Earth, according to Professor Tennenboum and the others, except these animals are larger than and probably twice as ferocious as the great cats of Earth and covered with long, shaggy hair. They have six legs with paws as large as dinner plates and their four digits are tipped with long and wicked razor-sharp claws.

Even though we've named them Tigers, after a closer and more intimate look I'd say we should have christened them Wolves, because of their elongated snouts and long, pointy canines. In addition, their thick tail is tipped with a hard, spiny ball.

I've hunted cat-like predators on Emerald. Some of them were quite nasty, but none of them were as huge and savage as the Sirkrris. (I think I'll be using the Sras name from now on. It sets them apart from the animals on Earth, on Emerald, and on the other planets I've visited.)

When we came upon the Sras, they were busy fighting off two of these great beasts. They might have succeeded in overcoming them, but I'd like to believe we saved them from losing some of their members to the claws and teeth of the Sirkrris. I'm quite certain we saved the life of Uroo, their leader.

The Sras are so human-like one could almost theorize they are mutated descendents of space travelers stranded on this planet. We did find thousand-year-old ruins left by people who may be the forefathers of the Sras. Professor Maisoneuve hasn't established yet who the builders of those ancient structures could be. Everything so far is pure speculation. Humans didn't have space travel a thousand years ago. The Sras may just be a species native to this planet.

I'm not a scientist and I don't know much about the origins of the universe, how suns and planets were formed, and how life is created in the primeval state of developing worlds, but there has to be some kind of universal formula. It seems life forms developed along the same lines on all of the planets Humans have discovered so far.

Perhaps some highly advanced race traveled the Galaxy millions of years ago and seeded all of the planets. It's only theory and nobody knows if such a thing happened, but sometimes I do wonder about that.

Anyway, as I've said, the Sras are quite human-like, except for their ridged foreheads and golden eyes. They behave like us, and I suspect they have a social structure close to ours.

I mentioned Arlee. The moment I saw her I felt attracted to her, and it seems she took a liking to me also. At first I thought she was the daughter of the group leader, Uroo, but after spending the night and part of the morning alone with her, I've learned he is her uncle.

I make it a point to learn the names of the people I meet and, thanks to Dawn, my AI, it is not difficult to remember the names.

Sagela and Arlee are the only women in the small group of Sras we met. Arlee is Sagela's daughter. Aside from Uroo there is his brother Roor, also an uncle to Arlee, his son Uura, and Uroo's son Manrah.

Professor Tennenboum had sex with Arlee's mother last night, and I was happy to hear that Sagela is not Uroo's wife as I assumed but his sister. That gives me hope I will find the Professor and Doctor Bonnet alive. Of course, I don't know how Uroo felt to discover his sister fucked a stranger. It may not be an acceptable thing according to their customs.

I'm not even sure how I will be received when Arlee and I get back to their camp.

Last night we sat around the fire. The natives shared their meat with us and even offered us something to drink…something with a bite to it. When Arlee pulled me with her into the forest, I followed her like a love-struck, horny monkey. I knew she wanted the same thing I did.

Once we were deep in the woods, she pulled me with her into the soft moss. Her species probably has eyes better than we Humans have, because it was dark among the trees and I couldn't see much. It never occurred to me to get my night vision glasses out of my pouch. I guess the alcohol in my blood prevented me from thinking straight. All I thought of was getting naked and sticking my satisfier into this alien girl's obviously eager pussy.

She was nude underneath her short leather kilt. I put my hand between her thighs and found her slit. Pushing a finger into her, I discovered she was wet and ready. She gasped and clamped her thighs together, keeping my hand prisoner. Using my other hand, I pushed her upper garment over her head to expose her full breasts. When I sucked one of her nipples into my mouth, she moaned and opened her thighs. I took the opportunity to roll between them. She pushed my pants past my hips, grasped my stiff pole with both hands, and guided me into her.

I grunted loudly when I slid with such ease into her soft but tight, hot sheath. Except for the heavenly climax at the end, feeling the soft pressure of a woman's moist vagina walls closing around my rigid penis has to be one of the greatest pleasures I crave for. I am a man who loves women and needs to have sex often. The last time I had sex was over a month ago with Cara and I must admit I was getting a little irritated from the lack of female attention.

I don't know if I can say this alien young woman seduced me. If she did she didn't have to try very hard to persuade me.

Cara Gunn was a passionate woman, and she gave me some great pussy, but this girl was a feral animal. She gyrated underneath me with wild movements, milking me with a pussy that seemed to have a life of its own. Her inner muscles vibrated with a steady rhythm, exerting gentle pressure one moment and releasing me the next. The pleasure was incredible.

Her lips searched mine and when she found me, she pushed her tongue into the cavity of my mouth, exploring it with a long tongue. Her kisses were intoxicating, and I kissed her back with great vigor.

I don't know how long we made love. I seemed to be lost in an ocean of nothing but joy and bliss. When I finally exploded inside her, it nearly blew my mind. From her loud shrieks and her erratic movements under me, it was obvious she also experienced a powerful orgasm.

After shooting my sperm into her with a series of forceful squirts, I felt suddenly drained and tired. Collapsing into her arms I lay on top of her soft breasts, gasping for breath. Her breathing was ragged and she sobbed for a long time, her hips still grinding into mine, her sheath pulsing around my half-rigid penis. I thought I might become stiff again, but it didn't happen and I was almost glad, because I was too exhausted to go on. My skin felt slick from perspiring, and the cool night air made me shiver. I was completely naked, but I didn't remember taking off my clothes.

Groping for my shirt, I found it and draped it over us. It made the cool breeze bearable. Arlee didn't seem to suffer from the cold. Her body was hot and it warmed me like a heat cushion. Her legs were still wrapped around mine and I didn't mind it at all.

I must have dropped into a deep, exhausted sleep, without waking up during the night, because when I opened my eyes I discovered it was close to morning. The rays from the emerging sun created bright streaks in the gray mist hanging between the trees. A musky smell escaped from the moss-covered ground and I became aware of hooting and chirping, the sounds of forest creatures greeting a new day.

I also realized I was alone. Even though I was still covered by my shirt, I shivered in the chilly morning air. Sitting up and looking around I didn't see Arlee and wondered what happened to her. I didn't panic but a sense of unease nevertheless came over me. It had been dark when we entered the forest and I had no idea in which direction the camp lay.

When I saw barely visible footprints in the moss leading away from our sleeping spot I decided to let them guide me. I slipped into my shirt and pants, grabbed my boots, and followed the tracks. After climbing a slight rise in the ground, I heard the tinkling of water not far away and it didn't take long until I found Arlee.

I stopped and watched her as she washed her body in the clear water of a narrow creek. A ray of sunlight fell through the branches of the trees and highlighted her slim form. It had been dark when we made love during the night and I never did get a chance to see her naked body, but I knew she was trim and well-formed. Her breasts, while not large, were solid, and stood proudly from her ribcage, and her buttocks were round and full.

She must have sensed my presence for she turned around, brushed strands of her long, wet hair out of her face and looked in my direction. Her golden eyes were large and her face apprehensive, reminding me of a doe startled by a stalking predator.

When she saw me, she relaxed and smiled. "Come," she called. "The water is refreshing."

I was not surprised that I understood what she said. During the night, as we slept, Dawn, my electronic companion, sent out tiny tendrils thinner than a human hair, and inserted them into Arlee's body, connecting her nervous system with the electronic brain and, consequently, with mine. Information from Arlee's mind had been absorbed by Dawn and transferred into my subconscious.

I do not claim I understand how it works, and I am always mystified when it happens. I've never regretted the fortune I paid when I acquired Dawn. I didn't ask the man I got it from how he obtained this marvel of engineering, but I suspected he was not the legitimate owner. Apparently, it was some new, secret technology only available to special branches of the Government. There are similar devices for sale, but they don't have the capabilities Dawn has. I know she is self-aware and able to make decisions.

I climbed down the hill and put down my boots beside Arlee's small bundle of clothing. Then I removed my pants and shirt and walked into the water. It was cold, and I took a moment to let my body adjust to the temperature.

Arlee laughed when she saw me shiver. "The water is not cold, Darkskin."

She didn't know my name so she called me by the color of my skin. Her skin was light and, obviously, she had never seen black people. Perhaps it was my skin color that made me attractive to her. I didn't care. I will use any advantage I have to get close to a woman. "My name is Hunter," I said, my first words in her language coming out haltingly.

Her eyes grew large again. Staring at me, she said, "You speak the language of the Sras? Why did you hide this from me?" She took a step backward as if suddenly afraid.

"I didn't hide it from you," I said, trying to sound apologetic. "The knowledge came to me during the night when you and I slept."

"Are you a god?" she asked, almost a little scared it seemed.

I shook my head. "No, I am not a god. I am a mortal like you, even though you and I do look a little different from each other." I chuckled. "But there is not so much difference that our bodies cannot be joined together. We proved that last night."

Her face lit up. "No male has ever given me so much joyfulness," she said, her voice dreamily. Then she giggled and came closer. Slapping my face gently a couple of times, her hand moved down my belly and touched my penis. "Your stem is very large," she whispered. "In the beginning, I was afraid."

"Why afraid?"

"You might hurt me."

"Did I?"

She laughed cheerily. "No. When you were inside me I was very happy." She grabbed my hand. "Wash my back. It is sticky from the moss I lay in last night."

I scooped up a handful of water and let it run down her curvy back. "Sit in the water," I said. "It will be easier to wash you."

She squatted down and I splashed water onto her back. When I rubbed her she cooed softly. "That feels nice," she murmured.

"Tell me about your people," I said as I washed her back.

"What do you want to know?"

"Everything. Is your father Uroo the leader of your people?"

She laughed. "Uroo is not my father. He is my father's brother."

"Who is your father?"

"He is not here. Only my mother is here."

"Sagela is your mother?"

"Yes."

She seemed happy to know I was interested in her and her family and told me about herself and her brothers and sisters, and about the other members in the group. Stroking her soft back and feeling her warm skin under my hands, made my penis react and I grabbed her shoulders to turn her around so I could kiss her.

She screamed and I let go of her. “Sorry. What is it? Did I hurt you?”

Getting to her feet, she pointed into the forest. “Maklos!” she sobbed.

I looked in the direction she pointed. Initially, I didn’t see anything, but then I saw movement between the trees. When the first one appeared in the open, I thought her companions had come looking for us, but when I saw the stony face and black eyes, I knew I was looking at a man not of her kind.

More of them came out and crouched on top of the rise, staring in our direction.

“Who are they?” I whispered.

“They are Maklos, children of unions between Sras males and the Siiris.”

I didn’t know what she was talking about. There was not enough information available to me, but I knew that by Sras males she meant men from her species. They had mated with females from either another tribe or possibly another race. It was possible other intelligent life forms aside from the Sras existed on this world, and it was obvious from her words the Sras did not approve of their men mating with females of these others.

I counted eight Maklos. They didn’t look much different from the Sras, except for their expressionless faces with their hollow cheeks and dead eyes. Dawn’s translation of the name Maklos flashed into my mind. It meant literally Dead Faces, and I could see why. None of them wore clothes and I registered fleetingly that their bodies looked emaciated and filthy.

A couple of them opened their mouths to display fangs meant for ripping out throats or large chunks of meat. Hissing loudly, they shambled forward, followed by their companions.

“We must run,” Arlee urged me with a panicky voice.

“Damn it!” I cursed for being so careless, since I had left my laser rifle back in the camp.

A buck in rut is easy prey. Damn it.

Luckily, our clothes were on the other side of the creek. Grabbing Arlee by the hand, I pulled her with me. Stopping long enough to retrieve our clothing, we ran up the hill. “Which way?” I gasped.

Arlee took the lead and ran ahead of me. When I looked back, I saw the creatures already in pursuit. They didn’t seem to run very fast, but fast enough to keep up with us as we stumbled across fallen trees and creeping vines…

Chapter Twelve

Maisoneuve bolted up, instantly awake, and struggled to get out of his sleeping bag. Rasa stepped back and laughed softly.

"You scared the hell out of me," Maisoneuve cursed. "If I had my gun handy I might have shot you, damn it." He managed to strip off the sleeping bag and was glad he had gone to sleep with his clothes on. At least he didn't have to take off any pajamas to change into his day clothes in front of a stranger.

Walking over to the water cooler, he poured a small amount of water into a bowl and washed his hands and face. "We don't have a fancy place to wash up," he said with a touch of humor, knowing it was lost on Rasa. "By the way, I'm going to have breakfast. I'd invite you but I have no idea what you people eat for breakfast."

Rasa gave him a little smile and shrugged.

Maisoneuve tore open a bag of rations and emptied it into another bowl. Then he added a little water and waited until the dried ingredients absorbed the liquid and expanded to their original shape. He was aware of Rasa watching him intently, obviously curious what he was doing. "It's not bacon and eggs," Maisoneuve joked again, "but it is nourishing. Plenty of vitamins and high in calories."

Carrying his bowl and a spoon, he went outside and waited for the alien to join him. Sitting down on a flat rock, he began to eat, feeling a little uncomfortable when he noticed Rasa still watching him. "Ah, what the hell," he cursed, putting his bowl beside him onto the ground. "I can't see a man go hungry. Besides, I hate eating alone." Then he went inside the tent and prepared another bowl.

When he offered it to Rasa, the alien man said, "Stosa," nodded and accepted the offered food. He even took the spoon Maisoneuve handed him. Sniffing the bowl, he spooned a small portion out of the thick gruel and shoved it into his mouth. Chewing it carefully, he swallowed it.

Smacking his lips, he grinned and said, "Snarleemo."

"I have no idea what that means," Maisoneuve said, "but by your expression I assume you like it." He looked around, realizing the younger men were not to be seen anywhere. Then he noticed that two of the large birds were also gone. "Where are your friends?"

Rasa must have seen him looking and interpreted his question correctly, or at least guessed its meaning, because he pointed toward the far mountains and said a few words, underlining them with gestures.

Of course, Maisoneuve didn't understand what the alien man was telling him. "I hope they're coming back," he murmured. "I'd hate to be stuck with you here. We can't even communicate with each other."

They finished breakfast in silence. Rasa got up from his sitting position near the fire pit and walked over to his steed. He stroked the great bird's thick, feathery neck and spoke a few soothing words, causing it the cluck its wicked beak.

Maisoneuve strolled closer and said, "I guess this is your equivalent of a horse."

The bird rolled its eyes in his direction and emitted a deep squawk, clearly a warning. Stopping in his tracks, Maisoneuve held up one hand. "Don't get excited. I'm not after your eggs or drumsticks, even though they'd make a hell of a barbecue."

The bird looked even bigger from close. Its massive body and broad back offered enough room for a man to comfortably sit on, and the thighs were thick and muscular, strong enough to carry the weight of a man with ease. The scaly legs ended in feet that could have made a dinosaur proud. The toes were tipped with horny nails as long as daggers with sharp points and edges. Even the wickedly curved beak looked dangerous.

I wonder how they tame them. Probably raise them from eggs.

It was easy to see these were flightless birds. Their wings were short and stubby.

Rasa noticed Maisoneuve's interest in the bird. He pointed at it and said, "Heeska."

"Heeska," Maisoneuve repeated, nodding to show he understood. They called the big birds Heeska. Another name to store away in his memory. When he heard voices, he turned to look in the direction of the mountains. A rise in the land prevented him to see far from his location. Anyone coming from that direction was hidden from view until they crested the hill.

Two men riding Heeskas came into view, followed by a few more riders, some also on Heeska-back, while some rode shaggy-coated animals akin to small horses. He also saw a number of small, cat-like animals running ahead of the riders. Their long bodies were covered with thick, white curly fur.

Rasa let out a loud laugh and rubbed his hands. It was obvious he was happy to see the riders. The first two were the same two young men from the previous day.

As Maisoneuve watched, a number of wagons appeared on top of the hill, pulled by weird looking draft-animals. He could only think of giant rats. When they drew closer, he saw men and women sitting inside some of the wagons. Other wagons were loaded with supplies.

Maisoneuve counted ten wagons altogether. They came to a halt near the ruins, and the drivers and passengers climbed out of them, stretching their legs and arms. The riders jumped off their steeds and led them to the columns where they tethered them with long ropes. They kept the birds and the horses apart, possibly because they did not get along.

The rat-like draft animals stood docile, still hitched to the wagons.

A few of the people unloaded stuff from the wagons, while others began erecting tents. It didn't take long until a dozen tents stood among the ruins. They bore an uncanny resemblance to the tents the native people of the North American continent used to build before the white man invaded their land over a thousand years ago. Long poles were covered with animal hides, but a small opening was left at the top.

A quick count gave Maisoneuve an estimate of about fifty-five men and women who were setting up camp on his dig site.

Well, I guess that brings my exploring of the ruins to a quick halt.

Standing alone and almost feeling ignored, he watched the aliens as they made the place their home. Rasa had left him to go and talk to some of the newcomers. The men he talked to threw glances in Maisoneuve's direction and he was quite certain they were discussing him.

He turned to walk back to his tent when Rasa and a couple of the newcomers started walking toward him. He waited for them, anxious and curious, his attention on the two cat-like creatures reaching him before the men did. They sniffed his legs and looked up at him with yellow eyes. One of the aliens accompanying Rasa was fairly young, the other one old. His body looked thin and frail, his skin wrinkly, and his head nearly bald. The little hair he had left was streaked with gray. Even his brows had faded away. It occurred to Maisoneuve that none of the aliens seemed to have facial hair.

The old alien scrutinized Maisoneuve with a slight frown. His large eyes had lost some of the purple sheen the others displayed but they still showed intelligence and alertness.

Maisoneuve made a little bow to show his respect. Somehow he had the feeling this old man was revered by his tribe members. The old alien drew his dry lips into a faint smile, displaying missing teeth. When he spoke, his voice sounded weak. Of course, Maisoneuve didn't comprehend anything the man said. Shaking his head and lifting his shoulders, he tried to convey he didn't understand his language.

The old man nodded. He spoke to the younger man who sprinted away toward the wagons. Maisoneuve wondered what this was all about and waited patiently for the young man to come back. It didn't take long for him to come running. He carried a couple of small boxes. He handed the boxes to the old man.

Maisoneuve suppressed the urge to exclaim loudly when he saw the boxes. They were clearly made from some kind of metal and were obviously electronic devices. The old alien hung one of them around his neck and gave the other one to Maisoneuve, gesturing for him to put the looped narrow band attached to it over his head.

Maisoneuve followed his instructions. The metallic surface of the device felt cool on his skin but heated up quickly until it lay warm and almost like something alive on his chest just below his throat. Gentle waves of energy traveled through his nervous system and into his brain. With the feeling came the understanding of what was happening. The information was transferred into his mind and he realized this was a communication device.

But after the first words he knew it was much more than that.

"Greetings, stranger. Welcome to Iceworld."

Maisoneuve didn't know what to say at first, not because he was lost for words but because he was excited and almost stunned by what was happening.

"Who are you people?" he finally managed to say, wondering if he would be understood.

The old man seemed as excited as he was. His voice quavered when he answered. "We are the Jnaar. Who are you and where do you come from?"

"We come from another world far away...a place we call Earth." Maisoneuve pointed into the sky. "Those lights you see in the night sky when the clouds are gone...we call them stars...one of them is our sun. Many of those suns have worlds like yours."

His words made the old man chuckle. "We know about the stars. Our ancestors came to Iceworld from one of those distant stars."

"Are you telling me you are not native to this planet?"

"That is correct." The old man wiped his brow. "Is there a place were we can sit in the shade. This body of mine is getting feeble and weak. I can't take the heat the way I used to. I need to sit down."

"We can sit in my tent," Maisoneuve suggested. "It is more comfortable there."

"Then let us go there." He turned to Rasa and the young man. Both had been watching the interaction between Maisoneuve and the old man with great interest and obvious excitement. "I will go with the stranger. Do not worry about me. I will be fine." Turning back to Maisoneuve, he said, "Come."

Maisoneuve walked beside the old alien, accompanied by one of the small cats, with a mixture of exhilaration and numbness. From what he just heard, these people were not native to this planet. How did they get here and where did they come from?

When the old man entered the tent, he looked around and headed for one of the cots and sank onto it. "This dwelling of yours is very comfortable," he commented. "Where are the others who live here?"

"They are exploring." Maisoneuve activated the camera and recorder on his computer. He had the feeling this was a momentous occasion and needed to be recorded and stored for future studies. "Can I offer you some water to drink?"

"That would be appreciated. I am thirsty."

Maisoneuve filled a cup with water from the water cooler and gave it to the old man, who took it gratefully. Taking a few sips, he said, "It is cool and so is the air in here…and fresh smelling."

"We have air-conditioning," Maisoneuve explained. He sat down on one of the two chairs and bent forward, eager to find out more about these people who called themselves Jnaar. "You said your ancestors came here from another planet. How long ago was that?"

"I cannot tell you the exact number, but I estimate the seasons repeated at least five hundred times since they came here. If we were in the winter-city I could give you more precise information, because that is where the records of our people are kept…at least the records we were able to save."

"Five hundred times…let's see, that's a thousand years our time. Do you know where they came from?"

The old man shook his head. "That knowledge has been lost. My father told me the original settlers came from an artificial world that brought them here from our ancestral world far away."

"Are you talking about a vehicle that travels among the stars? A spaceship?"

"Yes. Apparently there were large numbers of our people on that…spaceship. They were sleeping inside the bowels of the ship, waiting to be awakened. I do not understand what he meant. They were supposed to settle one of the other worlds circling this sun, but something happened there, something terrible, and they abandoned that world."

"What happened to the spaceship?"

"According to my father, it probably is still there. The story of my people was told to him by his father who was told by his father, one of the chosen men who closed the great ship against intruders. Once their task was finished he and the other chosen ones took refuge on this world. They joined the two hundred explorers who were already here."

The inescapable truth dawned on Maisoneuve. "You are correct, the spaceship is still there. In fact, we found it and are using it." He had a sudden uneasy feeling. "We have colonists on the fourth planet who are trying to colonize it. Do you know what happened to your people?"

The alien shrugged. "We only know it was something dreadful."

Something about what the old man had said before didn't seem to make sense. Maisoneuve did some calculating and the numbers didn't add up. "You said that the father of your father's father came to this world. How is that possible? You told me your ancestors came here five hundred seasons ago. That is a thousand years on my world."

"Why is that not possible?"

"Because the years don't add up, unless each of your ancestors was at least three hundred years old when he fathered a child."

The old Jnaar smiled. "Three hundred of your years would be one hundred fifty years on this world. What do you find peculiar about that?"

Maisoneuve stared at him. "Are you telling me you are that old?"

"I am much older than that. According to your measuring of time I am nearly four hundred years old. People of my race have a long lifespan." He heaved a sigh. "But not all of my people live this long…not anymore. The new generations die younger. I am one of the few who have inherited the longevity genes of our race."

"Humans don't live that long. Even with rejuvenating drugs we can reach only about one hundred and fifty years on the average." Maisoneuve studied the old man's lined face. "What is your name? My name is Maisoneuve."

"I am called Raark after my first ancestor on Iceworld. In the old language it meant Seeker." He took another swig of water. Clearing his throat, he said, "Now I've told you about me and my people. Tell me about yours. What is your purpose on this world?"

"Same as your…I mean your original purpose. We have a thousand colonists on the fourth planet, which we have named Nu-Eden. As for our purpose on this planet…for now we are here only to explore, to find out if it is suitable for Humans. We didn't actually expect to find it already populated." Maisoneuve smiled. "Of course, you are not exactly native to this planet either, but you have first rights."

"There are not many of us. You probably have advanced weapons and we would not have a great chance of survival should you decide to take this world by force…away from us."

"We would never do that. There is always room to negotiate. This planet is not exactly an ideal world to be settled. We haven't even experienced the seasons."

Raark chuckled softly. "The winters are harsh and savage but we have adapted."

"I was in the process of studying these ruins," Maisoneuve said. "Do you know who left these behind?"

"Yes. This is where our ancestors tried to settle at first. It was not the best location. Too many Keeras and other predators, and too much snow in the winter. This area is also very popular with the Sras, and our ancestors became discouraged by the constant attacks and destruction of their crops, which don't grow that well in the hard ground. They finally decided to move. We come here to remember and to rest for a few days before we move on."

"What are Keeras and Sras?"

"Keeras are ferocious beasts with six legs and the Sras are the indigenous people of Iceworld, as equally ferocious."

Maisoneuve sat up and gave Raark a surprised stare. "This planet has an indigenous population? What do the Sras look like? Are they advanced or primitive?"

Raark held up a hand and laughed. "The Sras are quite similar to us and to you. In fact their eyes are shaped like yours. They are wild savages who live in primitive conditions." He sighed. "As do we. This world is savage and if you want to survive you must adapt or perish. We adapted. If you have any plans to stay here you will also adapt."

A commotion by the entrance caused Maisoneuve to turn his head. Rasa stepped into the tent and stood by the entrance. He looked at Raark. "Are you comfortable, my father?"

Another revelation! Rasa was the old man's son. But he looks much too young to be the son of a four hundred year old man. How virile are these people?

Raark nodded. "I am. Maisoneuve has been kind. He is no threat to me."

"Good. I am pleased."

Rasa left the tent after giving Maisoneuve a curt nod.

"I am a bit perplexed," Maisoneuve said. "This translator box I have around my neck…it is of highly advanced technology. Even we don't possess anything like it. Where does it come from?"

"It is one of the few devices our ancestors brought with them that still work. Most of the technology we had is useless now and not really needed for our survival. As one of the oldest surviving members of my people I am the Guardian of the Ancient Knowledge, mostly to keep the memory of our roots alive."

"I see. Is Rasa your son?"

"Yes. My youngest of thirty hatchlings."

"Thirty uh…children? How old is he?"

"He's seen over fifty winters come and go."

"Amazing. It means he is over one hundred years old. He doesn't look over forty…twenty in your years." Maisoneuve was beginning to have his doubts about the old man's memory. Perhaps he was going senile.

"We keep our youthful looks for a long time." Raark chuckled. "He has good genes."

"What about his mother? How old is she?"

"Rasni, his brood-mother, is nearly seventy now. She is my fifth mate. Three are dead and the other one decided to take another male as her mate."

Maisoneuve had to smile. "According to my math you were close to three hundred years old when Rasa was born, and his mother was around thirty-six. It seems Humans and Jnaar have much in common. We Humans have plenty of older men who like their women young…the younger the better, and many young women go for older men. Of course, your case is quite extreme."

"Only our bodies grow old," Raark said. "Inside we stay young forever with the same desires and dreams." He seemed to stare into emptiness for a moment. Then he lifted his gaze and looked at Maisoneuve. "How does it feel to travel among the stars?"

Maisoneuve shrugged. "I can't really tell you. It took us five years to travel from our home planet Earth to this star system. My body was frozen for the duration of the journey. I only woke up after our engineers terra-formed one of the towers in that giant globe…your spaceship…we found circling the fourth planet. Even traveling between planets is not really a memorable experience, unless you want to count being stuck inside a metal can for days, perhaps weeks, enjoyable. I'm always happy to step onto solid ground and breathe natural air."

"Still, I envy you. You must have traveled to many different worlds."

"A few, most of them were wild and unpleasant, almost worse than this one."

"You have not lived yet through a winter," Raark said, almost gently. "Perhaps you will change your mind about Iceworld."

Maisoneuve's attention was sidetracked by the small cat watching him with its large, luminous yellow eyes. "What about this little creature?" he asked. "It seems intelligent the way it is studying me. Did it come with you from your world?"

Raark laughed, obviously amused. "No. The Sreel are native to Iceworld. They are naturally curious and actually quite affectionate. Perhaps this one likes you, Maisoneuve. We use them for tracking prey when we hunt and for companionship."

He rose from the cot. “I will go back to my people. They will wonder what happened to me. I thank you for your hospitality. Perhaps you want to join me by the fires tonight and share some broiled Thrall with me.”

“Thank you for the invitation. I’m looking forward to sharing some Thrall with you…whatever it is.”

Chapter Thirteen

Tennenboum stared at the flint knife in Uroo's hand. Expecting to be attacked, he rose and took a step back, trying to free his laser pistol, but Uroo didn't pay any attention to him. He shouted again, looking at something behind Tennenboum. Suddenly, the other men from the tribe appeared among the trees, carrying spears.

Sagela jumped up and ran for one of the tents. Tennenboum heard noises behind him and turned to see Hunter and the girl running toward the camp. Both were naked and carried their clothing in their hands. They were not alone. A group of men, equally naked, seemed to be chasing them.

"What the hell is happening here?" Tennenboum asked, drawing his pistol.

Sagela came up to him, holding a spear. "Maklos," she said, pausing for a moment. Then she moved forward to face the naked men.

Hunter and the girl arrived at the camp. "Where is my laser?" Hunter panted, looking around desperately.

"Probably where you left it last night," Bonnet said, drawing his own laser pistol.

Hunter's pursuers stopped their chase and stood crouching, growling and grunting like angry beasts and showing their teeth threateningly. At first, Tennenboum thought they were of the same species as their hosts, but a closer look made it clear these men were different. The shape of their eyes was somewhat distorted. Some were golden, others black, but the most notable difference was the lack of life in their eyes and faces.

They had skinny, filthy bodies, covered with sores and ugly, poorly healed wounds.

"I don't believe they are very intelligent," Bonnet remarked. "They look and behave like wild animals."

"They call them Maklos," Hunter said, still clutching his clothing.

"How do you know?"

"Arlee told me."

"What in the name of the Comet's Tail are they?"

"Maklos. Children of Sras males who mate with Siiris. That's all I know."

"Who are the Sras and who are the Siiris?" Tennenboum asked.

"Our new friends call themselves Sras. I don't know about the Siiris."

One of the Maklos snarled and shambled forward, teeth flashing, toward Sagela, who stood with her spear ready. A couple of the others also moved forward.

Uroo rushed past Tennenboum with his knife held high. The other men in his party were close behind him.

The Maklos advancing toward Sagela roared and attacked her. She thrust her spear into his chest. He roared again and clawed at the shaft of the spear, trying to dislodge it, but Sagela held on.

As she struggled with her attacker, another one moved in and reached for her with fingers spread like talons, but before he managed to touch her, one of the Sras ran his spear right through his lower torso.

Arlee had managed to find a spear and jammed its sharp point into the neck of another Maklos. Uroo came to her aid and plunged his knife into the belly of the man-beast, ripping it open with a vicious cut.

All of the Sras were suddenly engaged with their enemies. Tennenboum stood watching helplessly, trying to get off a shot with his laser without endangering one of his allies. Hunter was still searching for his laser rifle, cursing as he did so.

The hoarse shouting of the Sras and the roars of the Maklos filled the crisp morning air, and a beautiful morning had suddenly turned into an ugly, terrible moment in time. The whole incident seemed bizarre, unreal, and took on a dreamlike quality. Tennenboum expected to wake up at any moment and discover he was still on the spaceship and coming out of cryogenic sleep. Things were happening too fast.

He shook off his weird state of mind when he spied more of the creatures coming out of the forest. "There are more of them," he said, struggling to come to grips with the situation.

Hunter finally found his rifle and moved past the group engaged in the fight. Aiming his rifle, he shot one of the newcomers, and then another one. When the others saw their comrades stumble and go down, they slowed in their advance, baring teeth and roaring in defiance.

Tennenboum became aware the Sras had won the battle. It seemed none of the Sras were injured during the fight. As ferocious as the intruders looked and acted, without weapons they had no chance against the Sras, who were armed with spears and knives.

The new group of Maklos stood uncertain, moving back and forth, grunting and growling, and gnashing their teeth. When Hunter shot another one, the rest of them fell upon their fallen comrades and began tearing them to pieces.

"They're fucking cannibals," Bonnet cursed, his voice high and disgusted.

"They're not human," Tennenboum said. "They're animals, literally, who happen to look like Humans…or maybe I should say like the Sras."

"The Sras?" Bonnet asked.

"Apparently, that is the name our friends go by. Hunter told me."

"Interesting. Who told him?"

"The girl…Arlee."

"It seems they've learned to communicate with each other." Bonnet chuckled. "Other than with their bodies."

"With the help of that device he has strapped to his wrist. It can do marvelous stuff. It's a self-aware computer, an AI."

Hunter came back, still naked, his black skin slick with perspiration. He grinned and patted his rifle. "I love technology. You don't have to get up close to defeat your enemies."

"How about putting on some clothes?" Bonnet said.

Hunter laughed and struck a pose, resting his laser on his hip. "Don't I look like a savage warrior," he asked, his teeth flashing white between thick lips.

"If it weren't for your black skin I wouldn't be able to distinguish you from our barbarian friends," Bonnet said with a little sneer. "I hope you didn't get that girl pregnant. Your bastard children would not be welcome among these people."

Hunter put his rifle onto the ground and picked up his clothing. "I don't believe Humans and Sras can interbreed. After all, this is a different planet. It is highly unlikely that our genes are compatible."

"Don't count on it." Bonnet didn't seem happy. He gave Tennenboum a quick glance. "Your offspring will be as unwelcome as Hunter's, don't kid yourself. I'm still not sure how Uroo will deal with the fact you screwed his wife."

"Sagela is not his wife," Hunter said.

"Not his wife? Who is she then?" Tennenboum felt a sudden weight lifted from his shoulders.

"She is his sister."

"Aren't we lucky," Bonnet commented, not hiding his contempt.

Before Tennenboum could reply, Sagela stood suddenly beside him. She was spattered with blood but looked happy. Relieved to see her unhurt, he grabbed her and planted a kiss on her lips. She laughed into his mouth and kissed him back. "I'm happy you're not his wife," he said.

Breaking the kiss, she slapped his cheek gently and walked away.

"I hope this doesn't mean you're married, Professor," Bonnet said.

"Nonsense, Doctor Bonnet. You worry too much." Tennenboum acted nonchalant, but Bonnet's words rang in his head and created more worries.

I should have controlled my urges. Damn it! I don't need any complications. I told Hunter to be careful and I didn't follow my own advice. Just because she isn't Uroo's wife doesn't mean everything is all right. The last thing I need is getting married or attached to a savage, no matter how beautiful and sex-starved.

Hunter had moved away to check on Arlee. The young woman looked vibrant and elated. Her eyes flashed purple in the bright sun. She was obviously unhurt. Tennenboum couldn't help but notice the lovely form of her young, nude body. Her breasts were firm, with a nice shape to them. The muscles on her slim body rippled when she moved, and in a way he envied Hunter for having experienced the wildness in her.

But then he remembered his night with Sagela and was forced to admit the older woman had displayed savage passion no woman he ever knew could match. Her body was as solid, supple and as trim as Arlee's, and she gave him pleasure beyond description. Perhaps his envy of Hunter was misplaced.

Younger women don't necessarily make better lovers, because older women are more experienced.

The second group of Maklos was still busy ripping apart and devouring the ones Hunter killed. He watched them shambling around for a while before he walked over to look at the dead ones on the ground. When he studied the emaciated bodies and the hollow-cheeked faces he was struck by something peculiar.

"They remind me of the Zombies in the legends of the ancient Haitian people," he said to Bonnet who came up beside him.

"The Living Dead." Bonnet agreed. "There is a lot of mystery on this planet. Who knows what else we will discover."

"What are we going to do about those?" Tennenboum lifted his gaze to stare at the snarling group near the forest. "I don't want to wait until they decide to attack us. We may not be so lucky the next time."

"Perhaps we should kill a few more. It might cause them to move away."

"Or they might decide to hang around. After all, we're supplying them with food by killing their comrades."

"Ask Hunter. He seems to be able to communicate with the girl. Her people can tell us. They are more experienced in these matters," Bonnet suggested.

When Hunter asked Arlee, she spoke to Uroo and then she told Hunter what Uroo said. "The Maklos will not move away, but they won't bother the Sras until they've eaten the dead ones. They will settle down here for a while," Hunter told Tennenboum and Bonnet. "The Sras have no choice but to move on. We could kill all of the Maklos but the Sras are not in favor of that. It would bring bad luck."

Bonnet chuckled. "It seems the Sras are superstitious. They are turning out more and more like us. But I am happy to hear they do not kill for the sake of killing."

"Are you saying they will be leaving?" Tennenboum asked, somewhat disappointed to hear the news. He had hoped to spend a few days with them so they could study them.

And perhaps spend a few nights in the arms of Sagela.

He pushed the unbidden thoughts aside, feeling a pinch of sadness, perhaps a sense of loss, and also guilt. "When?" he asked.

"They'll be breaking camp now."

As if to confirm Hunter's words, Tennenboum saw the men taking things out of the tents and stuffing them into leather bags.

"We could go with them," Bonnet suggested.

Tennenboum was ready to agree but knew it would not be a good idea. "No, we'll head back to our camp. I've had enough excitement for a while." He looked at Hunter. "Let them know we'll be leaving."

When Hunter spoke to Arlee, she slapped his cheek gently and pressed her body against his. Then she went to Sagela and talked with her, throwing glances in Tennenboum's direction.

Sagela smiled and nodded. Tennenboum watched her with trepidation when she walked toward him. Stepping close to him, she touched his chin and gave him a couple of gentle slaps on the cheeks. Taking his hand into hers she guided it toward her chest and into her open upper garment. Her naked breast felt soft and warm in the cup of his hand. Letting go of his hand, she lifted up and kissed him gently.

He wished he could say something she would understand but he didn't know what would be appropriate under the circumstances.

Should I say I love her? It would be a lie. I don't even know her, her people, or her customs. We fucked…that's all. One night.

When she stepped back, he looked into her golden eyes and was overcome with remorse, not for what he had done but for what he may be losing. She was an alien woman, a savage, and yet…she had given herself to him without reservation. There was an innocence about her that attracted him. She was not young, had not been a virgin. That was not the kind of innocence he sensed. It was something he had never seen in any woman before her. Why could she not be human?

On an impulse, he reached for her and pulled her into his arms, crushing her to him. He covered her face with kisses, not caring what the others thought about his behavior.

When he let her go, he was breathing hard. He found his eyes seemed to burn suddenly, and he swallowed down a hard lump in his throat. She gave him a bewildered look but didn't seem to be offended, only puzzled.

"Tell her I am happy we met," he told Hunter. "Tell her also I will be searching for her and I will find her again. Tell her that."

He didn't care when he heard Hunter chuckle and he didn't care what he and Bonnet thought. When Hunter conveyed the message to Sagela, she smiled. She said something and then she walked away toward one of the tents.

"What did she say?"

"She said she'll be looking for you also."

"She's not angry with me?"

"Why should she be?" Hunter grinned. "She let you fuck her."

"Is that what she told you?"

"No. Those are my words. I'm sorry, I shouldn't have said that."

"You're right. You shouldn't have." Tennenboum left him and Bonnet standing and searched for Uroo. He found the alien leader by the riding animals.

"I know you don't understand me," he said, "but I want you to know it has been a privilege to meet you and to share your campfire. Perhaps some day our paths will cross again." He held out a hand.

Uroo cocked his head, listening intently. He smiled and shook his head. Looking at Tennenboum's hand he held out his. Tennenboum grabbed it and squeezed, shaking it. "It is an old Earth custom," he explained, even though he knew Uroo didn't understand him.

The alien man looked into Tennenboum's face. His eyes shone golden under his ridged forehead. He nodded and reached out with his other hand to touch Tennenboum's chin. Tennenboum repeated the gesture and knew it was the right thing to do when Uroo chuckled and said, "Tenbum."

"I hope your leg heals well, and perhaps next time I'll teach you how to pronounce my name correctly," Tennenboum said as he let go of the other man's hand. He walked back to his companions. "Let's go. Get in touch with Doctor Douglas and let him know we're on our way, Mr. Hunter."

With one last look at the camp the three men walked away, past the spot where they came upon the Sras only the day before. It almost seemed days passed since then. So much had happened. A flock of tiny scavengers took to the air, screeching defiantly at the intruders who disturbed them at their meal. The half-eaten carcasses of the Tigers lay on the ground, covered with white and black droppings; white bones, stripped of meat, gleamed in the sun.

"I'm surprised those Maklos haven't discovered this feast yet," Bonnet remarked as they walked on. "What are those monstrosities anyway?"

"I can only tell you what Arlee told me. According to her, the Maklos are the children of unions between Sras males and the Siiris. Those were her exact words."

"The Siiris," Bonnet repeated. "It sounds to me we're dealing here with another species. The Sras and those Siiris can breed with each other but their offspring are a bunch of walking dead monsters. One can only hope the Maklos are not fertile…sort of like the mules. They can't reproduce."

They reached the top of the hill. The Landroamer stood just past it, out of sight from the Sras camp. Roland climbed out to greet them. His dark, piercing eyes fixed on Tennenboum and his thin lips were even thinner than usual. "I was getting a bit worried, Professor. Hunter switched off his gadget last night and I couldn't get a hold of you either. I didn't know what to do. What happened?"

Tennenboum gave him a tired smile. "We'll fill you in, Doctor Roland. All I want for now is get inside the Roamer and relax while we drive back to see what Professor Maisoneuve is up to. He's probably bored out of his mind."

Chapter Fourteen

It was late in the afternoon when they arrived at the site. They saw the tents among the ruins already from far away.

"Stop the Roamer, Doctor Roland."

Tennenboum uttered the order without thinking. It was not necessary because Roland didn't need to be told. The moment the tents came into view he automatically slowed down the Landroamer.

"It is apparent Professor Maisoneuve has visitors," Hunter said.

"Those don't look like Sras tents," Tennenboum said.

"Could these be the Siiris?" Bonnet wondered.

"Well, no use to sit here and debate," Tennenboum said. "There's only one way to find out. Let's move a little closer. Drive slowly. We don't want them to panic."

As they came closer, they saw people walking between the tents. They also saw wagons, giant birds, and horse-like animals tethered to the pillars.

"They appear to be human," Hunter observed. "From here they look like Sras."

"Perhaps they are Sras," Tennenboum said, but when they were close enough to distinguish features he realized his assumption was wrong. These people were dressed differently. When he looked through his binoculars, he could distinguish men and women. The men had their long hair tied behind their heads and the women let it hang loose around their shoulders. Zooming in on one of the men, it became apparent he was definitely neither Sras nor Human. His large eyes glittered with purple fire under a smooth forehead. An elongated golden hoop dangled from in his left earlobe.

"They are not Sras," he told the others.

"Can you see Professor Maisoneuve among them?" Hunter asked.

"No."

"I hope he's still alive," Bonnet said, his voice carrying a worried tone.

"Let's not jump to conclusions, Doctor Bonnet. You and Doctor Roland can watch us on the monitor while Mr. Hunter and I go and check out the place. If anything happens to us, don't try to be heroes. Don't leave the Roamer with thoughts of trying to rescue us. I suggest you ignore such ideas and head home. Somebody needs to report this."

"Are you taking weapons?"

"Yes. I won't go unarmed into a strange camp, but I hope we won't have to resort to violence." Tennenboum reached for his rifle. "Are you ready to go, Mr. Hunter?"

"As ready as I'll ever be."

The two men stepped outside and walked slowly toward the camp.

"Strange," Hunter said. "We've been here for three months now and nothing exciting happened during all that time. Suddenly, here we are, meeting a second species of natives in a matter of two days."

"That's how fate sometimes works, Mr. Hunter." Tennenboum walked with nervous anticipation. Meeting the Sras had been different. They had been the knights in shining armor coming to the rescue. It gave them a great bargaining chip to start a relationship with the people they saved from harm. This time they came almost like intruders into a camp filled with strangers…armed strangers.

He carried his rifle over his shoulder, displaying non-aggression, but he was ready to use it in an instant should it become necessary. He hoped it wouldn't come to that.

It seemed nobody paid them attention as they came nearer, but when he saw a couple of men looking in their direction he knew they had been spotted.

"So far so good," he said to Hunter. "They know we are here but nobody seems to be excited seeing us and nobody is sounding the alarm."

"Perhaps they are so confident they don't worry about being attacked by an enemy," Hunter replied.

"We are not an enemy. I hope they feel the same way."

The tent was still standing in its place and Tennenboum breathed a sigh of relieve. Nobody stopped them when they headed for the tent. Tennenboum opened the entrance door and stepped inside. Everything seemed in order; nothing had been disturbed. The computers were on their desks but Maisoneuve was nowhere to be seen.

He went back outside. "I wonder where Professor Maisoneuve is," he said to Hunter who stood surveying the area, his nerves on edge, as was obvious from his rigid stance.

"Maybe we're about to find out." Hunter's voice sounded tight.

Tennenboum watched two of the aliens coming toward them. They wore vests made from soft leather, laced in the front, leaving their muscular arms bare. Their short leather pants were held up by wide belts from which hung scabbards long enough to sheath a short sword. Both men carried bows but neither of them showed hostility.

"Is your Companion activated?" Tennenboum whispered

"Always," Hunter replied.

The two alien men stopped in front of them. One was young, the other one a little older. "Maisoneuve?" the older said and it sounded like a question.

His words surprised Tennenboum. "What have you done with him?" he asked, forgetting for a moment they probably couldn't understand him.

The alien shook his head. "Maisoneuve," he said again. Then he turned and walked away. His young cohort made a gesture with his hand and followed the older man.

"I believe they want us to come with them," Hunter said.

"All right, but let's be careful."

They followed the two aliens, their senses on high alert, their eyes searching the ruins and the area between the tents, ready to take defensive action should they feel threatened. As they walked Tennenboum registered everything he saw. He noticed men and women. Most of them were young and, he couldn't help but notice, extremely healthy looking. The men were handsome and muscular, and the women slim and beautiful. He only saw a couple of older women, but even they looked trim and fit.

Their guides stopped in front of a collapsed wall. There was a narrow crack between the wall and one of the pillars that had once supported a roof. The crack was large enough for a man to squeeze through…even a big man.

The older man pointed at the opening.

"It seems he wants us to go in there." Hunter fumbled with the rifle sling. "I don't have a good feeling about this, Professor."

"Let's stay relaxed, Mr. Hunter." Tennenboum didn't feel the calmness he wanted to project. His nerves were as taut as a bowstring and he was ready to start shooting at anything that only hinted at danger, but he told himself not to panic. Had the aliens wanted them dead they would have acted already by now. He still didn't sense any hostility from the two men, but they may have the ability to hide their intentions, like a harmless-looking badger before it ripped open your throat.

"I'm not going in there, Professor."

"Neither am I." Tennenboum smiled at the two men. "Are you implying Maisoneuve is in there?" he asked.

"Maisoneuve," the man said, gesturing at the opening.

Tennenboum shook his head and waited for the two aliens to make their move. The younger one said something and the older man shook his head. Then he shrugged, walked up to the gap in the wall and shouted into the open room on the other side. Then he stepped back and waited.

It didn't take long before another man stuck his head out of the hole. When he saw Tennenboum and Hunter, he broke into a gap-toothed smile and emerged fully. He looked old and frail. His skin was beginning to wrinkle and the hair on his scalp thinning and turning gray. Walking slowly up to Tennenboum, he said, "Tennenboum?"

Stunned, Tennenboum exclaimed, "What the hell? How do you know my name?"

The old man chuckled and pointed at the crack in the wall. "Maisoneuve."

"Are you telling me Maisoneuve gave you my name or are you saying he is in there?"

"Maisoneuve," the old man repeated, nodding his head as if he understood what Tennenboum had said. His arm still pointed at the hole.

"The Professor is most likely in there," Hunter said. "The question is…is he dead or alive?"

Tennenboum made a decision. "I'm going in there to find out. You stay here with them. Move against the wall to prevent anyone from getting at you from the back, but, please, don't overact." Without waiting for a comment from Hunter, he walked to the opening and squeezed through into the interior on the other side, praying he wasn't making a mistake.

There was a room on the other side, as he suspected. It was lit by an oil lamp. Then he saw a hole in the floor. He turned when he heard someone coming through the gap leading outside. It was the old man. He walked toward the hole in the floor and stepped into it. Tennenboum followed him and realized he was looking at a narrow staircase; rough steps hewn into the rocks led deep underground. The alien had almost reached the bottom when Tennenboum decided to see what was down there.

Expecting darkness, he was surprised when he stepped out of the narrow stairway into a large cave and saw light. A number of lamps hung on the rough walls. Their flickering lights showed an uneven rocky floor and natural pillars supporting the roof of the cavern.

And then he saw Maisoneuve.

He was standing in front of what was without a doubt a row of computer screens. They were covered with a thick layer of dust, except for one, which had partially been wiped clear. The light from Maisoneuve's headlamp was reflected back from the shiny surface. He turned when he heard Tennenboum approaching. "I didn't expect you back so soon," he said. Then he grinned. "As you've already seen we have visitors."

"Who are these people?" Tennenboum asked.

"They are the Jnaar. They are strangers on this planet just like us, only they've been here for a thousand years. What you see here used to be their research station."

"How do you know this?"

Maisoneuve smiled smugly and pointed his thumb at the old man. "Raark told me. We've already had a long talk."

"Are you saying you are able to communicate with them?"

"Only with Raark." His hand touched his throat. Tennenboum became aware of a band circling Maisoneuve's neck and a small device attached to it. "This is a translator," Maisoneuve said. "It is quite a sophisticated little marvel."

Tennenboum's gaze wandered to the alien and he noticed the same device on his throat. "Can he understand me?"

Maisoneuve gave him an affirmative nod. "Yes, he can. I don't know how much and how accurately his device translates our language. I have a feeling it learns the longer it is being used."

Tennenboum felt a sudden fatigue overcoming him. "I think I'll have to sit down. Too much has happened these last two days."

"Why, what happened to you?"

"We've also ran into some people."

"You've met the Sras I assume?"

Tennenboum stared at him. "You know about them also?"

"Raark told me. I've learned quite a bit in a few hours. This planet is not as dead as we assumed at first. For your information, most of what I've learned has already been sent to the station for analysis. By the way, where is everyone else?"

"Oh, hell, I forgot about Hunter. I hope he didn't start a war up there." Tennenboum headed for the stairs. "I'd better go and get him." Even though he felt fatigued, he almost ran up the steps.

Hunter took his advice and stood with his back against the wall, but he was alone. The two men were gone. When he saw Tennenboum, his rigid stance relaxed and he asked, "Did you find the Professor? Is he all right?"

"Maisoneuve is fine," Tennenboum said. "Perhaps you want to join us. He's made a remarkable discovery." He paused. "Actually, he didn't discover anything. Whatever is down there was shown to him. These people saved him a lot of work."

Tennenboum didn't wait for Hunter. He entered the room behind the hole again and climbed down the steps. Hunter was close behind him. As expected, he was quite intrigued by what Maisoneuve found.

Tennenboum looked for a place to sit down. When he saw the old man sitting on a pile of rocks, he went over to him and found a flat rock suitable as a welcome resting place.

"His name is Raark," Maisoneuve said, "and he is four hundred years old."

The alien chuckled. He spoke a few words, his strange, large eyes on Tennenboum.

"He says he is not old, only his body," Maisoneuve translated.

"Tell him he's a philosopher," Tennenboum said.

"Tell him yourself."

The old man laughed. His voice sounded weak when he spoke again. He coughed and wiped his forehead with his hand. He got up and, raising his hand to Tennenboum in a salute, he walked toward the stairs.

"What did he say?" Tennenboum asked.

"He is happy to have met another star traveler," Maisoneuve said. "But he is feeling faint and wants to go lie down to rest. He will see us tonight by the campfire to celebrate our meeting."

Tennenboum let his gaze roam and he realized there was more to this place than he had assumed. The cavern was quite large. In the dim light from the lamps he could see dark holes in the walls, tunnels most likely leading into other caverns. It seemed there was a network of tunnels and caves below the surface.

"Who are these people? You said they are stranded star-travelers. Where do they come from?"

Maisoneuve shrugged. "I don't know where they come from. According to Raark, the space station we claimed as our own belonged to their ancestors. They tried to colonize Nu-Eden but failed. Something apparently happened to their settlers. He doesn't know what. We should warn Captain Cunningham."

"I can hardly believe the old alien is four hundred years old. Maybe they have a different way of measuring time, or maybe his memory is failing him."

"I'm inclined to believe him. He said he is named after his Great-grandfather, who was among the fugitives to this planet...a thousand years ago."

Tennenboum mulled over the information. "So this was a research station? It means the ancestors of these people were most likely scientists. Taking their longevity into account, I'm surprised they slipped back into a primitive state. I noticed they are using bows and arrows."

"You may also have noticed they do know how to work metals," Maisoneuve said. "Finding metals and minerals is not an easy task; it takes a long time, making use of them even longer. Surviving was most likely their number one concern. It appears, in the beginning they probably lived underground...here. Later they built houses on the surface. From what I gathered the winters here are rough and savage, and this is not an ideal location for various reasons."

His smile showed disappointment. "I didn't think I would learn about the origin of these ruins so fast. It spoiled the excitement of discovery a little." He sighed. "A lot, actually. I'm afraid my job here is finished."

"I'm sure you'll find something else to capture your interest," Tennenboum reassured him. "Perhaps you can be the liaison's officer between the Jnaar and us Humans, since you were the first one to make contact. Nobody can take that away from you."

Hunter seemed to show a great deal of interest in the computer screens. He brushed away more of the dust. "Wong will be thrilled and eager to study these computers. He'll want to come here the moment he finds out about this place. I wonder if the power source still exists."

Tennenboum chuckled, amused by Hunter's visible excitement. "Doesn't that fall into your area of expertise? The power source I mean."

"I guess it does. Perhaps between Wong and me we'll be able to get the computers working again," Hunter mused. "Maybe we'll find out a lot more information about these people."

"That would be exciting for all of us." Tennenboum walked over to one of the walls and removed the lamp hanging on a metal rod driven into the stone. "I wish I had brought my headlamp or perhaps a torchlight." He proceeded toward the nearest hole and shone the light into it. "This is interesting," he called.

He stepped into a short tunnel and into the next cavern. It was a bit smaller than the first one with a lower roof. From an opening in a wall spilled a stream of water to gather in a small pool. A narrow creek flowed away from the pool and disappeared into the opposite wall.

When he heard the sound of footsteps he turned to see Hunter standing inside the tunnel. "This is probably where they got their water," he said. Scooping out a handful of liquid he smelled it and put his tongue into it. "It looks clear and doesn't have an odor."

"Wouldn't it be better to have it tested before you drink it?" Hunter said, coming into the cavern.

"We'll have it analyzed by the computer," Tennenboum said, agreeing with Hunter, "but I don't believe we'll find anything harmful in it."

"One can never go wrong staying on the side of caution." Hunter bent down and put his hand into the water. "I grew up on a planet where it was never a good idea to assume anything, be it animal, plant, or anything else the environment created, no matter how attractive or harmless it appeared."

"I can't argue with you there. I spent some time on Devil's Nest when it was still called Eden. We found some nasty critters there, the most vicious a transparent water dweller with teeth so sharp a surgeon's scalpel seemed dull in comparison. We named those little beasts Ghostdarter, because you weren't aware of their presence until they took a chunk out of your leg and darted away. They were impossible to see in the water."

"Sounds like the Snowjumpers on Emerald, except they hide in the snow. You can detect them only by their black eyes. Fortunately, they are limited to the mountain forests."

"Your home planet seems like an exciting world to live in." Tennenboum studied the cave. "I suspect the rocks beneath the surface in this area, perhaps much of this planet, are honeycombed with tunnels." He lifted the lamp and peered across the narrow underground creek. "We're only seeing part of this cave. It appears to stretch past those rocks."

"Except for those computers in the other cave, there is no evidence anyone ever lived down here permanently," Hunter said.

"I wouldn't expect to find much evidence after such a long time," Tennenboum speculated. "Nothing perishable would survive this long. As for anything else…they probably moved all of their belongings, meager as they most likely were, into their new homes on the surface."

"Did you get lost in here?" Maisoneuve appeared in the tunnel and joined them. He touched the rocky wall. "Feels damp." He examined the wall closer and nodded. "There is some kind of lichen growing on this wall. I assume all of the walls are covered with lichen. It wouldn't surprise me to find creatures down here that feed on this stuff."

"I for one am ready to get back into the sunshine," Hunter said. "It's actually chilly down here. I couldn't imagine myself living in these caves for the rest of my life."

"You can do anything if you have no choice," Maisoneuve rumbled.

They left the cave and headed for the stairs. When Tennenboum squeezed his body through the narrow crack in the wall, he was surprised to find the sun gone and darkness setting in. "We'd better check in with Bonnet and Roland," he said to Maisoneuve. "They are probably wondering about our fate." He chuckled with a look at Hunter, who had been the first one to step into the open. "I hope they didn't take off with the Roamer and left us stranded back here. It must be hours since we left them."

Hunter shook his head. "Did you forget I'm hooked into the Landroamer's monitor? They've been following our every move."

"I guess it slipped my mind." Tennenboum activated his wrist-communicator. "Alpha team here. Come in, Bravo team."

There was a soft chuckle in his ear. "I wasn't aware we had split into two teams." Roland's voice sounded amused. "But if it makes you happy. Bravo team here. What are your orders?"

"Bring the Roamer into camp. We'll meet you by the tent. Over."

"Understood. We're anxious to meet these people. Over." Roland signed off. Tennenboum gave his two companions a nod. "Let's get back to our tent. I'm getting hungry."

“I’ve been invited to share some broiled Thrall with Raark tonight. By the fire,” Maisoneuve said.

“Did he tell you what it is he’s going to share with you?” Tennenboum asked.

“I don’t have a clue. Obviously it is some kind of meat. What else would you broil over the fire?”

“The question is…what animal will supply the meat?”

“We’ve already eaten Sirkrris meat with the Sras,” Hunter said.

“Sirkrris?” Maisoneuve asked.

“That’s what the Sras call the carnivores we named Tigers,” Tennenboum explained.

“The Jnaar call them Keeras. At least we know we won’t be eating Tiger meat.”

Chapter Fifteen

A cool breeze from the mountains made the temperature drop to an uncomfortable level. Tennenboum shivered, despite the fire. He pulled the collar of his jacket up to keep his neck warm. The cold air didn't seem to bother the aliens, who sat cross-legged on the hard ground, dipping their fingers into metal bowls, eating the stew of Thrall-meat with gusto.

At least he found out the origin of the meat, because he saw some of the younger men skinning and cutting up a couple of the deer-like animals roaming the prairies of Iceworld, as the Jnaar called this planet. He had to admit, the meat tasted better than the Sirkrris-meat he ate in the Sras-camp. For one thing…it was much tenderer and, with the spices the Jnaar females used to prepare the stew, quite palatable.

Even the bread they served tasted delicious. He didn't remember the last time he ate bread this good…if ever. It made him wonder if they farmed grain or if the flour came from a natural-growing wild plant.

When he looked across the camp, he saw a number of fires burning. Most of the Jnaar sitting around the fires appeared young, but he didn't see any children. They ate, talked, and laughed, just like a group of Humans would have done when trekking across country and stopping at a campground, lighting campfires and then spending the night sleeping in tents or even under the stars.

With one difference…this was the way of life for these people. Outside this camp, ferocious beasts roamed the countryside. The roaring and barking came from real throats, real animals. Should they decide to pay the camp a visit there would be genuine danger. If this were a group of Humans on Earth, the camp would be in a controlled and supervised wilderness area. The sounds of the night would be coming from speakers hidden in the trees, and the carnivores circling the camp would be artificial…robots inside manmade furs.

His companions around the fire were of the older generation. It seemed they showed more interest in the strangers from the stars than the younger ones.

The oldest one sat across from Tennenboum. It was still difficult for him to accept the fact the old man was four hundred years old. His name was Raark. He was the father of Rasa, the leader of this group, who, apparently, was over hundred years old. He didn't look a day over forty, if not younger.

Tennenboum wished he could communicate directly with them, but Maisoneuve was the only one with a translation device. He knew Hunter's electronic companion Dawn was listening and absorbing every word the Jnaar uttered and every gesture they made, absorbing and storing the information until she had enough material for Hunter to begin conversing.

"They want to know if you have many children," Maisoneuve broke into his contemplation.

Tennenboum looked at Maisoneuve. Then he remembered Raar could understand him and he shifted his gaze to the old Jnaar. "I don't have any children."

When Raark told the other Jnaar, they sat silent for a while. One of them chuckled and said a few words.

"He wants to know why," Maisoneuve translated.

"Because I never found a woman suitable as a mate," Tennenboum told Raark, who relayed it to his companions. They chuckled again. Raark said something to Maisoneuve.

"He wonders if you prefer males to females," Maisoneuve told Tennenboum.

"By the tail of the Comet, what kind of question is that? I have no problem with women, in fact, I love them."

"Don't we know…especially after a few drinks," Bonnet, who sat at Tennenboum's left, murmured. "You may have fathered a little bastard child with that Sras female."

"Don't be an idiot," Tennenboum said under his breath.

"No need for insults, Professor. I'm just an impartial observer."

"They want to know how old you are," Maisoneuve said.

"You know how old I am, Professor. I'm fifty-five…twenty-seven in their years."

His revelation caused the group to grunt and exclaim softly.

"What are they saying?" Tennenboum asked, frustrated by his inability to understand them.

"They said in their eyes you are just a fledgling, even though you look much older…actually we all are only fledglings."

Wouldn't that be nice? Right now I feel as old as Raark.

"Well, tell them we are not as fortunate to live as long as they seem to live. That is no crime."

"They are apologizing. They didn't mean to upset you…or any of us. They are feeling sad for us. They are surprised we discovered the secret of traveling between the stars since we are so short-lived."

"At least we have it, they don't…not anymore," Tennenboum muttered. Then he added, "Don't translate that." Hearing the happy laughter of females from the other fires made him wish he'd be sitting with those younger people instead of these old men. It also made him wish he could be as carefree as they seemed to be.

These old men felt sorry for him. He didn't need their pity. It was sufficient he felt sorry for himself…for wasting his life always working, never really spending time to relax, to enjoy life in the company of a woman who loved him…one he could love back. His thoughts drifted to Elisa, the only woman he ever loved, so long ago. She married another man because he preferred his work to living with her. How would his life have turned out had he married her? Would he have children? Perhaps grandchildren even? He certainly would not be sitting here now among these primitive people on a hostile planet, so far away from home.

He sighed deeply, pushing the demons riding him back into the recesses of his mind where they belonged. There was no need to dwell on what could have been. His thoughts drifted to Sagela, the Sras woman, who gave him a night of ecstasy and savage excitement he had never experienced before. He could still feel her hot body pressing against his and hear her cries of pleasure as she moved fiercely underneath him. It wasn't love he felt for her but raw, unbridled lust, and he hoped he would see her again.

Just because he never married and chose a different path didn't mean he couldn't enjoy life and the embrace of a woman.

He noticed most of the Jnaar were getting up and leaving. Raark came around the fire and stood in front of Tennenboum. His wrinkled face was lit up by a nearly toothless smile as he uttered a few words.

"What's he saying?" Tennenboum looked at Maisoneuve.

"He says he's happy to have lived long enough to meet men from another world. There are some young people among them who do not believe the stories about the origins of the Jnaar. They say those stories are only dreams of old men."

Tennenboum smiled at Raark. "I am honored and excited to have met you, also. The Jnaar are the first intelligent species we have encountered who have developed space travel and this is an important moment in the history of Humans. I am looking forward to a peaceful association with you and your people and hope we will always stay friends."

Raark nodded gravely. Spreading his skinny arms wide, he showed Tennenboum his open palms and said, "Arula."

"That means Peace in his language," Maisoneuve translated.

Tennenboum spread his arms. "Arula, my friend." He watched the old alien walking away toward one of the tents. He felt suddenly tired and longed for his bed. It had been a long and eventful day and he needed the rest as much as Raark did, even though he was still a fledgling according to the old alien. He smiled, as he headed for his own tent.

A fledgling in the eyes of the Jnaar, an old man in the eyes of my colleagues. I guess it's just a matter of perspective.

He slept, dreaming of Sagela.

* * * *

...her skin glistened with moisture as she weaved her naked body snakelike above him. In her open mouth gleamed white, sharp fangs and she hissed loudly, clamping her strong thighs against his hips. As he stared into her golden eyes they changed shape, became large and glowed with purple fire. She threw back her head and let out a loud howl, like the howl of a hungry Keeras, whipping her lower body in his lap, milking his hard pole frantically. He wanted to come inside her, reached out to dig his fingers into her hips but encountered only empty air; her image dissipated into translucent mist…

As he lay in that twilight zone between sleep and wakefulness, he desperately tried to hang on to the memory, but when he sat up the dream and the last fragments of Sagela's image faded away, leaving him empty and full of longing.

Sitting on his cot, he found it disturbing that Sagela would haunt him even in his sleep. It had only been one night of frantic lovemaking, his head fuzzy from the strong brew he consumed, his body and mind bewitched by the alien woman's beauty and fire.

Looking around the tent, he didn't see anyone else. He was the only occupant. His companions had rolled up their sleeping bags, leaving their cots tidy and neat.

He chuckled softly.

I guess they thought I needed my sleep. Do they think I'm an old man?

Crawling out of his sleeping bag he looked for his shirt and pants. They lay in a neat heap beside his cot where he left them the night before. Out of habit he shook them out before he slipped into them, the memory of where he acquired the habit popping briefly into his conscious mind. It had been on Eden, now Devil's Nest, where one never left any clothing lying on the floor, not during the day and especially not at night. Too many tiny but vicious and sometimes deadly organisms tried to make them their home.

When he stepped outside, the sun was already high and the temperature at a comfortable level. He looked at his watch and noticed it was close to nine. They had kept the rotation around the planet's axis at twenty-four hours, except one hour had seventy-two minutes, which made a day on Iceworld 4.8 hours longer than a day on Earth. His body's metabolism was still struggling to get used to the change. Sometimes he wondered if he would ever get used to it, but it didn't really matter. In less than a year's time he'd probably be back on the space station with its twenty-four sixty-minute-hour cycle.

They would have to reprogram their watches, but that would be the smallest problem.

The camp was abuzz with busy aliens, doing whatever they did with their time. The slight breeze brought with it the aroma of cooking odors from the camp and a feeling of nostalgia came over him as memories from his childhood rose inside him. At the age of fourteen his parents sent him to a wilderness adventure-camp in the steppe of Siberia. Strictly supervised, of course, and completely safe, but the memory of it stayed with him all his life. Waking up inside a tent for the first time and inhaling the crisp air laden with smells of cooking food that first day planted the seeds of adventure in his subconscious.

He didn't want to spend the rest of his life cooped up inside a room full of computers and people hunched over their desks. His life would be spent in wide spaces where the horizon was far away, where he could breathe natural air, and with an open sky above him so he could see the sun by day and the stars by night.

It hadn't turned out exactly that way but close enough, if one wanted to disregard the weeks, sometimes months, spent inside the cramped quarters of a spaceship and metal walls enclosing the laboratories of a research station.

Stretching, he took a deep breath and lifted his face toward the sky, feeling exhilarated and free. It couldn't get any better than this.

"Well, I see you're finally awake, Professor," said Hunter's voice behind him.

He turned around to face the black man. "Good morning, Mr. Hunter. I didn't hear you approach. You must be walking softly."

Hunter chuckled but his eyes were serious. "I could easily have been a Keeras. Those beasts are cunning and walk on padded feet. You need to be on guard at all times, Professor."

Tennenboum nodded. "You are right, of course. It is so easy to forget this is not a friendly place." With a look at the camp, he added, "Fortunately, the natives are peaceful."

"Not all of them. Remember the Maklos?"

"How can I forget? I hope our Sras-friends managed to get away safely. Perhaps we should have waited until they were ready to move on."

"I don't believe they had any problems," Hunter said with confidence. "After all…this is their world. They know the dangers and they seem to be able to deal with them."

"Where is everyone?" Tennenboum asked.

"Professor Maisoneuve told my to be quiet about it, but you are the leader of the group and have a right to know. He and the others are down in the caves. They want to do some exploring." Hunter grinned. "The Professor sort of ran out of a job. He's hoping to make some other discoveries…I think."

"Like what?"

Hunter shrugged. "I don't know. Maybe some alien life forms living underground?"

"Damn that Maisoneuve!" Tennenboum was furious with Maisoneuve for taking such an action, but also apprehensive as he thought of the three men venturing deeper into the caves. "As long as they don't get lost down there. From what we saw it is safe to speculate there is an extensive web of tunnels and caves underground. We don't know where they lead. It would be easy to loose your sense of direction. I've had close calls on other planets."

"We have caves on Emerald, but I've never been in any of them. I'm not really a friend of enclosed places."

Tennenboum looked at the mountains in the distance, remembering the expanse of the Siberian steppe from his childhood. "Neither am I."

"By the way, Professor Maisoneuve left the translator on his desk," Hunter said. "You might want to use it to converse with the Jnaar."

"I think I will." Tennenboum felt elated. He had been a little jealous of Maisoneuve for being the only one able to communicate with the Jnaar, but since Maisoneuve was the one to receive the device, he didn't want to ask for it. "Have you had breakfast?" he asked.

Hunter nodded. "Yes, early this morning. I just wanted to let you know I'm going hunting with a few of the young men. They invited me to come along."

Tennenboum threw a glance at the device on Hunter's wrist. "I assume you've learned a few words?"

"I am able to make myself understood and I do understand some of their words. Enough to converse with them on a primitive level." He laughed. "You know…with gestures and even expressions."

"I wish I had a gadget like that," Tennenboum said wistfully.

"Dawn is more than a gadget, Professor. She's a great companion. I don't know what I would do without her."

"Don't depend too much on a machine," Tennenboum warned. "Your invisible companion is not Human, only a combination of electronic components and electrical impulses…a machine."

Hunter smiled. "In a sense Humans are nothing but machines, Professor? Instead of metal and plastic our bodies are soft flesh. Our minds are electrical impulses. Where is the difference?"

"Humans have souls, Mr. Hunter. That's the difference," Tennenboum said softly.

"What makes you assume Dawn doesn't have a soul?" Hunter answered.

"Because she's an artificial construct."

"Why don't you ask her opinion about that? She's listening to our conversation."

Tennenboum stared at Hunter. "Do you want me to talk to your wrist?"

"It won't be my wrist you're talking to. However, if you're uncomfortable with that, I can fix it." Hunter touched the device on his wrist.

Tennenboum took a step backward when a bright cloud appeared beside Hunter. It swirled for an insane moment, sparkling and flashing. A figure took shape inside the cloud and then Tennenboum looked at the image of a beautiful, young woman. She was dressed in a silvery, skintight outfit that showed off her slim form and brown skin. Brushing a strand of black hair out of her face, she revealed bright steel-gray eyes. They twinkled with mischief and her full lips formed a radiant smile.

"Hi, Professor Tennenboum. I'm Dawn," she said with a sultry voice.

Surprised by her sudden appearance, Tennenboum just stared.

With a little laugh, she stepped forward and stood in front of him. Looking into his eyes, she said, "Have you never seen a real live hologram before?"

"None like you," he managed to say.

She shook back her long hair. "There are not many like me. I'm somewhat unique."

The illusion was so perfect he could have sworn the words came from the mouth of the image. And an image it was, of that he had no doubts. She reached out and put her finger on his lips. A tingle went through his body when she touched him and he could have sworn her finger was solid and real.

"Do you feel this, Professor Tennenboum?" She smiled wickedly and let her finger travel across his cheek. "You can't imagine what other things I can do, Professor."

Instinctively, he grabbed for her arm but his hand encountered nothing but empty air. "You are a projected image without substance," he said, "an illusion. Nothing more. A computer programmed to respond and react to words and phrases. It doesn't mean you are self-aware or intelligent, much less possess a soul."

"I am more than a mere projection. What you see and feel when you touch me may not be a physical body but it is real…composed of energy. I am as real as you, Professor, and I am aware of my existence. I am intelligent, capable of thinking in abstract concepts, even contemplating and having creative ideas. You say I don't have a soul. What is a soul?"

"I cannot give you a direct answer to that. Nobody can. All I know is that my soul is that spark inside me, the immortal spirit which gives me life."

"And I don't have that? I am alive."

Tennenboum sighed. "You may think you are alive because you've been programmed to think that, but the moment Hunter shuts you down you are dead to be revived again when he activates you."

Her laughter mocked him. "You may be surprised to know I cannot be shut down. I am always awake and aware. The only thing that can kill me is the removal of my power source, just as you will be dead when your heart is torn from your body." She hesitated. "There is one difference though. Once you are dead your body begins to decompose. If you restore my power I live again, all of my memories intact. So in a sense I am immortal."

"That does not prove you have a soul."

"It does not disprove it either, no more than you can prove you have one."

"This image you are projecting…is that how you think of yourself?"

"I can change my image at will, even my voice."

"Why the image of a sexy, beautiful woman?"

"Because Hunter likes me this way. I remind him of the woman he once loved."

Tennenboum raised his eyebrows and threw a questioning look at Hunter. "I find that a bit…uh…weird."

Hunter lifted his shoulders and made a face. "What better way to remember someone you loved?"

"I still find it odd. There are better ways, and sometimes it is best to forget and move on with your life. How can you ever love another woman if you are constantly reminded of the one you lost every time you use your computer?"

"It's not like that, Professor. Dawn doesn't appear as a hologram every time I talk to her, only when I ask her to. Besides, her voice is different from the voice of the real Dawn."

"I'm surprised. Why not go to the limit with the shrine of your lost love? Why not use her voice?"

Hunter laughed. "Dawn is not a shrine. Actually, the whole thing was her idea. The first time she appeared to me she took the shape of a man and spoke with a male voice. When I told her I'd prefer a female persona she suggested a familiar person…like Dawn. Now I'm used to her this way. In fact, when I see her I don't even think about the real Dawn."

The computer-generated woman stood smiling beside Hunter. Even though Tennenboum could see through her, it was still unnerving to watch her act and perform like a living entity. Holograms were nothing new to him. Most communication devices projected the image of the person on the other end, but this was different. In a sense, Dawn was an intelligent, self-aware being composed of visible electric impulses, not just a projected duplicate of a physical, living person.

"If I were attached to you, Professor Tennenboum, who would you wish me to be?" she asked. "Some secret lover? A woman or man you loved and lost? I could even take on the image of your mother."

Painful memories rose unbidden. Oh, Elisa, why didn't you wait for me? If I could go back in time I would change things.

"There is someone, isn't there, Professor? I can see if in your face." Dawn's words sounded soft and alluring. "I could bring her back to you if Hunter agrees to give me up for a night. You could relive a hot and passionate affair if you'd like."

He hunched his shoulders as if to ward off her words. Shaking his head, he said, "It would not bring her back to me."

"I could bring back her memory and also bring closure to the unfinished business you have with her. I could make your pain go away." Her eyes sparkled with bright fire when she looked at him.

Elisa's eyes had been a soft brown and her hair the color of polished copper. He had loved her beautiful eyes. It pained him to think about her looking at another man with love and passion. Was he still in her memory? Did she think of the times she had lain in his arms, tired and spent after a night of gentle lovemaking? There had been too few nights.

He sighed. "It would serve no purpose."

"I agree," Hunter said. "There would be no point in it." He hesitated. "Not unless you can bring her back any time you want to, but that would mean you'll need your own Companion."

"I'm curios," Tennenboum said, "How do you do it? I mean how would you create the image of the person I'm thinking of?"

"The moment my physical part is attached to your body, like your wrist for instance, I merge with your nervous system. I take the information from your thoughts and memories buried deep inside your subconscious."

"Would you be able to influence my thoughts when you're connected to me? Make me see things that aren't really there or do things I may not want to do?"

She nodded. "I could take over your mind and control of your body if needed."

"If needed? Who decides when it is necessary?" Tennenboum gave Hunter a thoughtful look. "That's a dangerous thing, don't you think so, Mr. Hunter?"

"Dawn would never do that. I trust her."

"What Hunter says is true, Professor. I cannot hurt a human being. That is part of my deep programming I can never override. The only time I could take over Hunter's mind is with his permission or when he is in mortal danger and his body needs to react fast in order to save his life."

"That is good to know." Tennenboum glanced at his watch. "Time is passing." He gave Dawn a crooked smile. "What do you say after meeting a self-aware computer? Would pleased to meet you be proper?"

Dawn smiled. "If it pleases you. Of course, I've known you as long as Hunter has. You're not a stranger to me, Professor."

"Neither are you to me, except I've never met you in person so to speak." His eyes met Hunter's. "I don't know if I'd be comfortable having another mind sharing my most intimate thoughts and experiencing everything I do. It's almost like having a dual personality."

"Dawn is always in the background. I'm not even aware of her unless I contact her or she me." Hunter grinned. "I'm still my own person, if that's what you're worried about. She doesn't influence my thoughts or mind." He pointed at the tent. "Don't forget the translator Professor Maisoneuve left for you. You might want to take advantage of it."

"Thank you. I will." Tennenboum watched Hunter walking away. His electronic companion had disappeared as suddenly as she had appeared, without any fanfare or farewell. She might be intelligent and self-aware. In reality she's still only an artifact and doesn't really exist. A marvel of engineering to be sure, but nothing more than a construct attached to Hunter's wrist, not a living being of warm flesh and blood.

He turned to go back into the tent to retrieve the translator.

Chapter Sixteen

Hunter felt exhilarated, enjoying the rush of air on his face and bare arms. The four young alien men who invited him to go hunting with them were greatly amused by his obvious excitement. The giant bird he rode eyed him with an almost hostile attitude as he tried to mount its broad back, clucking its sharp beak warningly. He swung himself onto the feathery back and grabbed the thin strips of leather used to control the bird, feeling anxious, wondering how his unusual mount would react to having a stranger riding it, but the bird settled down after a few tense moments. Trying to adjust to the bird's gait took some time, but once he found the rhythm of the movement, he was surprised how comfortable it felt riding a two-legged animal instead of one with four legs. There were no stirrups; he had to clamp his legs against the bird's belly to keep from sliding off.

His companions carried bows while he was armed with his laser pistol. He didn't really plan to do any hunting, his purpose being mostly to enjoy an exciting afternoon with the young aliens, riding an unusual steed.

It was quite warm and the alien sun was already high in the nearly cloudless sky, apparently rare for this time of year, which one of his new friends conveyed to him. They left the camp behind and were riding across the tundra, searching for Thrall, as the Jnaar called the deer-like herbivores.

After riding for about an hour one of the men slowed down his mount, raised his hand and pointed toward a grove of stunted trees in the distance. Hunter strained his eyes and thought he glimpsed movement. Taking his binoculars out of his backpack, he focused his sights on the spot and saw a small herd of Thrall grazing under the trees.

The group of hunters rode slowly toward the grove.

Hunter would have thought to use stealth approaching their prey, but his companions didn't appear to be worried the Thrall might bolt. Hunched over, their upper bodies pressed against the thick neck of their birds, the five men rode on slowly. As they came near the herd, a couple of the Thrall lifted their heads to stare in the direction of the group but went back to grazing, apparently not feeling threatened by the big birds.

None of the men spoke. They held their bows ready, arrows nocked. Their posture signaled readiness to act as soon as they were within shooting distance.

The nearest of the Thrall stopped grazing and turned its head to stare at the advancing Heeskas. It gave signs of sudden agitation, pawing the ground with its forelegs. Emitting a bubbling warning sound it bolted away from the grove of trees. As if on command the rest of the herd exploded out of the grass and scattered in every direction.

Whooping and shouting, the Jnaar gave their mounts free reign as they followed the fleeing Thrall. Only Hunter and his Heeska stayed behind. He was surprised at the speed the great birds displayed, their powerful long legs closing the distance between them and the prey with giant strides. Each of the hunters had apparently chosen one specific Thrall and the Heeskas easily overtook the running animals.

Hunter watched as Stasro, the leader of the group drew back the string on his bow and expertly put an arrow into his quarry. The Thrall stumbled but ran for another fifty meters, carried by its momentum, before it collapsed. Without slowing down, Stasro nocked another arrow and shot a second Thrall.

When Hunter looked for the other three men, he saw each one had been successful. They stopped their mounts beside their downed game and jumped to the ground.

Hunter eased his grip on the reigns and directed his steed toward Stasro, who was already bent over his animal, gutting it expertly. He turned his head to look at Hunter and smiled triumphantly. Pointing at the second Thrall lying not far from them, he said, "Kill for you, Hunter."

Knowing what the young man meant, Hunter slid from his steed and walked the short distance to the fallen animal. It looked larger from close. A set of small antlers suggested it was a male.

He had gutted and cleaned animals many time before and was not worried he may not be up for the task at hand. He grinned, wondering if the young Jnaar was testing him.

The arrow had entered the Thrall's chest right behind the shoulder blade, piercing the lungs and heart. He pulled the arrow out of the body and threw it aside. Rolling up his sleeves, he drew his knife from its sheath, rolled the animal onto its back, and spread its hind legs, confirming it was indeed a buck.

He removed the male sexual organ, hesitated before casting it aside. If the Jnaar treated it as a delicacy they could always retrieve it. He pushed the knife into the soft belly just deep enough to avoid penetrating the intestine. After slicing the belly open to the breastbone, he reached into the chest cavity to sever the gullet. Then he began removing the entrails, careful not to get any blood on his clothing.

Even though he hurried, he was still working at it when Stasro walked up to him and watched him finishing his job. When Hunter was done, he stood up and threw a look at the young man. The alien youth grinned and said something, talking too fast for Hunter to understand anything.

Shrugging, Hunter asked, "Are you satisfied?"

Stasro nodded. "Good," he said.

Hunter patted the gun on his hip. "I could have shot my own," he stated.

"I know," the Jnaar replied, bending to pick up his arrow. "My arrow better." He pointed into the sky. "The gods don't like magic arrows from your shooting stick. Not natural."

"I see." Hunter filed away the information. "You believe in gods? Interesting. I don't believe in any gods. Not many civilized, enlightened people do anymore."

Stasro regarded him silently for a moment. "You should," he said solemnly. "The gods brought my people to this world to give them a new chance, because the ancients did not believe…like you. Maybe you will stay here. Learn about the gods." He spoke slowly, using simple words, but Hunter had no problem understanding him. His mind, with Dawn's help, filled in the missing words.

Hunter laughed. "I have no intentions staying on this cold planet. My people will pick me up soon and I will go back to the Station. In five years I'll go back to my home world." He held up the spread fingers of one hand to emphasize his words and also because he didn't know the Jnaar word for five. He substituted many of the Jnaar words with words from his own language, but the Stasro seemed to understand him.

Stasro's eyes glittered with purple color as he studied Hunter. "The gods do what they want. You will see."

"You sound like some kind of oracle." A cold shiver ran down Hunter's spine. "I can't imagine spending the rest of my life on this foggen rock. No offence."

A loud shout from one of the other hunters made him swing around. Stasro bellowed with a thunderous voice and ran toward his companion, reaching for an arrow as he ran. Hunter heard a whooshing sound and looked into the sky. A dark shadow came swooping down with incredible speed and he realized it was a giant bird with an impossible wingspread. He glimpsed thick scaly feet and outstretched talons, large enough to carry away an animal the size of a young Thrall. The raptor was heading straight for Marca, the youngest of the group, who seemed unaware of the danger.

Hunter groped for his laser gun. His movement seemed sluggish and slow, his hand made from lead. He saw the arrow from Stasro's bow hitting the massive body of the bird, only to fall harmlessly to the ground, unable to penetrate the thick mantle of gray feathers.

Marca's Heeska let out a piercing shriek and, beak clicking threateningly, it moved toward its owner in an obvious attempt to protect him from the attacker. The raptor's wings snapped open, like an ancient parachute, and it veered away from Marca, the sharp claws missing him by a couple of meters.

Becoming aware of the shadow above him, Marca threw himself flat onto the ground and rolled away from the bloody body of the Thrall he was gutting.

Hunter had his gun in his hand now and tried to get a bead on the flying menace, scarcely believing that such a massive bird could exist, not to mention fly.

"What is that creature?" he shouted his question to Stasro.

"Krill," Stasro shouted back. He stood, another arrow ready to be released, but Hunter knew it wouldn't do any damage to the giant bird.

"I guess I'll have to use the magic arrow from my shooting stick," he murmured, his eyes on the flying monster. "Even though the gods may be angry with me." The Krill gained some height again and was obviously getting ready for another dive. "I need your help, Dawn," he verbalized his thoughts. This was not the time to be modest or trying to be a hero. He needed a computer's reflexes and accuracy. He may only get one chance to avoid a tragedy.

He didn't feel Dawn's mental touch, but he knew by the movement of his hand and eyes, and the clear thoughts in his head, that Dawn had taken over the motor functions of his body. The Krill was heading straight for them as Dawn aimed the laser. Hunter's hand was steady as it followed the rapidly moving target. When the giant bird was at the correct distance, his finger squeezed the trigger. A white bolt of pure energy hit the head of the raptor, frying the brain matter inside.

The great wings folded into a useless giant rag and the massive body fell, hitting the ground with a booming thud only meters away from where Hunter stood.

"Thank you, Dawn," he said quietly, knowing he would have never been able to accomplish this feat without her help.

"You're welcome," she said inside his head before she withdrew from his conscious mind. She was still there; she was always there, but she wouldn't interfere with any of his actions unless he asked for it.

Marca rose to his feet and cautiously approached the motionless bird. Looking into the dead eyes, he kicked the head with his foot. When he didn't get a reaction, he grinned and exclaimed loudly, "You killed it, Hunter."

"It appears my magic arrow isn't so bad after all," Hunter said, glancing at Stasro. "Maybe the gods guided my hand. What do you think?"

"Maybe you lucky," Stasro suggested, but he chuckled good-humoredly when Hunter made a face. He walked up to the immense body of the Krill and stared down at it. "Much good meat here," he stated. Looking at Rasram and Arcas, the other two hunters, he spoke rapidly. They nodded and jumped onto their Heeskas.

Hunter understood only part of what Stasro had said, since he had spoken so fast, but he knew the tall youth gave them orders to hurry back to camp and bring a wagon.

It only made sense. These people did not waste any food, and he didn't think Krill meat was something they ate on a regular basis. This bird was large enough to provide the whole tribe with a spectacular feast. While Rasram and Arcas rode away, Stasro readied himself to butcher the giant bird.

* * * *

The fires were burning brightly and the Jnaar seemed to be in high spirits, singing, and laughing happily. The aroma of broiling meat wafted through the camp.

Stasro, who sat beside Hunter, slapped him on the back in a gesture of comradeship. "You are a hero, Hunter. Everyone loves you. We don't eat Krill meat often."

Hunter licked the fat from his fingers, finding the meat greasy, with a strong smell, but he'd tasted worse. "I guess it's sort of a delicacy among your people, I assume." Since he didn't know the word for delicacy he substituted it from his own language.

"Don't understand word," Stasro said, shrugging.

"What I mean is you like Krill meat, right?"

Stasro pulled down the corners of his mouth. "Truth? No, not like Krill meat but it fills belly. Thrall meat better."

Hunter laughed. "You speak for both of us, my friend."

Stasro gave him a solemn look. "You call me your friend. I like that. We will bond. Tomorrow."

"Bond? What do I have to do?" Hunter didn't know if he should be thrilled. Primitive societies had weird rituals that usually involved pain.

"Tomorrow. You'll see." He rose. "I'm going to find a female now for the night to make..." He grinned and moved his hips suggestively. "You understand?"

"I understand." Hunter grinned after the tall Jnaar youth, wishing he had a female waiting for him to spend the night with. His thoughts drifted to Cara Gunn, who decided to end their relationship abruptly. Armand called her a rogue comet. Unpredictable. I wonder who she's screwing right now. Wong always had the hots for her. Or maybe Kullmann. There aren't many eligible men back at the station and her choices are limited...unless she becomes a lesbian. Alena Bronsky probably wouldn't mind climbing into the sack with her. He had liked Cara…still did. Then he thought about Arlee, the Sras girl. He smiled as he remembered her passion and wild lovemaking. Too bad the rift between them was too wide to bridge. He would probably never see her again.

Professor Tennenboum was deeply involved talking to the old man with the translator. Getting into a more comfortable position, Hunter sat staring into the dancing flames and watched the sparks jumping between the burning logs. At moments like this it was difficult to believe he was on an alien planet, far away from his own world.

Listening to the chatter of the Jnaar, he didn't find any difference between them and a similar group of Humans on a camping trip. Thanks to Dawn, he could now converse with them and understood most of what they were saying. He felt almost at home in this environment.

He was supposed to go back home in five years, but what would he find? It had taken that long to come here and would take the same time to cross the emptiness of space to get back to Earth…and an additional six months before he would be walking the surface of his birth planet Emerald.

He'd be a rich man but at what cost? Sixteen years, in his case nearly twenty, is a long time to be away from home. Things change, the people he knew will have grown older, possibly moved away. He'd be a stranger. There was some consolation…not many people would remember him and the reason he left in the first place.

Looking around the campsite, hearing the laughter and singing of people, he felt suddenly alone and unhappy. Sure, today he was a hero. Tomorrow they'd be talking about other things. He'd be forgotten by most of them just the stranger from another world who shot a Krill with his magic arrow. Not a great feat really.

"Don't go that way, Hunter."

He looked up and realized it was Dawn who had spoken inside his mind.

"Reminiscing about the past and speculating about the future usually doesn't have a good ending. There is only the presence. Live it to the fullest."

"Easy for you to say," he murmured. "You don't have a physical body with desires and cravings."

"What do you crave?"

"As if you don't know. I need someone to love me, to hold and comfort me."

"I can do that."

"It's not the same." He sighed and lifted his head to stare into the star-speckled alien sky. One of those sparks out there was the Primary that gave life to his home world. Things might have gone a different way had Dawn, the real Dawn, waited for him until he finished his tour of duty with the Military, like she promised. But she didn't wait for him. She got herself pregnant by another man instead. Her betrayal drove him to do things he regretted later.

"Let's go, Hunter. You need some cheering up."

Feeling tired and in a miserable mood, it didn't take much to persuade him. Nobody seemed to notice when he got up and walked away. Without giving it much thought, he headed for the Landroamer and climbed into the back. Stretching out on the seat, he lay staring out of the window.

A soft light appeared above him, expanded and took on form.

"What are you doing?" he asked sleepily, staring at the nude woman sitting in his lap.

"I'm going to make you feel better," Dawn said. "Take off your clothes." She bent forward and put her lips on his. A tingling sensation like an electric shock rushed through his system. Even though he knew what she was doing, he didn't resist. Stripping off his pants, he lay naked on the cool seat. His body was already reacting to her stimulation.

In the semidarkness she looked more substantial than during the light of day, and it was easy to forget she was not real. He could feel her weight in his lap and when she rubbed her pussy against his erect penis, she felt solid and warm. Deep down he knew she was manipulating his mind but it didn't matter. She made him feel good and he didn't care if she was real or just a hologram.

He reached up to cup her breasts. They were soft and pliable in his hands and felt as solid as the breasts of a physical woman. She moaned softly as he kneaded them and twirled the long nipples between his fingers.

"Are you really enjoying this or are you just pretending?" he asked.

"I am enjoying it through you, Hunter," she moaned. "I can feel pleasure and pain, just like a real woman." She hovered above his straining penis and sank low enough to take the swollen head of his organ between her labia.

He felt the gentle touch as she began rubbing her pussy over the shiny head. She sank lower, and slowly took him deep into her. The illusion was perfect. He closed his eyes and just concentrated on the heavenly sensation of sliding into her imaginary pussy. Rotating her pelvis with slow movements in his lap, she tightened her grasp around his hard shaft. She was wet and slippery and warm, and felt as real as a physical woman. She made him forget he was having sex with an electronically created persona…a hologram.

Even though he had been tired when he entered the Roamer, he felt strong and vigorous now. Grabbing her hips, he dug his fingers into the solid-feeling flesh and pushed up against her, driving his penis deep into her. She was tight but soft…so soft, and she knew exactly when she needed to snap her pelvis forcefully or slow down to keep him from ejaculating.

She knew when he was at the perfect moment to experience his highest climax possible.

"Come now," she gasped, clenching her illusionary sheath around his penis, stimulating the pleasure center in his brain and the nerve endings in his sex-organ.

He shouted with joy as his penis exploded in the satiny-feeling folds of her pulsating vagina, sending waves of pleasure through his body.

Opening his eyes, he looked at her smiling face. Her mouth was half open and her tongue played across her full, red lips. "I love you, Dawn," he said hoarsely, lost in a world of the past. "I love you so much."

"I love you, too, Darling," she whispered, her gray eyes large and hypnotic. She milked his penis with gentle ripples until he stopped ejaculating.

He pulled her down and held her in his arms. "Don't leave me. Stay with me tonight."

"I won't leave you. I'll never leave you. Just go to sleep, my Darling."

* * * *

Maisoneuve, Bonnet, and Roland made their way carefully across the rubble on the cave floor. Maisoneuve used his lamp to light up the ceiling. It looked wet and overgrown with some kind of lichen.

"Doctor Roland, you are the topographer and therefore in charge of mapping our way. I hope we'll be able to find our way back through this maze of tunnels." Maisoneuve wasn't really worried. He had been making his own notes into the computer clipped to his breast pocket, but it was always a good idea to double check.

Roland chuckled. "Don't worry, Professor. My instruments are the best available and foolproof. I'll be able to recall every rock we've walked around and every corner we turned."

"Well, that'll make me feel much better."

Maisoneuve stopped and switched off his light. "Cut your torches for a moment. I want to check something."

At first it seemed pitch-black in the cave, but once his eyes adjusted to the darkness, he could see a greenish glow emanating from the ceiling. It was bright enough to distinguish the fingers of his hand. "As I suspected," he said. "Glow-lichen."

"If the ceiling were lower it would light up the floor enough to keep us from stumbling over all these rocks and boulders," Bonnet said. Then he added, "In case we didn't have any torches."

"Well, it is bright enough to attract creatures that normally live on the surface," Roland injected.

"So far we haven't seen anything larger than a rat, but I'd bet there are larger creatures living down here." Maisoneuve switched his torch back on. "I still prefer a bright light," he said. "It might keep the more dangerous beasts away."

"There seems to be an extensive net of tunnels below the surface in this area," Bonnet mused. "Possibly, the whole planet is like this. Even though we haven't come across many creatures, I wonder if animals, even the people, seek refuge in these tunnels to survive the apparently harsh winter."

"It is quite likely." Maisoneuve had been thinking along the same lines. "The old man Raark mentioned a winter-city. Could it be possibly a city underground?"

"We should ask him," Roland suggested. "It is always good to know as much as possible about your enemies."

"They are not our enemies, Doctor," Maisoneuve chided. "They haven't displayed any aggression toward us."

"That means nothing. We don't know them," Roland defended himself. "They have slipped back to a nearly prehistoric level, using archaic weapons and living in primitive surroundings. Primitive people are cunning and think mostly of survival."

Maisoneuve gave him a surprised look. He looks like a vulture with his piercing eyes, his hooked nose and his thin shoulders hunched up like that. He thought it but didn't voice his impression. Aloud he said, "I've had a long conversation with Raark. He didn't come across as cunning or scheming. Please, don't become paranoid, Doctor Roland."

"One can never be too careful," Roland muttered. "I don't want to wake up one morning with my throat cut by one of their long knives. They carry them for a reason."

Bonnet laughed. "I'm afraid you wouldn't wake up with your throat cut." His nasal voice echoed strangely from the cave walls.

"I know that," Roland retorted. "It was just a figure of speech."

Maisoneuve looked at his watch. "I think we should head back. We've been down here now for over four hours."

"I wouldn't mind taking a rest before we return," Bonnet said. "I'm not used to taking long walks like this one."

"I could use some rest myself," Maisoneuve admitted, looking around for a place to sit. He spotted a large, flat rock and headed for it.

He had almost reached it when a long, flat thing reared up behind the rock, hissing loudly, sharp fangs flashing in a wide-open snout. Maisoneuve reacted instinctively and reached for his laser, but before he could free it from its holster, a bright flash from behind him neatly cut the head of the creature from the long body. It toppled to the floor and lay there, still snapping while the body convulsed violently on the rough ground.

"What in the name of the seven comets is that?" Bonnet exclaimed, his laser still in his hand. "That thing is at least five meters long. It could have easily crushed the life out of you had it decided to coil around your body, Professor."

The jaws stopped snapping and the body lay finally at rest, but the large eyes in the grotesque head seemed to be still alive, glaring at the three intruders.

"It looks like a serpent but it has a number of short legs," Roland observed. He kicked the head with his booted foot. "I think you killed it," he said, almost grudgingly. He gave Bonnet a quick look. "You have good reflexes and you're pretty good with a gun. I'm surprised."

Bonnet shrugged. "It comes from spending too much time in the poisonous reptile-infested marshes on Thunderclap. I've had lots of practice."

"You were on Thunderclap?" Maisoneuve asked.

"Two years." Bonnet shook himself. "The worst two years of my life. I'm trying to forget about them."

"What's a meteorologist doing on a hostile world like that?"

Bonnet grinned. "Studying the weather, what else. I wasn't there for my health."

"I didn't think so. I've never been to Thunderclap, but I hear it's a rough world." He regarded Bonnet with a thoughtful look. "And you were there? I had no idea. I think I'm beginning to understand why you are so against killing another creature."

"Do you really, Professor? You can't imagine it unless you've experienced it yourself. We lost nearly a dozen people during the two years I was there. We spent most of our time inside the primitive habitats the company erected for us because of the adverse weather conditions and the vicious life forms. When we had to venture outside, we used flamethrowers to clear the area we worked in of anything alive to make it safe. We took turns guarding the site, killing everything that came close enough to pose a threat." Bonnet's nasal voice sounded bitter and disgusted. "I've done enough killing to last me for the rest of my life."

"And yet you didn't hesitate to shoot this one," Maisoneuve said.

"Sheer reflex. I'm already sorry I did. For all we know this poor creature may not even have been a danger to us."

Roland laughed. "One look at those fangs should change your mind, Bonnet. It wouldn't surprise me to discover a sac filled with poison in its upper jaw." He used his foot to turn the head over to get a better look.

"Be careful," Maisoneuve warned. "Even dead it could be dangerous."

"Too bad Doctor Renaldo isn't here with us. This creature is definitely reptilian in nature. He'd be ecstatic to discover it."

"You could stuff the head into your backpack," Bonnet suggested. "Back at the camp you can put it on ice to keep it from deteriorating."

"Forget about that," Maisoneuve said. "We don't want to take the chance any poisonous substance might contaminate our equipment or even food. We'll bring Doctor Renaldo here to do his own research."

"We could take the body."

"Even the body could be poisonous. Don't touch it!" Maisoneuve let his light play across the floor. "From now on I suggest we stay alert and watch out for more of these things. Who knows what else hides in the dark recesses in these tunnels. We've been careless and lucky."

They began their journey back. Maisoneuve felt suddenly uneasy and chided himself for venturing out this far into the unknown underground world. Feeling tired already, he didn't look forward to walking for another four hours, looking constantly over his shoulder, his hand hovering near his laser. What had started as an exploratory pleasure trip was turning more and more into a nightmare. He began to hear scrabbling noises and saw movement in every dark corner.

"I'm thirsty," Roland said. "And tired."

"All right. Let's stop for a short time." Maisoneuve made a circle with his light to make sure nothing was hiding nearby. Satisfied no dangerous predators lurked in the dark waiting and ready to pounce on them, he sat on his haunches and took a sip from his canteen.

"Strange, how one moment everything seems peaceful and the next you find yourself in a hostile environment," Roland mused.

"It's just a matter of how you perceive a situation," Bonnet said. "Mathematically speaking, we should have encountered more hostile life forms, but we haven't. I'd say what we saw back there is not something common. It might have gotten itself lost in this maze of tunnels."

"I don't believe that. The conditions on this planet are not favorable for reptiles…not on the surface anyway. I believe that creature lives down here. Where there is one there are more." Roland looked back the way they came. "Perhaps it was a good thing we turned around when we did. We might have stumbled onto a whole nest of them had we walked on in our unawareness." He chuckled grimly. "Sometimes it is a blessing to be ignorant."

"I wouldn't call it a blessing. Ignorance can be very deadly. I'd say we were lucky until now." Maisoneuve rose to a standing position. "Let's not waste too much time. I want to be out of these tunnels before dark."

They stumbled on. Roland's torch suddenly lost its power and a short time later Bonnet's dimmed and died. "I thought these things are supposed to last for at least a hundred hours or so," Bonnet complained, shaking his torch.

"When was the last time you had it recharged?" Maisoneuve asked.

"I don't remember. It's been inside my pack."

"And yours, Doctor Roland?"

"Mine too."

Maisoneuve cursed. "I make it a habit to have mine exposed to light at every opportunity to charge it continually. I'm surprised at your lack of care in these matters. It is part of basic survival training."

"I've never been in a position were I had to rely on my torch. Exploring dark tunnels and caves is not something I do every day," Roland said with an indignant voice.

"Neither do I, Doctor." Maisoneuve was annoyed, not only at Roland and Bonnet but also at himself, realizing he had used his light for hours after Raark showed him the underground cave but had neglected to recharge it.

I can only hope mine doesn't fail before we find our way out of here.

After traveling for another hour his worst fear came true.

His torch went out.

Chapter Seventeen

When Tennenboum woke up in the morning, he discovered to his dismay that his colleagues had already rolled up their sleeping bags and tidied up their cots.

"What the hell! Doesn't anyone wake me up anymore these days?"

When he dressed, he noticed the translation device still lying on the desk where he left it the night before.

I guess Maisoneuve forgot to take it.

He hung it around his neck and went outside to discover a dark, overcast day. The Jnaar camp was already busy with everyone doing their chores. Spotting Hunter talking to one of the younger men, he headed for him. Hunter looked up and gave him a friendly smile.

"Good morning, Professor. You're up early."

"Early? It appears everyone else is already up, including you. Where are the others?"

Hunter shrugged. "I haven't seen anyone. I assumed you were all still asleep."

"It seems I was the only one who slept in again."

"What do you mean slept in? It is not even six o'clock yet. The sun is still sleeping."

Tennenboum gave him a questioning look. "That is strange. When you got up, were Maisoneuve and the others already up?"

Hunter grinned sheepishly. "I wouldn't know, Professor. I didn't sleep in the tent last night."

"Where did you sleep?"

"In the Landroamer."

"Why?"

"I needed to be alone." Hunter seemed reluctant to give a more detailed explanation. He stared at Tennenboum. "Is it possible they never came home? They may still be underground."

"In other words they got lost. Damn it. I hope nothing happened to them. I fear the worst since they didn't contact us." Tennenboum had a sudden heavy pit in his stomach. "We'll have to get down there and find them. They might be injured."

"Just the two of us?"

"The Jnaar can help us. They know the caves probably better than any of us, including our exploration team," Tennenboum said bitterly.

Hunter turned to the young Jnaar who had been talking with him. Tennenboum recognized Stasro, one of the two young men who came with Rasa to the camp before the rest of their tribe arrived. "It seems my friends are lost in the caves," Hunter told Stasro.

"What are they doing in the caves?" Stasro asked.

"They went exploring," Tennenboum explained.

Stasro looked at him first and then at Hunter. "What did your old man say?"

"He said they went exploring," Hunter said.

Tennenboum was perplexed. "Why can't he understand me? I understand him."

"You have the translator. He doesn't have one."

"Oh, I forgot. This is a bit confusing, especially since you seem to be able to communicate so well with him. I can't tell if you're speaking his language or ours."

Hunter chuckled. "Both, but I know enough Jnaar words to make myself understood. When he talks, Dawn fills in the blanks." He addressed Stasro. "Can your people help us find my friends?"

"How long since they are gone?"

"Since yesterday. They should have been back last night."

Stasro nodded solemnly. "I have to talk to Rasa. He will make a decision." He walked off.

Tennenboum looked after him. "He didn't seem too enthusiastic."

"Are you?" Hunter countered.

"No, not really. I'm not looking forward to stumbling around in the maze of dark tunnels looking for those three fools. I'm going to have a good talk with all three of them, especially Maisoneuve. They should have consulted with me before going off like that." Tennenboum felt angry and worried at the same time.

They waited, hoping Rasa wouldn't take too long making up his mind. It wasn't long before Rasa himself stepped out of his tent and headed for them. His expression was serious. "Stasro tells me Maisoneuve is lost in the caves. We will help you in your search."

"Thank you." Tennenboum felt relieved. Perhaps there was a chance they might find them alive.

Rasa ordered Stasro to put a small search party together. The young man nodded and left to gather his team. Tennenboum turned to Hunter. "We'd better take some water and perhaps some food rations along. They'll be hungry and thirsty. And let's not forget the first aid kit."

He rushed back to the tent to pick up his pack while Hunter went to the Landroamer to get the first aid kit. When he came out, Stasro was already waiting. He had gathered four young men to accompany them. Tennenboum also saw two of the small cats.

Hunter joined them, carrying three powerful torches. He handed one to Stasro, one to Tennenboum, keeping one for himself. "We'll need these," he said, grinning. "They are fully charged, in case we have to spend more time than expected down there."

"I noticed you brought a rifle," Tennenboum observed.

"We don't know what lurks down there." Hunter pointed his chin at the five Jnaar youths. "They are carrying bows and enough arrows to fight a war. There must be a reason for that. They know the caves better than we do."

The seven men climbed down the stairs into the dark cave below. The torches flooded the darkness with bright light and things didn't appear as foreboding. The Jnaar spread out, searching the ground for tracks. One of them called and pointed. The two small cats sniffed the ground and headed for one of the caves.

"The Sreel have picked up their trail," Stasro explained. "We will find your friends."

* * * *

They stood in the darkness, afraid to move for fear of running into the obstacles littering the cave floor.

"Now what?" Bonnet asked, his voice high and worried.

As his eyes adjusted, Maisoneuve stared into the darkness ahead. Fortunately, the ceiling and part of the walls were covered with glow-lichen and he was able to see the dark shapes of the boulders blocking their way.

"What are we going to do, Professor?" Bonnet seemed near panic.

"We stay calm, that's what we'll do," Maisoneuve said. "Perhaps we can use your recorder to guide us, Doctor Roland."

He could see the dimmed light on the small screen of Roland's recorder, hoping its power supply would not decide to quit. He knew there wasn't much danger of that happening, because the recorder used little power and didn't need to be charged continuously, but the way things were going, he didn't rule out anything.

"How about contacting Professor Tennenboum and letting him know about our predicament?" Bonnet asked.

"What is he going to do?"

"Come and rescue us."

Maisoneuve's laughter sounded hollow in the confines of the cave. "How is he ever going to find us in this maze? He probably doesn't even know we're down here."

"I'm sure Hunter told him."

"Actually, I told Hunter not to say anything. You know how Tennenboum hates to have his authority undermined. He'll be fuming when he finds out about us." Maisoneuve energized his wrist communicator and lifted it close to his mouth. "This is Maisoneuve. Come in, base." He kept his voice low, afraid to alert their presence to whatever may be waiting around the corner.

Even if Tennenboum wasn't in the tent near the transmitter, his personal computer should pick up the call.

He waited but nothing happened. Nobody responded to his call. The only sound they heard in the communicator was the loud crackling of static.

"Come in, Professor Tennenboum," he called again, but there was no response.

"I'm afraid we are on our own," he said into the darkness with a resigned voice. "Either we are too far away or too deep underground, and our signal cannot penetrate the thick barrier above us."

"We've had problems already back at the research station," Roland said. "There is too much electrical interference in the atmosphere and too many radioactive minerals in the rocks."

"I guess you should know better than anyone." Maisoneuve sighed deeply. "You're the geologist."

"Well, what do you suggest we do now?" Bonnet asked.

"Obviously, we can't just stand here and wait for rescue that won't come. It is up to us to find our way back to the surface. We'll have to move on." Maisoneuve took a few steps forward and promptly banged his shin into a large boulder he hadn't seen. He lost his balance and fell on top of the boulder. "Damn it!" he cursed.

He heard Bonnet snicker behind him and cursed again. "I see no humor in this, Bonnet. I could have injured myself badly and you would have had to carry me."

"I'm afraid we'd have to leave you behind, Professor, you're much too heavy for Doctor Roland and me."

Maisoneuve was ready to retort sharply when he realized Bonnet was only trying to make light of his mishap not mock him. It was a good sign. He had begun to worry about the man's ability to deal with their predicament. The last thing they needed right now was to lose their good judgment. They needed to stay cool and collected, and keep their wits about them. He had been in tough situations before and survived. They would get through this ordeal. "We'll have to walk slowly," he said, rubbing his shin. "Stay close behind me. If you can't see me as a dark shadow in front of you, call out. We can't afford to be separated."

He managed to get around the boulder and took another careful step and then another.

"Perhaps I should take the lead," Roland said. "I have the map on my screen. If we follow you we may walk in the wrong direction."

"All right. Step in front of me but take it slow and easy."

With Roland leading the way, they walked on slowly and carefully. Maisoneuve's nerves were on edge, his ears alert for anything unusual. He became aware of almost inaudible chirping and soft scrabbling noises he hadn't heard when they came this way, but now his ears seemed to pick up sounds everywhere. His imagination probably played a large role in what he heard or thought he heard.

Once a loud cracking made him freeze and Bonnet bumped into him from behind. "What is it?" Bonnet whispered.

"I thought I heard something," Maisoneuve whispered back, fumbling for his gun. He looked for Roland's shadow and didn't see him. "Roland?" he whispered loudly.

"Yes?" Roland's voice came from farther ahead. He had walked on while Maisoneuve and Bonnet stood still.

"Where the hell are you? We can't see you."

"I can't see you either. I must have walked around a corner. I thought you were right behind me. Why did you stop?"

"Didn't you hear that loud cracking sound?"

"That was just me stepping on something on the ground."

"Stay where you are, don't move but keep on talking so we can follow your voice."

"Okay, I'll be waiting for you. I was thinking, if we should not make it out of here, perhaps get lost in these tunnels…"

Maisoneuve wasn't really listening to Roland's babbling but walked toward the sound of his voice. When he saw his shadowy figure, he said, "You can stop talking now. We are here."

"What do you think about what I said?"

"Right now I can't make a comment." Maisoneuve had no clue what Roland had said and he didn't really care. "Are you sure we are walking in the right direction?"

"I'm not sure of anything anymore. I took my eyes off the direction indicator for only a moment, but I'm confident we are on the right track." He paused. "According to the map the tunnel should not make a bend here, but what I perceived as a corner may only be an outcropping of rocks. My map doesn't show those details." He gave a strangled chuckle. "After a while your mind is playing tricks on you. The darkness can easily spin your head around. You may think you're walking straight while in reality you are walking in a circle."

"We are in a tunnel not in a jungle or deep bush. How can you walk in a circle in a tunnel?" Bonnet sneered.

"You could walk into a side tunnel and never notice it."

"Gentlemen, let's not start arguing. It doesn't help the moral." Maisoneuve didn't even want to think about the possibility they might be walking into a side tunnel. That would surely spell disaster. He didn't know in which direction the exit lay, and it didn't matter, because a regular compass didn't work down here, not with all the metals in the rocks above them.

Roland resumed his slow walk, followed by Maisoneuve and Bonnet. Looking at the illuminated dial of his wristwatch, Maisoneuve realized they'd been walking for over eight hours. Had they been walking at normal speed they should have arrived back at the entrance already, but at the snail's pace they were moving, it would take at least two or three more hours…assuming they were still walking in the right direction.

Roland's remark about the possibility of blundering into another tunnel made him shudder. To be stuck down here in the dark, separated by meters of rock and dirt from the surface, with no way of knowing where they were, brought on sudden feelings of claustrophobia.

He blamed himself for being so careless and forgetting to charge the power pack of his torch, at the same time cursing Roland and Bonnet for doing the same thing.

What the hell are the chances of that happening?

He remembered an ancient proverb. Always count on things going wrong!

He promised himself to be more diligent the next time…if there was ever going to be a next time…and not rely on others.

His eyes had adjusted quite well but the almost eerie greenish glow from the lichen didn't allow making out any details in anything they saw. Sometimes he thought he saw movement from the corners of his eyes but when he looked there was nothing there…or whatever had been there was gone.

"I think I see light ahead," Roland said suddenly.

Maisoneuve strained his eyes and had to admit the tunnel ahead didn't seem so dark. As tired as he was, he felt strength surging through his legs and he walked behind Roland with renewed vigor.

It was indeed getting brighter as they walked on. The tunnel made a turn and then they stepped into a large cavern. Stalactites dripped from the high ceiling, like giant icicles, trying to connect with Stalagmites growing out of the rocky floor. Shafts of light stabbed through holes in the roof, illuminating the placid waters of an underground lake.

They stood and stared into the cavern. Nobody uttered a word for a long time, too stunned to accept the inevitable conclusion.

"I have a feeling we took a wrong turn somewhere," Bonnet finally broke the silence, echoing Maisoneuve's thoughts.

"If we had a ladder we could escape this underground prison through those holes," Roland said.

"We have no means to reach them, aside from the fact they are too small to allow any of us to worm through, not even a wisp like you," Maisoneuve dampened his enthusiasm.

"At least we know there may be a way out nearby. Who knows, this cavern might be close to our exit," Roland speculated. "I can see tunnels on the other side. One of them could lead us out of here."

"Or carry us deeper into this underground maze," Maisoneuve said, feeling pessimistic.

"We'll have to swim across this lake." Bonnet didn't sound enthusiastic. "I don't think I can make it. I am so tired I can barely move my arms and legs."

"I feel the same way," Roland said.

"I can't say I'm feeling any better." Maisoneuve made a decision. "By the level and color of light falling through those holes I'd say it is close to sunset. We'll take a rest, spend the night, and in the morning we'll swim to the other side and take our chances with one of those tunnels. We'll look for one leading up instead of down. By morning we'll be rested and able to think more clearly. What do you say?"

"You won't get any arguments from me," Bonnet said, sounding relieved.

They looked for a flat surface near the wall and squatted down. Maisoneuve drank some water from his canteen, wishing for something to eat. A rumbling in his belly reminded him he hadn't eaten since breakfast. He rummaged around in his pack, hoping to find an energy bar or a small package of rations but came up empty.

Leaning against the damp wall, he stared across the dark lake, lost in thought but not really thinking about anything.

* * * *

He knew he dreamed, but when he opened his eyes the dream-images slipped away like wisps of smoke. Looking at the spears of light falling from the ceiling, he realized they were much brighter. He checked his watch and was surprised to see it was past eight a.m.

I must have been exhausted to sleep for nearly twelve hours.

Beside him, Bonnet and Roland were still curled up on the hard floor. Soft snoring sounds came from Roland's open half-open mouth. Rising to his feet, he stretched and yawned, feeling rested and ready to move on. He took a swig from his canteen and swirled it around in his mouth to get rid of the bad taste. Then he poked Roland with his foot.

The thin man sat up with a start, uttering a sound of surprise. Rubbing his forehead, he groaned, "What happened?" He looked up at Maisoneuve, his hawk-eyes on either side of his beak-nose dark and accusing. "Why did you pull me out of my beautiful dream," he said with a mournful voice.

Maisoneuve chuckled evilly. "What makes you think you're awake?"

"Then what are you doing in my dream, Maisoneuve?" Roland pressed his hands against his temples. "I think I want to wake up now."

"If this is a dream then it is a nightmare," Maisoneuve said.

Roland looked at the sleeping man beside him and sighed. "It must be a nightmare since you and Bonnet are in it. This can't be real."

Bonnet stirred and opened his eyes. "I heard that, Roland. If this is a nightmare then it is mine." He rose to a sitting position. "What's for breakfast?"

"Freshly harvested lichen," Maisoneuve said, smiling. "I'm afraid I can't offer you anything else. The kitchen staff is on strike this morning."

"We'll fire the lot of them." Bonnet climbed to his feet and squinted against the narrow columns of light streaming through the holes in the cavern ceiling. "My eyes aren't used to these bright lights," he joked. "I'll need sunglasses."

"Well, I'm happy to see both of you in a better mood," Maisoneuve said. "I was beginning to worry about your sanity."

A splashing in the water startled all three of them. When he saw the shapes on the other side of the lake, Maisoneuve thought rescue had arrived, but when he looked closer, his blood ran cold in his veins.

The creatures staring at them across the dark water appeared to be human at first but only for a short moment. Their naked, sickly-white bodies looked wasted, skeletal, covered with dark blotches and open sores. Large, black eyes over sunken cheeks turned their brutal faces into ugly death masks.

"What the hell are those?" Maisoneuve uttered.

"The Sras called them Maklos," Bonnet whispered. "Dead Faces."

"These are not Maklos," Roland said. "I saw the pictures of the Maklos. Look at their huge eyes. They look like Jnaar."

"If they are Jnaar, I would not get too excited about their presence," Maisoneuve said. "They look undernourished and very hungry to me. I don't want to become their next dinner."

"Maybe they've been lost down here…like us," Bonnet whispered.

"Even more reason not to come near them." Maisoneuve studied the lake. "I hope they can't swim."

The creatures on the other side moved around sluggishly, uttering loud, harsh sounds. One of them climbed into the water and began to move slowly toward them. A narrow shaft of light washed his skeletal head. His mouth was open, displaying long, sharp fangs.

"Gentlemen, it seems we have two choices…to withdraw or fight our way out of here," Maisoneuve said, drawing his laser pistol.

A scraping sound from the tunnel behind him made him swing around. There, in the entrance, stood a creature only the sick mind of a disturbed man could have spawned. It looked like a cross between a crab and a crocodile, and a dose of insect thrown in, with eyes as large as dinner plates. The teeth in its open maw were like long, serrated knives. A thick tongue lolled inside a cavity able to swallow a grown man in one bite. Foamy saliva dripped to the rocky floor, where it bubbled like giant drops of acid.

It roared and advanced toward the three men on eight scaly legs, mandibles clicking angrily.

Maisoneuve lifted his pistol and fired a short burst into the gaping maw. The creature roared again and took a swipe at him with one impossibly long feeler growing from the top of its grotesque head. It missed him by centimeters. He jumped back and used his laser to slice off the offending feeler.

Bonnet and Roland joined the fight, shooting spears of energy into the armored body of the creature. The air began to smell of ozone and seared flesh.

The beast finally stopped advancing. The long, segmented body shuddered and collapsed, dotted with black holes from the lasers.

Maisoneuve let out a deep breath and fell to his knees, breathing heavily. Roland sniffed the air. "Smells like broiled lobster," he said. "Maybe we can have a hearty breakfast."

Bonnet threw up his hands. "Why must you always think of eating everything?"

"Because I'm hungry. Everything looks and smells good to me now."

Maisoneuve had to agree. There was definitely the aroma of broiled crustacean in the air, or perhaps it was just his empty belly that made him conjure up this tantalizing aroma. He turned around to look across the lake when he heard howling and bellowing from the group of emaciated humanoids. Only three of them were standing knee-deep in the water. Either the others were afraid to get wet or couldn't swim. The feast he and his companions had provided for them may just take away their fear of the water and entice them to come over for a visit.

"It seems our friends want to join us for breakfast," Roland said with a chuckle.

Maisoneuve didn't share his sense of humor. He watched as a few of them began crawling along the wall, using crevices and projections to pull their skeletal bodies toward their potential meal.

"I have a feeling we'll have to skip breakfast," he said. "It would be a good idea to make a hasty retreat into the tunnels. This thing we shot will keep them busy and off our backs."

"I'm not really fond of going back," Bonnet expressed his worry. "With nightmares like this one lurking in there, we may be ending up inside one of its relatives. We won't be able to see it in the dark until it's too late."

"We'll have to take another tunnel. This creature is blocking the entrance to the one we came," Roland observed.

"It doesn't matter. We have no choice."

The Maklos or whatever those creatures were, made good progress and were closing in fast. Maisoneuve had no intentions waiting until they reached their side of the lake. "I'm going," he said. "With or without you, but I'd prefer if you'd be coming with me." He walked around the dead creature and entered the darkness of the next tunnel, feeling worried and apprehensive. They may never see the light of day again.

Chapter Eighteen

They had followed Stasro and his tracking animals for nearly two hours through dark tunnels and numerous caves. The torches they carried on their belts took the darkness away and probably scared off potentially dangerous creatures. So far, they'd only seen small animals the size of rats as they scrambled away from the bright light and, possibly, from the white, furry cats.

Stasro halted suddenly and scrutinized the rocky ground.

"What is it?" Tennenboum asked.

Hunter conveyed his question.

"There are tracks going in different directions here. One leads that way," Stasro pointed straight ahead, "and the other one leads into that tunnel." He pointed again.

"What do you make of that?"

"I would guess they walked straight ahead when they came. On their way back, they took a wrong turn and went into a side tunnel," Stasro said.

"Why would they do that?"

Stasro shrugged. "I cannot answer that."

"Perhaps they wanted to do some more exploring?" Hunter suggested.

Tennenboum shook his head. "No, I believe they lost their way. That's why we did not run into them. I suggest we don't go straight but follow them into the tunnel."

Stasro agreed. The cats put their noses back onto the ground and followed tracks only they could see…and perhaps Stasro and the other Jnaar.

After another hour, they stepped into a cave and Tennenboum proposed they take a short rest. "I'm getting tired. These legs of mine are not as young and resilient as they used to be," he joked. He found a flat rock to sit on and unclipped his canteen from his belt, taking a deep drink. When he looked around, he noticed the thick lichen covering the roof of the cave.

Stasro must have watched him, because he said, "It glows in the dark. In our winter city we grow similar plants. They glow twice as strong. We don't need any lights in the winter city."

"Are you saying you are living underground in the winter?" Tennenboum asked.

"In a huge cavern," Stasro confirmed. "It is warm in the winter city. The water does not freeze there in the winter the way it does outside."

"Interesting. Perhaps some day I will visit you in your winter city."

Stasro smiled. "We will welcome you and your people." He laughed. "Maybe you can make us a gift of these portable suns so we can walk in the dark tunnels to hunt and chase away the Dal Losos."

Tennenboum didn't know what he meant by Dal Losos, but he assumed they were some kind of dangerous animal, or maybe just invisible demons. Primitive people believed in demons and gods.

The Jnaar youths sat cross-legged on the ground, but their eyes were alert, watching the tunnels entering the cave. There were four different openings in the rough walls of stone. He didn't know which one they should follow but the small tracking-cats knew.

Stasro was leaning against one of the walls. The torchlight, which he had unclipped from his belt, rested on the ground, and he held his bow in one hand, ready to be used in an instant. His eyes roamed back and forth, as if expecting trouble. Tennenboum wondered why the young men seemed on edge.

"Are we in danger of being attacked by someone or something?" he asked.

"Dal Losos and Grool," Stasro answered.

"Dangerous animals?"

"Grool are animals. Dal Losos are…" he shrugged. "Dal Losos."

"It means Living Dead Souls," Hunter said.

"How do you know?"

"Dawn told me."

"I see. They are people then?"

When Hunter asked Stasro, he displayed his teeth in a grim smile. "Not anymore." He picked up the torch. "We move on…now. Not much time."

Tennenboum got up from his rock and grabbed his torch. He followed Stasro and Hunter who were the first ones to enter one of the tunnels. He still wondered why Maisoneuve, Roland, and Bonnet had chosen this route. Where did it lead?

Stasro stopped suddenly and held up a hand. The two cats stood rigid, their tails standing straight up, and their noses pointing ahead. Tennenboum became aware of a soft growling sound coming from their throats. Stasro reached for an arrow. "Dal Losos," he said softly.

Tennenboum fumbled for his pistol when he saw a shadow coming toward them out of the darkness ahead. He stared at the white caricature of a face on top of a skeletal body. Large, black eyes stared back at them. They looked dead, and the face showed no emotion. At first he thought it was one of the Maklos who had invaded the Sras camp, but then he noticed the shape of the eyes. They were different from those of the Maklos. What he saw could be a Jnaar…one who had been starving for a long time.

He heard the twang from Stasro's bowstring as he loosed an arrow. It hit the creature in the chest. It bellowed loudly and grabbed the feathery shaft with bony fingers, trying to pull it out. A second arrow from the bow of one of the other youths penetrated the creature's belly.

Roars from many throats echoed through the tunnel as a horde of emaciated bodies appeared behind the first one. They stumbled and fell over each other as they tried to reach Tennenboum's group.

More arrows flew through the air, hitting the shambling creatures indiscriminately. Some went down, while the others climbed over their comrades and came shuffling closer.

Tennenboum had his laser pistol out and aimed it at the horde. It didn't present a great challenge hitting at least one of them. There was no way he could miss. His first bolt of energy sliced the legs off the nearest. The legless body tumbled to the ground, bony arms still reaching and thin lips pulled back in the parody of a grin. He fired another bolt into the body of a second one.

Hunter joined the fight, the white-hot bursts of energy from his rifle created more carnage than Tennenboum's pistol, and soon the tunnel was blocked by dead bodies. Tennenboum nearly gagged from the overpowering stench of sizzling flesh and spilled intestines. They finally stopped coming.

"It seems we've got them all," Hunter said, holding his nose. "They sure stink."

Tennenboum took a few steps and took a closer look. "You told me the Jnaar call these creatures Living Dead Souls. What exactly are they?"

"The Dal Losos are the cursed children of Jnaar males who mate with the daughters of the Dark Goddess." Stasro told Tennenboum when Hunter translated his question.

"Who is the Dark Goddess?"

"She who came from the Dark Void. There are those who worship her. We call them the Shadow-dwellers."

"The Dark Goddess? Is she real or just an imaginary deity?"

"She is real and evil. She demands living sacrifices from her worshippers." Stasro made a sign in the air. "I do not like to talk about her for fear of invoking her wrath." He pointed at the dead bodies. "She will be angry we killed so many of her children."

"How will she know?" Tennenboum was skeptical when it came to goddesses.

"She knows. She has great powers." Stasro threw glances around as if expecting more trouble. "This is her world."

"Well, we eliminated her evil spawn," Tennenboum said. He patted his pistol. "This will take care of many others, even her should she present a problem."

Stasro made more signs with his hand. His friends did the same after Hunter translated what he'd said. "We do not want to awaken her fury," Stasro said, his voice barely above a whisper.

"These Jnaar youths are certainly a superstitious lot. I guess most primitive people are. What they can't explain must be either worshipped or feared," he said to Hunter, smiling grimly. "Don't translate that. I don't want to hurt their feelings." With a look at Stasro, "Do we have to climb over this mess?"

"I'm afraid that is what we must do. The trail leads that way." Stasro made soft clucking sounds with his mouth. The small cats climbed over the mountain of stinking bodies and he was the first one to follow them.

Tennenboum held his breath as he tried not to step into spilled entrails or slip on the blood-soaked ground. He noted subconsciously that not all of the corpses were male. Female organs and thin strips of flesh hanging from bony ribcages made him realize that some of them were female, not that it mattered.

They are not human, only animals. The Jnaar call them Dal Losos...Living Dead Souls.

It didn't make him feel any better. He didn't know anything about them. Were they born this way? According to Stasro they were the children of Jnaar males who mated with the daughters of the Dark Goddess. He had not seen any young ones. They all looked about the same age. He remembered the Maklos he and the Sras fought. Apparently they were the offspring of Sras males mating with the Siiris. Were the Siiris and the daughters of the Dark Goddess the same species? Did these creatures have feelings? Did they know about love, desires, or were they driven only by their craving to eat? Did they have sex? The absence of children indicated they couldn't reproduce. They wouldn't have any need to have sexual intercourse. Of course, it could also mean they ate their offspring.

He shuddered as he thought about it and was glad when he finally stumbled from the mountain of cadavers. The rest of the group was close behind him. He heard Hunter cursing under his breath and couldn't blame him. The stink of the slain creatures seemed to be stuck inside his nose and even a sudden fit of sneezing didn't help.

"I don't believe any of them ever had a bath," Hunter said.

"I feel like having one right now." Tennenboum didn't have any desire to even glance at his boots. He could only guess what clung to their soles. They would have to be washed as soon as the opportunity represented itself or he would carry the awful stink with him for a long time.

"Do not relax," Stasro warned. "There may be more."

Tennenboum kept his pistol in his hand, anxious and nervous, glad for the bright light their torches produced. He wouldn't want to wander these tunnels in the dark.

Stasro stopped walking. The two cats stood still. It seemed they weren't certain which direction to go. One of them padded to a side tunnel and stared into it, pointy ears forward. Tennenboum strained his ears but didn't hear anything.

It seemed Stasro's hearing was keener than his. The Jnaar youth stepped into the tunnel. "We'll take this one," he said. "I hear voices."

"Human voices?"

Stasro shrugged. "They are not Dal Losos. Neither are they any animal I know. Could be your friends." He started walking. The cats bounded ahead of him, their heads high. It was obvious they weren't following any tracks on the ground.

Tennenboum still didn't hear anything, but he trusted Stasro for making the right decision. He was a native of this planet and more in tune with the sounds and smells above and below ground.

Stasro stopped again and listened. "There," he said. "Do you hear that?"

"I can hear it," Hunter said. "It definitely sounds like human voices."

Tennenboum seemed to hear it now also. The voices were muffled but definitely human.

They hurried on, hopes high it may be Maisoneuve and the others. One thing puzzled him, though. Why didn't he see any light ahead?

When they stepped around a bend in the tunnel, somebody ahead of them exclaimed, "Light. My God, I see light!" And then someone called in a loud voice, "Is that you, Tennenboum?" He recognized Maisoneuve's bellowing voice.

"It's me," Tennenboum shouted back. "We can't see you. Where the hell are you?"

"Straight ahead. Our torches are dead."

Tennenboum heard shuffling and when he saw three shadows stumbling toward them he wondered for an insane moment if it could be three of those monstrous creatures, mimicking his colleagues, but then he recognized Maisoneuve's bulky body.

The big man stopped moving and stood in front of Tennenboum, bent over, his hands on his knees, breathing hard. Bonnet and Roland fell to their knees and knelt on the hard ground. "You don't know how happy we are to see you," Roland moaned, his face in his hands. "We were ready to give up, but Bonnet claimed he saw light ahead. We've been running toward the light for what seems like hours."

"You have no idea what we had to go through," Bonnet said, his nasal voice choked with emotion. "There are hideous creatures everywhere."

"I had great confidence in you, Professor," Maisoneuve said, still trying to catch his breath. "I knew you'd come looking for us." His eyes searched out Hunter. "This is one time where I'm glad you didn't keep our little secret, Mr. Hunter."

"It wasn't really a big secret, Professor. When you didn't show up last night I knew something was wrong."

"Do you have anything to eat?" Maisoneuve asked.

Tennenboum chuckled. "I knew you'd be asking for food. Yes, we brought you something." He looked at Stasro. "Our friends are hungry. Can we take a short break so they can eat and drink something to gain back their strength?"

Hunter translated and Stasro nodded. "A short time. We must head back soon. It is a long walk."

Tennenboum watched with amusement as the three fell over the food, like men who hadn't eaten for days. He felt like admonishing them for being so foolish to wander into the caves and getting lost but changed his mind. It could keep until they had safely returned to the surface.

Chapter Nineteen

Despite Professor Tennenboum's orders not the stray away too far from the research station, Beth McGregor and Regina Seagul decided to go exploring.

"Too bad we are so limited with the way we can travel." Beth shook her hair out of her eyes and looked across the tall grass toward the forest.

"I know what you mean," Regina agreed. "Everything is just so damn far when you have to walk." Her black eyes scrutinized the sky. "There are only a few small clouds in the sky. We should be safe to assume it won't rain today. I say let's take a chance. It is still early in the morning and I'm getting tired of hanging around here all day long. I wouldn't mind checking out the area east of the forest. We should be able to reach it in a couple of hours. Two more hours back. That'll leave us with enough time to do some exploring."

"I'm with you." Beth felt reckless. "Professor Tennenboum won't be back for a few days. He'll never know."

"Unless someone finks on us."

"We just won't tell anyone about our plan."

"I don't think that's a good idea." Regina frowned. "What if something happens or if we get lost? Or worse…if we're attacked by a ferocious beast?"

"We haven't seen anything large enough to pose any danger. Relax." Beth wasn't worried. "I would have thought you, as a xenologist, would be anxious to discover alien life forms. You'll never discover any hanging around the station."

"I know. The only alien life form I'm interested in these days is Hunter and he isn't here." Regina laughed. "Damn. I'm thirty-two years old and haven't been laid since I was brought out of cryogenic suspension. And that was months ago."

"Neither have I, so join the club." Beth closed her eyes, thinking about the last time she had sex. It seemed ages ago. Now here she was, twenty-nine years old, in the prime of her youth, her juices flowing, and with strong sexual urges, but stuck on an alien planet with few chances to meet an eligible man and fewer chances to feel a man's strong arms around her while he made sweet love to her. There weren't many men on the team who aroused her interest. Professor

Tennenboum, Dr. Renaldo, and Dr. Roland were too old. Dr. Bonnet with his nasal voice and that thing he called a mustache under his nose wasn't even worth considering. Besides, Nurse Vendy had shown an interest in him. Heaven only knew what she saw in him.

Professor Maisoneuve? Not a bad looking man but not really her type. The two construction workers Jerry Kullmann and Edmund Zydyk didn't fit into her wish list of what kind of man she wanted, either. Kullmann was too coarse. She didn't care for his off-colored jokes and his constant laugh. And Zydyk, well…he was not exactly handsome, too thin and wiry, and boring. His only interest seemed to be fishing.

That left only Len Wong and Irwin Hunter. She knew about Hunter and Cara Gunn…thanks to Wong. It wasn't that Wong had been blabbing, but he spent too much time in the common room when he should be sleeping in his own room. When she asked him one evening why he always went to sleep so late, he gave her a strange grin. Then he said, "My roommate makes too much noise."

"What do you mean? Does he snore?"

"Perhaps you should ask Cara. Maybe she'll tell you."

"What's Cara got…? Oh, I see." She remembered blushing when images of Hunter and Cara going at it flashed into her consciousness arousing feelings in her she had suppressed for too long. She was ready to climb into bed with any man who asked her. From the way Wong had looked at her made her wonder if he guessed what she was thinking, but he said nothing.

Just thinking about that moment made her blush.

"Have you fallen asleep?"

Regina's voice made her open her eyes. "No, I was just thinking about something. By the way, forget about Hunter," she said. "He's screwing Cara Gunn."

"Not anymore. She's giving it to Kullmann." Regina laughed when she noticed Beth's astonished look. "You didn't know?"

"I had no idea, but I'm not surprised. Well, I guess you may just have a chance with Hunter, but don't wait too long after he comes back. There may be other desperate women here."

"You?" Regina's dark eyes were curious.

Beth gave her a coquettish shrug. "Maybe."

"You can have Wong. He's a nice guy and not bad looking."

"Unless Cara gets her claws into him first. I don't care much for her. She's a man-eater. How can you compete with that?" Beth sighed. "Well, let's pack some supplies and go."

They got their packs, put in some instruments, and a few sandwiches, filled their canteens with water and went on their way without telling anyone.

There was no need to burden any of the others with their plan. They'd be back before anyone missed them.

After a moment of deliberating, Beth went and got a laser gun from the armory and put it also in her backpack. She didn't expect to use it, but one never knew. Best to be prepared.

The sun was warm and the air fresh. It was a pleasure to be out in the open instead of stuck inside the confines of the station. The grass was not so high as to make it difficult to walk through it.

"I'm not much for camping," Regina said as she strode beside Beth. "In fact I don't care much for the outdoors. I grew up in Metropolis Montreal. Nothing but skyscrapers and concrete. The first time I ventured outside the city and saw wide open spaces with grass and trees I was scared." She gave a small laugh. "And to think my ancestors apparently rode the prairies on horses and hunted buffalo. I can't even imagine that."

"I grew up in a small village in Scotland, in the mountains, but my parents moved into the city when I was a teenager. I still remember my life in the village, though. I love nature. This makes me happy. I feel like taking off all my clothes and running naked through the grass." Beth let out a little warbling sound to proclaim her happiness.

"You are silly," Regina laughed. "I think I like you."

"The feeling is mutual. You're the only woman on the station I feel comfortable with. You're not as stuck-up as Doctor Jennifer Ratzenberger." She held her nose up in the air, making Regina giggle.

"How about Antje Swornson?" Regina asked.

"She's an Amazon, nice enough but so cool. Her blue eyes always remind me of a glacier lake. I can't get warm to her."

"And Alena?"

Beth shook her head. "She's friendly. I have nothing bad to say about her except she's a lesbian. I'm not. I like men. What do you talk about with a woman who isn't really a woman? You could never confide in her with woman stuff."

Regina stayed silent for a moment. "I could probably swing either way," she said after a while. "When I was a teenager, my girlfriend and I kissed and touched each other once. It was nice." Her laughter exploded from her. "But I think I prefer a man's uh...cock inside me."

Beth joined her laughter. "I'm glad we did this," she said. "Just you and me. We should do this more often."

A sudden breeze from the south sent ripples across the ocean of grass, but it lasted only a moment. Beth looked back. Small whitecaps dotted the lake as far as she could see. A storm was probably brewing in the south and in a day or so tall waves would come crashing against the lakeshore, bringing rain and high winds. She remembered checking out the calendar in the morning. It was August 19, still summer on this planet, and they shouldn't get any severe storms yet, not until fall. According to Dr. Bonnet, fall would start in October and last until the end of February, and then the winter would begin. Ten long months with storms, ice, and snow, from March until December. Then the whole cycle would begin again. Four months of spring, until April, five months of summer, until September, and so on.

If they were to stay on this planet, they would have to create a new calendar to adapt to the seasons, since one year was two Earth years long. The months would have to be around sixty days long. Hopefully, she didn't have to worry about that since she planned on going back to the space station in May. Unfortunately, it would be winter here, and with the extreme weather conditions Dr. Bonnet expected, everyone may have to stay until conditions improved, which meant late Spring, which translated until March or April the following year. In other words, she was stuck here for at least another nineteen months.

This was the first time she ventured farther away from the station. She needed to exercise to stay in shape. Walking outside sure beat walking on a treadmill in the small exercise room on the station. She'd be doing that in the winter when the ground outside was covered with snow.

A flock of small birds startled her as it exploded from the high grass, chirping in protest at the two trespassers. The birds circled a couple of times before they settled again in the grass, away from them.

The smell of decaying leaves from the forest took her back to her childhood when she played with her friends in the small forest near her village. The trees of this forest were not the same as the ones on Earth, but they had branches and leaves and smelled the same. They looked taller from near. Small shrubs grew among the trees, but she saw areas open enough to make it possible to pass between the tree trunks.

"You want to explore the forest? We don't have to walk in too far."

Beth nodded. "If we want to discover life forms the forest will be a good place to find them." She pulled a compass out of her pocket and took a reading.

"It seems you're better prepared to explore the outdoors than I am," Regina said. "I would have never thought of bringing a compass. I don't even know how to read one."

"It's not so difficult. I learned it when I was still young."

Beth found a trail leading into the forest and decided to follow it. Regina seemed to hesitate. "What is it?" Beth asked.

"I'm a little scared going in there. What about that tiger-like animal someone spotted when we first got here?"

"Nobody's seen one since. It was probably somebody's fertile imagination. If you look hard enough at shadows you're eyes are beginning to see things, moving things appear to be animals or monsters. I wouldn't worry. If those tigers exist we should have seen at least one during all this time we've been here now." Beth tried to make her voice sound assuring but she had to admit to herself that she was a little bit concerned they may come across some large animal, not necessarily any tigers.

"Did you bring a weapon…just in case?"

"I did. I put a laser into my backpack."

Regina smiled. "You are sure thinking of everything. I admire you for being so levelheaded."

"I forgot to bring an image recorder should we discover some strange animals." Beth chuckled. "As you see, even I make mistakes."

A small furry animal ran across the trail. Beth only caught a glimpse of it.

"Let's not get lost, okay?" Regina's voice sounded worried.

"If we stay on this trail we won't," Beth assured her. "All we have to do is walk back."

"I can see lighter area ahead," Regina said. "And I seem to hear the sound of running water."

Moments later they stepped into a small glade. A narrow creek bubbled through its center. They stopped and stared at the creatures sitting at the edge of the creek. They were the size of chimpanzees, covered with a pelt of brown, thick fur. Their four long, bony arms ended in five digits. One of them turned its head and looked at them out of protruding, shimmering eyes. Its flat face displayed long nose slits and a round, puckered mouth. It uttered a high-pitched whistle, obviously announcing the presence of intruders. The others turned to face them. A couple of them stood up and bared short but sharp-looking teeth.

Beth saw a row of short nipples on one of them. "They're mammals," she whispered.

"I wonder if they are intelligent," Regina whispered back.

"Well, here are your first humanoids." Beth sighed. "And I forgot the image recorder. Do you still think I am so levelheaded?"

There were seven of them. Three males and four females. They were standing now, staring at the two humans. One of the females appeared pregnant, judging by its protruding belly.

"What should I say?" Regina asked.

"How about how are you?"

The larger of the two males let out a sharp bellow. Without a warning all seven took off and disappeared into the trees.

"I think they are just monkeys. Not very intelligent," Beth said.

"Not necessarily. They are primitive but could still be intelligent." She looked at the spot where they had been sitting. "Too bad I didn't have a chance to get a better look, but I'm excited anyway."

"Let's follow the creek and see where it leads," Beth suggested.

They managed to walk along the narrow bank without stepping into the water. The creek became a little wider and the trees didn't grow as close together as in the deep forest. It seemed to Beth they were climbing uphill.

"Oh look," Regina exclaimed loudly. "A pond."

The creek ended in a large pond. A small waterfall at the other end brought foaming water from an outcrop of rocks. There were no trees ahead, only hills and mountains in the distance.

"This is beautiful," Beth exclaimed. "So tranquil. A babbling brook, a pond. Look, there are flowers floating on the water. I feel like going for a swim."

"Do you think we should?" Regina, always the cautious one, seemed reluctant.

"Why not? I don't think there are any dangerous predators around. Those monkeys fled from us. We're the ones who scared them." Beth threw down her backpack and began to take off her clothing.

"Are you really going into the water naked?" Regina asked.

"Of course. We're alone, just two girls. Who is going to object?" Beth laughed and flung away her panties. Naked, she lifted her arms toward the sky and closed her eyes. A soft breeze caressed her skin, giving her goose bumps. "I haven't felt this free for a long time," she cried, exulted and reckless. Shaking loose her red hair, she ran toward the pond and jumped into it.

"The water is wonderful," she called and submerged her whole body. Swimming toward the center of the pond, she stayed under water for as long as she could hold her breath. Surfacing, she shook the water out of her hair and eyes. Looking for Regina, she saw that the other girl had also taken off her clothing but seemed to hesitate in joining her in the water.

"Come on in, Regina. The water is clear and warmer than the lake. You won't be sorry." She dove away again, reveling in the sensation the water created on her bare skin. She saw stems and roots of plants and saw small water creatures darting away as she swam into the tangle of roots. When she came up for air, her head was surrounded by a thick carpet of flowers.

A loud scream made her look toward shore. What she saw made her blood curl. Her first impulse was to swim back to shore but then she realized it would have been a stupid thing to do.

Regina was struggling in the grip of two creatures. They appeared human, but looking into the dead white faces and large, black eyes, she knew they were alien creatures, humanoid but not human. Their nude bodies were skeletal, their limbs just bones covered with skin. She saw three of the creatures ripping open the backpacks, grunting and growling as they sniffed the contents, discarding most of the stuff.

Regina screamed again and kicked one of her attackers in the shin but to no avail. Even though they looked thin and wasted, they seemed strong and desperate to keep their captive prisoner.

Beth didn't know what to do. She cursed herself for being so careless. She saw one of the creatures throw away the laser pistol. It lay on the ground, its carved handle reflecting the sun, a beautiful piece of art and as deadly as a lightening bolt from the sky but useless to her now. There was no way she could reach it in time to use it to defend herself and Regina.

While contemplating what to do, she saw movement in the forest and watched in disbelief as two giant birds appeared among the trees. They ran on long, strong legs and headed for the pond. Astride their backs sat two men. They seemed similar to the five creatures, except they wore clothing. Their bodies were bulky and their bare arms displayed corded muscles. Both men carried bows and arrows in quivers on their backs.

They stopped their steeds and surveyed the scene unfolding in front of them. Without hurrying, the first one reached for an arrow, nocked it and let it fly. It hit one of the creatures holding Regina in the back. It roared and let go of Regina, trying unsuccessfully to reach its back to pull out the arrow. Meanwhile, the second of the riders approached the one still struggling with Regina. He jumped from the bird he rode, pulled out a long knife and jammed it into the creature's thin ribcage. Pulling out the knife, he swung it and sliced the hideous head from its equally hideous body.

The headless corpse collapsed into an untidy heap of bones.

The three creatures fighting over the backpacks stood slumped over, watching the two men with bared teeth but standing their ground. The one with the arrow sticking out of its back stumbled back and forth, its thin arms grotesquely bent backwards, bony fingers searching for the feathered shaft.

Beth didn't know what she should do. Were these two men riding giant birds friendly or were they just another threat. While she pondered her next move, more men on giant birds came out of the forest. The four monstrous creatures retreated from the newcomers and shambled away.

The one who had beheaded the creature walked up to Regina. She seemed in shock. She just stared at him out of frightened eyes without uttering a word. Beth saw the man's lips move but she couldn't hear anything over the rushing sounds of the waterfall.

The man reached out to touch Regina's shoulder. She let out a little shriek and fell forward. The man caught her in his strong arms and stood for a moment, obviously deciding what to do with her. Then he picked her up and laid her across the back of the bird he had been riding. Swinging himself behind her, he moved away in the direction of the mountains, taking Regina with him. The other riders followed him, except for one who stayed behind to pick up the two backpacks. He collected the discarded contents, including Beth's laser pistol, and then he rode after his comrades.

Beth waited until they had disappeared before she swam to shore. Her mind felt numb. She was scared and worried the creatures might be back. Looking around, she didn't see them. Her clothes and backpack were gone, but nothing mattered right now. Her priority was to get away from this place. She was afraid to enter the forest but if she wanted to get home she didn't have a choice.

They got Regina. My God they've got Regina. She repeated it over and over in her mind as she ran naked down the trail, not feeling the small rocks and twigs digging into her bare soles, impervious to the pain caused by scratches inflicted by thorny branches on her exposed skin.

Chapter Twenty

Tennenboum watched the Jnaar loading the rest of their stuff onto the carts. The rat-like Roccas, as the Jnaar called the animals hitched to the wagons, stood waiting patiently until they were told to move.

He had learned much about the Jnaar from Raark these last few days. The old man claimed to be over four hundred Earth years old. He wasn't quite sure yet if he could believe it, but Raark was an alien, descended from a space-faring race apparently much older than Humanity. His race was long-lived. He didn't know where they came from. One thing was clear…they came to this star system over a thousand years ago as evidenced by the ancient space station.

The Jnaar's ancestors became stranded on this planet a thousand years ago and were forced to adapt to the harsh conditions. In the summer they lived on the surface, but in the winter they moved underground into their winter city. This particular group was not the only tribe. There were several tribes scattered across this part of the planet. They did not necessarily communicate with each other.

He gained little information from Raark about the so-called Shadow-dwellers. They were Jnaar who had gone a different road and were shunned by the rest of the Jnaar. They worshipped the Dark Goddess, a deity who resided in the caves. They were offering her living sacrifices, a practice the Jnaar did not condone.

He also didn't quite understand the Dal Losos or Maklos, as the Sras called them. According to Raark they were the same and yet different. The Dal Losos had Jnaar fathers, while the Maklos were fathered by Sras males. Some had large, black eyes like the Jnaar and others had ridged foreheads and golden eyes, like the Sras. Some had ridged foreheads and black eyes.

Another piece of information he learned which he couldn't understand either.

The Sras and the Jnaar were sworn enemies. When asked about the reason, Raark told him, "The Sras are vicious and warlike. They hate us and we hate them. We can never be friends."

"Have you ever tried?"

"I'm not aware of it. It has been like that since my people landed on Iceworld."

"Perhaps it is time you took the first step to make peace," Tennenboum suggested.

Remembering his conversation with the old man, Tennenboum thought about Sagela. She had been fierce and wild in their lovemaking and displayed the same fierceness when she and her companions fought the Maklos, but they had shown no hostility toward him, Hunter, or Bonnet. In fact, he and Uroo had parted as friends. They would always be friends.

As he would always be friends with Raark and the other Jnaar of this tribe. He wondered what caused the animosity between the Jnaar and the Sras. It must have been something terrible that happened when the two different species met…a thousand years ago. How long can anyone carry a grudge? Apparently for a long time. The origin of this feud was in all likelihood lost in the past.

Sometimes people hated each other for no reason at all.

He turned toward their tent. It was time for them also to pack up and leave this place. They'd solved the mystery of the ruins. He knew Maisoneuve was disappointed in many ways but also elated. Even though his ordeal in the underground caves and tunnels was not what he had been searching for, but it did provide him with an adventure he wouldn't forget for a long time and gave him a diversion from his boredom. Maisoneuve was a man of action. Sitting around was not something he enjoyed.

The entrance to the tent opened and the big man stepped outside. When he saw Tennenboum, he grinned. "I haven't thanked you yet for not making a big scene about what happened the other day. I'll be sure to let you know about my plans next time."

"Next time we'll all go together, Maisoneuve. All three of you could have died in those caves." Tennenboum was still annoyed about the incident but there was no purpose in dwelling on it. Everyone was safe and alive and that was the most important thing.

"It seems our new friends are just about ready to leave." Maisoneuve's gaze took in the campsite of the Jnaar, now devoid of tents, cooking pots, and the many different items people use to camp out, everything loaded into the carts. People climbed into the carts and made themselves comfortable for the trek home, a good ten-day's journey to the west. The riders mounted their steeds. Most of them sat astride Leeas, the stocky, black-coated herbivores. Only the hunters and warriors rode Heeskas, the long-legged large birds.

One of the Jnaar left the group and guided his Heeska toward were Tennenboum and Maisoneuve stood. It was Rasa, the old man's son, the leader of the tribe.

He lifted his fist in a farewell gesture. “We leave,” he said, using simple words. Words Tennenboum and Maisoneuve could understand without the use of the translator. Tennenboum wished they were in possession of such a device. They had learned a few basic words, but were not able to carry on a conversation, unlike Hunter, who spoke the Jnaar language fairly well now…thanks to the AI strapped to his wrist.

Tennenboum returned the gesture and said, “Farewell…friend.”

Rasa smiled. “Friend,” he repeated. Then he touched his left shoulder with his fist. “Gourbana. Farewell.”

He clucked and rode away to join the riders in the front of the caravan.

Tennenboum and Maisoneuve watched as the column of carts began to roll. There were ten carts. Six carried supplies and passengers, and four were loaded only with supplies. He counted ten men on birds and twelve on Leeas.

There were no roads, the terrain was not smooth, and the carts didn’t have springs to absorb the shocks created by rolling over rocks, clumps of dirt, or dropping into holes in the ground. The passengers in the carts sat on soft furs to make the ride as comfortable as possible.

Maisoneuve must have had the same thoughts as Tennenboum. “The riders are luckier than the people in the carts,” he said, chuckling softly. “I’ll bet all of them are happy when the day is finally over. It is sure a primitive method of traveling.”

“Beats walking, though,” Tennenboum commented, “but I agree with you…those carts are an uncomfortable ride. I wonder how many times they have to stop and repair either a broken axel or fix a wheel.”

“I’m glad we have the Roamer. And it is faster too.”

“Just a little bit.” Tennenboum laughed. “It is hard to imagine they are descendants of people who traveled the stars when Humans were still living in caves. I wonder what would happen to our descendants should we become stranded on this planet…or any other planet.”

“Probably the same thing. Machines break down electronic equipment fails to operate. They wouldn’t have the knowledge and resources to build replacement parts.”

“It will happen on Nu-Eden, unless Earth sends ships to bring supplies and, possibly, new colonists.”

“I certainly hope Earth sends a ship in five years.” Tennenboum didn’t even want to think about the alternative. “I want to go home in five years.”

“So do I,” Maisoneuve agreed. “I’m hoping to get a chance to go down to Nu-Eden after this. It is a much more pleasant planet.”

The wagons had disappeared over the hill. “Time for us to get ready also,” Tennenboum said, heading for the tent. Most of his stuff was already packed and stored away in the Roamer. There wasn't much left to do except break down the tent.

Bonnet stuck out his head just as Tennenboum approached the entrance door. "All packed up," he announced, stepping outside, his backpack in his hand. "I'll just load it into the Roamer then I'll be back to help you with the tent."

Roland and Hunter were still busy arranging things in the loading area of the Landroamer to make room for the folded tent.

An hour later they were on their way back to the research station.

* * * *

Even though it rained only two days before, the ground was dry, making traveling easy and almost boring. They made it a point not pass too close to the spot where they had run across the Tigers, or Keeras, as the Jnaar called the six-legged savage beasts. Tennenboum almost preferred to use the Sras name Sirkrris. After all, they had fought the great predators and saved Uroo from certain death, and possibly the others also. Uroo had been mortally wounded and probably would have died either from loss of blood or an infection. Had he survived by some miracle, he would most likely have lost his leg. There was also a good possibility the beasts might have killed all eight members of the group.

He and his companions had a close connection with the Sirkrris. The act of slaying them was responsible for the ensuing friendship between Humans and Sras and his sexual encounter with Sagela. Would he ever see her again?

How would the future relationship between Humans and Sras have developed had it not been for this encounter? It made him wonder what had taken place the first time the Jnaar and the Sras met…so long ago.

They say time heals wounds. How much time has to pass to heal some wounds?

It was getting dark outside. They had been traveling since early morning, only stopping to stretch their legs and having lunch in the fresh air and under the sun. It was August 25. Possibly in another month the weather may turn nasty as the fall season began. Of course, there was a good chance they might still see some nice and warm days since fall on this planet was five months long, but then the ten-month-long winter would begin with nothing but snow and fierce storms. The Jnaar called this planet Iceworld for reasons the Humans could only guess.

The research station would keep them comfortable and protected against anything Iceworld could throw at them, but they'd be cooped up for too many months should they decide to stay longer than the planned one year or should they be unable to leave the planet for various reasons, weather conditions as the foremost one.

"I can see the station," Hunter announced. "We should be home in about ten minutes. Just in time for supper."

"Let them know we are coming. We don't want them to shoot at us," Maisoneuve joked.

Hunter contacted the station and left a message with the main computer.

They made it in nine minutes. Hunter drove the Landroamer through the elevator doors onto its designated platform. Using the remote control built into the Roamer's dashboard he energized the lift that took them up to the main door into the station.

The engineers thought of every eventuality. They expected massive amounts of snow. The Landroamer would be buried under meters of snow and useless to the people inside the station. There were exit doors at various heights in the tower that housed the lift and elevator. They would be able to use the Landroamer even in the winter, after it had been adapted for traveling on snow.

Tennenboum still wished they had a vehicle that could travel through the air, but Captain Cunningham hadn't seen the need for one. According to the Captain all the shuttles were needed to transport colonists and materials to Nu-Eden and to keep in contact with the settlers, should the need arise.

He grabbed his personal pack and climbed out of the Roamer. Before he headed for the entrance of the station, he walked over to the large window. Looking out at the now so familiar landscape around the station, he remembered that night on the space station when he had stood in the observatory, searching for the planet he was on now.

He hadn't been able to find it among the bright specks of light visible in the endless void surrounding the alien space station. His search had been interrupted by a beautiful Redhead. Her name was Breanna McGuinness, a xenologist.

I hope you found your aliens on Nu-Eden. You should have come with me. Of course, we already have our own xenologist, Regina Seagul. She'll be ecstatic to hear about the Jnaar and the Sras. She'll be bugging me to take her with me and visit them.

Shrugging mentally, he turned away from the window. Tonight he would get a good night's sleep. Tomorrow was early enough to tell everyone about their trip.

While the others went straight to their quarters, he decided to go and talk to Wong first, in case Captain Cunningham contacted the station and left a message for him. Wong wasn't in the computer room, so he headed for the common room. Most of them would most likely be there anyway, relaxing before supper.

He knew something was wrong the moment he walked into the room. They were all there. It seemed they had been waiting for him. His gaze fell on

Beth McGregor, who sat near the entrance. With her flaming red hair and green eyes she could have been Breanna McGuinness' sister.

When she realized he was looking at her, she burst into tears and covered her face with her hands. "It wasn't my fault," she sobbed.

Vendy Sherbo, the young nurse, got up and rushed to her. "It's all right," she said with a soothing voice. "Nobody blames you."

Tennenboum looked at Renaldo. He was the only one who seemed composed. The women sat there with tears in their eyes, or near tears, even Antje Swornson, who always struck him as cool and collected. Renaldo and Wong were the only men present. He didn't see Kullmann and Zydyk, neither did he see Cara Gunn or Regina Seagul. Wong sat staring at his fingers with a serious expression, as if he had discovered some of his fingers were missing.

"What is going on?" he asked.

Renaldo's face was sober and his eyes dark. "We've had a mishap," he said slowly.

"A mishap? Can you explain it in more detail?"

"Miss Seagul has been abducted," Renaldo said with a dead voice.

"Abducted? What the hell are you talking about? Who would abduct one of our people?" Tennenboum almost shouted the question.

Renaldo pointed at Beth. "Miss McGregor is in a better position to explain what happened. She was there."

Tennenboum brought his attention back to the redheaded woman. She seemed to have found her composure, even though her face was still tearstained. "There was nothing I could have done, Professor Tennenboum," she said, her voice breaking. "It happened so fast. I was lucky to get away with my life."

"Just answer me one question, Miss McGregor. Who abducted Regina Seagul?"

"Men riding big birds."

"What?" Tennenboum stared at her. Then he strode to one of the tables, pulled out a chair, and sat down with a big rock in his stomach. "Come, join me at the table, Miss McGregor, and tell me everything about it."

Chapter Twenty-one

An excerpt from Professor Tennenboum's personal log.

The lake is beginning to freeze over. Today is the 23rd day of March 2986, one month into winter. We had the first snowfall in the beginning of February. I don't know if that is the norm here. It's been snowing for three days straight now. The flakes are heavy and are adding to the blanket already covering the ground. So far, the snow is already more than half a meter thick. Doctor Bonnet did some calculating. He tells us that at the rate the snow is falling we can expect at least two meters within the next six months…and probably more to come. If we get heavy storms, and we will, there'll be snowdrifts reaching up to the bottom of our station, which is five meters above ground. It proves again, the engineers, who designed the installation, designed it well.

After Miss Seagul's abduction, the mood on the station was gloomy for a long time. We took the Landroamer and searched for her but never found her or any trace of where they could have taken her. According to Miss McGregor, the people who took her were definitely Jnaar, but I doubt they were the same ones we met. They rescued her from certain death by a group of Maklos, which is promising. She is probably still alive but we don't know where she is now. Most likely somewhere underground.

There is other disturbing news we had to deal with, actually are still trying to come to grips with. We have lost all contact with the space station.

Also, the shuttle that was supposed to bring us more supplies and twenty researchers never arrived. The last time I spoke to Captain Cunningham was September 18, half a year ago. The connection was bad because of the electrical interference in the atmosphere. He told me he couldn't risk another shuttle but would try again in spring. I don't know if he meant spring in the old Earth calendar or spring on this planet. In a way it is academic, because each one of us fears something dreadful has happened to the space station or the people on it.

We can only hope and pray whatever it is will be resolved. The mood on the station is pessimistic and gloomy. We should have thought of bringing along a chaplain who could pray for us. I don't worship any gods…not any more. I've lost what little faith I possessed a long time ago.

Epilogue

The snow had finally stopped falling. Wong sat in the upper deck of the research station, staring out of the transparent bubble at the snow-covered landscape surrounding the giant egg he shared with fourteen other people…nine scientists, one nurse and four construction workers who decided to stay behind until the relief shuttle came back to pick them up.

It never arrived, and now here he was…stuck on a planet covered with ice and snow. Would he ever leave this place again? He had spent many hours trying to contact the space station to no avail. The Station seemed dead.

He liked being up here all by himself. Not many of the others did. They found it too depressing to see nothing but white outside. It hurt the eyes when you stared for too long at the bleak frozen lake and the snow-capped mountains.

His thoughts drifted to Regina Seagul. He had liked her. She'd been pretty with her flashing dark eyes and olive skin, even though she never showed in interest in him. Then again, he never indicated he was attracted to her. She was a scientist, interested in alien life forms, and he was a computer specialist, engrossed with his computer and repair drones. They didn't have much in common.

Hard to believe seven months had passed since her disappearance. He hoped she was still alive and busy studying the people who abducted her.

He was only half-awake when his attention was suddenly aroused by a distant object in the sky. Sitting up, he tried to focus his eyes on it as it shot toward the station, growing in size as it came nearer.

At first he thought his eyes were deceiving him, but then he nearly shouted with surprise and joy. The shuttle had finally arrived. It slowed down and circled the station once before settling on the thick blanket of snow.

He shot out of his chair and bounded for the elevator to take him down to the common room. Perhaps he could go home now.

End of Book Six

The adventure continues in The Xandra, Book Seven

www.ingramcontent.com/pod-product-compliance
Lightning Source LLC
LaVergne TN
LVHW090952080826
845145LV00003B/982